A Second Summertime Courtship

The Hasting Sisters
Book Two

Sandra Sookoo

ARE YOU SIGNED UP FOR DRAGONBLADE'S BLOG?

You'll get the latest news and information on exclusive giveaways, exclusive excerpts, coming releases, sales, free books, cover reveals and more.

Check out our complete list of authors, too!

No spam, no junk. That's a promise!

Sign Up Here

www.dragonbladepublishing.com

Dearest Reader;

Thank you for your support of a small press. At Dragonblade Publishing, we strive to bring you the highest quality Historical Romance from some of the best authors in the business. Without your support, there is no 'us', so we sincerely hope you adore these stories and find some new favorite authors along the way.

Happy Reading!

CEO, Dragonblade Publishing

Additional Dragonblade books by
Author Sandra Sookoo

The Hasting Sisters Series
The Devil's Game (Book 1)
A Second Summertime Courtship (Book 2)

Willful Winterbournes Series
Romancing Miss Quill (Book 1)
Pursuing Mr. Mattingly (Book 2)
Courting Lady Yeardly (Book 3)
Guarding the Widow Pellingham (Book 4)
Bedeviling Major Kenton (Book 5)
Charming Miss Standish (Book 6)
Teasing Miss Atherby (Novella)

The Storme Brother Series
The Soul of a Storme (Book 1)
The Heart of a Storme (Book 2)
The Look of a Storme (Book 3)
The Sting of a Storme (Book 4)
The Touch of a Storme (Book 5)
The Fury of a Storme (Book 6)
Much Ado About a Storme (Novella)
A Storme's First Noelle (Novella)
A Storme's Christmas Legacy (Novella)

The Lyon's Den Series
The Lyon's Puzzle
The Lyon's Redemption

Dedication

To Ragene Anne Cope.
I would have loved to meet you, write books for you—and
with you.
You will always live on through stories.

CHAPTER ONE

May 15, 1817
Bromington House
Manchester Square
London

Miss Cora Hasting, second daughter of Baron Landover, frowned as she completed a sentence in the letter she wrote to her mother back in Bedfordshire, where all her sisters save one resided.

A wave of homesickness swept over her, and it took a few seconds to swallow back the tears. Missing her family, especially since her father's mind was deteriorating, was a constant battle, but because of that—amidst a few other things fate had thrown their way—it had been necessary for some of the Hasting sisters to take paid positions, which was the lot of many daughters of the *beau monde* whose families had fallen into reduced circumstances.

But that didn't mean she needed to enjoy it.

After another few moments of trying to appear cheerful and translate that into her letter so her mother wouldn't worry, she gave up the attempt. The words flowed even more smoothly. No doubt her mother would write back and implore her to come home, but that would only hasten the loss of Cora's ancestral home all the quicker due to unpaid taxes, and she couldn't allow herself to be a failure.

Or any of her sisters.

Especially since her older sister Amelia had married a viscount last month. The man's coffers were allegedly empty, which didn't help anyone's situation, but apparently it was a love match after much aggravation, and they'd wed in a small private ceremony that Cora had been fortunate enough to attend at Landover Manor. Her family had gathered round, and her sisters had dressed in their best gowns. For her father's sake, she had been glad they'd had the ceremony there.

A stab of envy went through Cora's chest, for though she didn't begrudge her sister the relationship—her viscount *was* sinfully handsome with a reputation to match—she'd assumed that by the time she'd reached the age of nine and twenty, she would have been married with a few children. Instead, she'd been jilted steps from the altar almost three and a half years ago, left with her reputation in tatters, a secret hope that had been dashed, and her dreams shattered.

There were no more Seasons out of necessity and there had been no more opportunities for her, for her family had retreated to Bedfordshire, and that had been that.

Until circumstances had become so dire the sisters were convinced the only salvation was to take paid positions and send coin home.

"Miss Hasting?"

She glanced up from the letter as a feeling of relief slipped down her spine as one of the upstairs maids came into the room. "Yes, Bridget?"

The young woman ducked her head, tucked a strand of red hair that had escaped its braid behind her ear and then wiped her hands on the stomach of her pinafore apron. "I'm finished with Mrs. Bromington for the moment and thought I would see if you needed assistance." She often had to double as a second lady's maid when the original one was overworked… or sent off crying.

"You are sweet to offer." Cora gestured the other woman into the room. "I've just about finished this letter so can afford the break. Where is, ah, Mrs. Bromington currently?" It didn't matter that Cora had been given Thursdays and Sundays off. Somehow, her charge demanded things of her regardless.

"She was on her way to the drawing room to meet her embroidery group."

"You mean her gossip circle." In the three and a half months since Cora had been Mrs. Bromington's companion, one thing she'd noticed was the cantankerous woman enjoyed gossiping, with anyone who would listen, and she enjoyed even more cutting people's reputations to ribbons with her sharp tongue.

"There is that." Bridget sneaked farther into the room and closed the door quietly behind her. "And she especially detests if there is a romance beneath her roof." Mischief sparkled in the maid's eyes. "Do you think she is opposed to intercourse as well?"

The question took Cora by such surprise that a bout of laughter escaped before she clamped a hand to her mouth. "Bridget!" It was an inappropriate topic of conversation, but one she never had anyone to share with before, which was why her friendship with the staff had blossomed.

To say nothing of the fact she was one of them within the paid position.

"What? It is a part of life, and a large part at that if a girl is lucky." Bridget flounced onto the trunk at the end of Cora's bed. "Can I help it if I think men are delicious?"

"The *right* men," Cora corrected with a raised eyebrow as she quickly finished her letter and then capped the inkwell.

"True, but the wrong ones have always been that too, more's the pity." The maid's grin was contagious, and soon Cora did the same. "What say you? Is there a man in your life? You have been in Town long enough to attract some sort of attention."

She briefly pointed her gaze to the ceiling before settling it on the other woman. "When would I have time for any of that?" Even though her employer couldn't hear, Cora lowered her voice. "Mrs. Bromington is an exacting taskmaster. She never allows me time alone when my attention should be on her."

"Oh, I am well aware, and you have it worse than the rest of us, but please say you will try. You have at least one pretty gown in your wardrobe, so you should at least enjoy yourself."

"Enjoying myself in the past caused far too many problems," she admitted in a near whisper. That particular scandal had been the real cause for the family hiding in the country and all the Seasons to halt. The dire finances her father had kept hidden didn't come out until much later. "I'm not certain I am strong enough to go through such a thing again, not even for a delicious man, for those are the kind who are the most irritating."

She'd hidden that shame from her parents and even from her older sister Amelia. The only sister who'd known or even suspected was her twin, Nora. That bond was unbreakable, even now when they were apart. Nora had agreed to stay at home to look after their parents when she and Amelia left for London. Familial gossip held that Nora wasn't all there in her upper stories, for she had trouble speaking and could hardly hear, but since the country doctors she'd seen couldn't understand why she was that way, they had proclaimed her deaf and dumb and said there was nothing anyone could do for her.

That had further put a strain on the family finances, but no one held it against her. Why should they? It wasn't her fault she'd been born differently from the rest of them. But according to Amelia, Nora only needed a creative way to communicate and be understood. It was merely a matter of finding it.

And knowing her older sister, Amelia would find it once the newness of her marriage wore off. If that were possible. She and her viscount husband were quite in love and walked the bounds of scandal when they were together.

Cora frowned as jealousy once more reared its ugly head. *I could have had that, but fate didn't think I needed it.* Not wishing to ponder her failed engagement, she let her mind linger on her twin. Nora was lovely, intelligent, clever, and resourceful. If given half the chance, she would turn London on its head and the world would open up to her, all because their parents refused to send her away to an asylum. For her sister's sake, Cora hoped all would be well, for no one deserved to be alone, especially if that state was forced due to being unable to speak correctly.

"Then don't expect forever." Bridget shrugged. She brushed at a smudge of dust on her apron. "Pursue fun instead." Whenever the maid was interested in a subject, her Irish brogue became more pronounced.

The sound of the other woman's voice wrenched her from those thoughts. "If only it were that simple." At least, it wasn't for her. Not now. Not after she'd known heartbreak and shame, love and loss, dreams and despair.

The maid blew out a breath as she shook her head. "Some days, I'm not sure I'm looking for marriage, but if the right man would convince me to let him beneath my skirts, have his wicked way, then I would ride him until the feeling of madness faded."

Oh, that feeling! How well did she remember such a thing? The wild rawness of being in a man's arms, of feeling his hard body moving against her softer one, the way kisses grew passionate enough to make her take leave of her senses, the frantic pressure that only broke when lips or hands or tongues bedeviled certain places on her body… A sigh of regret escaped her. But Bridget was correct. With the right man, that madness was like an addiction, and she would do anything to immerse herself in it again.

Almost.

Then she frowned. "What about the consequences? A woman cannot indulge in such things willy-nilly without finding themselves in scandal at least once."

"You worry too much." Bridget scoffed and there were secrets in her eyes that made Cora feel as if she were naught but a naïve innocent. "Have you not learned that there are many ways to prevent unwanted pregnancy?"

"I suppose I didn't think much upon it, even though I've

heard whispers…"

The maid tsked her tongue. "Some of my friends make their living on their backs. They have told me their secrets, and it's good knowledge to have. Titled men don't want by-blows. It's too complicated and embarrassing, even though the woman bears the whole of that burden. Middle-class men are only moderately better when it comes to children, and lower-class men can't provide for them."

"Where does that leave us?" It was appalling how much she didn't know regarding life, but her mother had been reticent to discuss such things, and only on the day Cora would have been married did she speak slightly of what happened in the marriage bed between men and women.

Except Cora had already anticipated that particular act, and she had adored heartily with the man she had assumed she would marry. According to her mother, it wasn't something to enjoy with abandon but to endure for the sake of reproducing.

Cora still didn't believe that.

"Women must look after their own interests lest we be branded as whores and turned out of society." She shook her head as a hardened look went through her expression. "There ain't no life in the poorhouses and workhouses, no place for a child to grow or thrive." The brogue was quite heavy. Obviously, this was a topic close to her heart. "We must take measures to prevent pregnancy to survive. Lord knows the men of the world don't care."

"You make an excellent point." Cora clasped her hands together on top of her letter. She wished she would have known that earlier in her life. Perhaps it would have saved heartache, shame, and embarrassment. "And it's something every woman needs to remember when swept away by pleasure…" Oh, when it was right, it was heaven, and there *was* no thinking beyond that fall. A woman wanted everything that man would give.

"While that is true, if a man is skilled in bed sport or if he plain loves you, I wonder if such things would matter?" Bridget shrugged. "We all must weigh how we will survive and move through life against that temporary madness."

The maid was far too wise for her years. "I thought I had that years ago." Cora sobered. Though over three years had gone by, her heart was still bruised, and some animosity lingered. "As it turned out, all he wanted was the bedding. Or else he was a coward, for he broke our engagement and fled, left me at the bloody steps of the church that morning." She met Bridget's gaze as she blew out a breath. "I had no recourse but to hide at my father's country estate. Coming here as Mrs. Bromington's companion is the first time I stepped back in London since my reputation was completely ruined."

"Oh, I didn't know that." Bridget assumed an expression of compassion. "I have never had such luck in bringing a man up to scratch, and well-off men don't want a maid."

"That's not true."

"Ha!" The other woman snorted. "I'm still here, so I'll wager it is, but if a man calls off on an engagement, he should have his stones in a vice."

A ghost of a grin curved Cora's lips. "I might have agreed with you at the time." Did she still wish revenge on Peregrine, wherever he was? No, she didn't, for she had forgiven him, but that didn't mean she'd forgotten what he'd done and how much of a coward he'd been.

"Well, it's for the best, truly, Miss Hasting," Bridget said as she stood and shook out her skirting. "Men are mostly trouble."

"I'll agree with you on that." Cora stood as well. It was always a joy to talk with the maid, and afterward, she didn't feel so alone in this position. "Ah, Bridget, why are men so wonderful and so aggravating at the same time?" She shook her head. "Besides, I rather doubt I'll be allowed to meet any eligible men let alone be in their presence long enough to have a proposal offered with Mrs. Bromington in the mix. She's rather demanding."

They both shared a laugh, for it wasn't a lie.

Bridget rolled her eyes. "We all hate her, Miss Hasting, but sometimes the devil you know is better than the devil you don't. There are much more horrible employers out there." Shadows appeared in her brown eyes as she shrugged. "She doesn't abuse us physically, and she doesn't have male relatives who abuse us girls in other ways. Many of my friends don't have that. This position is better than any I've had, if I can remember to ignore her dictates."

"Good advice. Perhaps I need to learn how to do that, as well as take gratitude into consideration." For far too long, she'd been resentful of having to take the paid position, of her father's dismal financial state, of being abandoned steps from the altar. It was time to take back control of her own life and find a path she wished to trod. "I'm sorry all the same. No one should need to fear for their position or whether they will be violated in the same."

"Thank you, Miss Hasting. You're a good sort."

"I sometimes wonder." She frowned. Working in a paid position had opened her eyes to many things, and it was vastly different from how she'd previously lived her life. It made her both appalled and thankful. And if the coin she gained each month could stave off having Papa selling Landover Manor, all the better.

"Compared to some other ladies of the Quality I've known; you are the best." She offered a bright smile. "Don't mind most of my talk, though. I would like to meet a stable man who thinks the world of me and wanted to marry me. Having wee ones with the ability to feed them is the only thing I've ever wanted since I was at my Gran's knee."

The ball of unshed tears rose in Cora's throat once more, just as it always did any time someone spoke of being a wife and a mother. "I can understand that all too well. There is something about wishing to see a child with the looks of both its parents, someone who will love you unconditionally." Tears welled in her eyes. "But you are correct. There is no point in bringing a child into this world if it cannot be cared for."

Answering tears pooled in the maid's eyes. "We can only hope for the best but accept what we're given. Sometime in there, fate might grant us happiness. Until then, there is work to do."

"You are so sensible." In many ways, Cora admired that, for she definitely was not. Perhaps because life had shown her nothing good came of being sensible.

"It keeps me out of trouble." The maid chuckled. "I should go belowstairs. Mrs. Bromington will no doubt call soon. She's already run Bess ragged."

"Sounds about right." Cora nodded. "Thank you for coming by. I am always cheered by our talks."

"I do what I can. We all need lifting at some point. And Miss Hasting?"

"Yes?"

"What you are doing here, earning coin for your father? That's admirable. I know you hate it here and dislike the position, but you keep on because you must. I hope your family is grateful for your sacrifice."

"Oh!" Heat slapped Cora's cheeks. "I hadn't thought about it in that way before, but is it truly a sacrifice if I've already tossed away my chances?"

"Only you can decide that, miss." With a wave, Bridget left the room.

"I'm afraid my days of deciding anything are long past," she whispered to herself as she returned to the small secretary in the corner of her room. She folded the letter and then slipped it into a matching envelope. Until the taxes on her father's manor were paid, being companion to the difficult Mrs. Bromington was her future. It didn't matter that the woman's attitude often left her and others on the staff in tears, for coin was more important than confidence.

Yet she couldn't help but wonder what had become of Peregrine Wetherford and if he'd found happiness with someone that he obviously couldn't see with her. Another wave of homesickness swept over her, and this time a touch of self-pity accompanied it. With tears in her eyes, Cora threw herself onto her bed, buried her face into her pillow, and wept for all the dreams that hadn't come true and for an uncertain and quite boring future where she felt trapped from familial obligation.

How can I endure months of this, let alone years?

There were no answers except that no one would come to rescue her, and there was no hero who would dash in, fight the dragon that was her employer, and then carry her off into the sunset for a happily ever after.

I need to stop reading those silly fairy stories I used to adore as a young girl.

Honestly, they were doing more harm than good, for life wasn't that simple.

CHAPTER TWO

May 17, 1817
The Albany
London, England

Captain Peregrine Wetherford once more threw a toy rabbit made from burlap so his beagle, Matey, could gallop out of the room in the chase of it. "That is the last time. I do have entertaining to attend," he called after the animal.

A half-hearted bark was his only answer.

"You spend entirely too much time shut away in this set and with that dog." This from his best friend Charles, or rather Viscount Maubrey. "If you aren't careful, you will become a recluse."

"As if that is such a bad thing." After grabbing a bottle of brandy from the sideboard, he crossed the room and joined his friend, dropping into a comfortable leather winged-back chair that matched Charles'. "My looks are rather upsetting in some circles, so I would rather stay tucked away for the peace."

"Bah. I would never have thought you a coward." The viscount took the bottle from Peregrine's hand, poured a measure of the amber liquor into his glass. "Don't try to deny it, for that is exactly what you are by hiding."

"I have no intention of denying it." With a frown, Peregrine relieved his friend of the bottle then poured some of the brandy into his own glass. After setting the bottle on a small round table at his elbow, he sighed and stared into the contents. "Being back in London is proving a trying endeavor."

"It needn't be."

"True, and it is something I must work through for myself." Unbidden, his left hand drifted to the same side of his face where the skin was scarred and puckered. He'd been injured while in His Majesty's service, and during a naval battle with a pirate vessel in the eastern Caribbean Sea, one of the cannons on his ship had been hit with a cannon ball. When it exploded, he'd been too close, had taken the brunt of the flying shrapnel. His cheek, the side of his neck, his ear had been the recipient of hot metal and burning bits. Some of that had penetrated his uniform, leaving scars and burn marks behind to decorate his shoulder and side. "I never wanted to retire so early from the navy."

I miss my ship, the men I sailed with, the familiar and mysterious undulation of the sea.

"I am well aware of that." Charles regarded him with a frown. Concern shadowed his eyes. "I was there. Hell, I was the one who scooped you off that deck and dragged you to safety while it seemed the world was burning."

"I remember." As if he could ever forget. Charles had been the chief navigator, which he'd done with aplomb, before he'd become the viscount after the unfortunate news that his father and older brother had perished in a carriage accident.

Eventually, the fires were put out on deck and the pirates' vessel fled. Since Peregrine's ship had been disabled enough to prevent any sort of speed until repaired, they'd been forced to let the criminals go. Since they were probably one of the last pirate vessels in the area after the English and American navies had run them out of existence a few years before, it was a given they would eventually be caught. Then things were a tad fuzzy regarding the events that had followed, and the only thing he remembered was the pain.

Later, they'd told him he'd suffered from a raging fever, a mild infection at various burn sites, and the crew had feared for his sanity, to say nothing of his future. On the lengthy trip back to England, Peregrine had no recourse but to fight for his life and heal the best he could. The ship's doctor had done the best he could under the circumstances, and by the time they'd pulled into port at Dover, Peregrine had been well on the way to healing.

With scars as his souvenir.

"Yes, well, despite your penchant for becoming the crab at times, you are still attractive, still retain your sense of humor when you let it out, and there is no reason you shouldn't accept at least half the invitations sent your way." Charles shook his head. "You have been back in England for six months, man. It's time to live again."

"I *am* living. The watch repair shop should open within the next month, and the addition of nautical instruments will bring in fellow navy men."

Charles blew out a breath. "Which gives you yet another place to hide as if you were a beast." He tsked his tongue. "That cul-de-sac buried two streets over from Bond Street will be the death knell of your life."

"No, it will give me an income, and at least it's a shop instead of a stall at the Exchange."

"There is that, but what of your personal life? There is more to living than peddling wares."

"Which I *am* trying to do by discovering if Miss Beaufort and I will suit. If so, then I shall ask to pay my formal addresses to her." In some annoyance, Peregrine took a sip of his brandy and winced when the liquor burned his throat. "That doesn't mean I need to spend every waking hour in the public eye of society."

Before he'd been injured and permanently scarred, each time he found himself in London on leave, he was a highly sought-after guest to any dinner party or society event. The addition of a military man regardless of what branch that man had served in was a certain way of guaranteeing success at a gathering. Once he'd retired from the navy, he'd taken speaking engagements about Town which netted him a decent income, but each time, he always wondered what the attendees thought of him and if the prevailing emotion was pity. That was something he despised above all else.

"Miss Beaufort, eh?" Charles shivered then took a sip of his own drink. "Isn't she rather young for you?"

"A bit." To his knowledge, the chit was one and twenty, which made her fourteen years his junior. "But she seems mature for her age, and her looks are lovely. She has tidy manners, and her family is of a decent sort."

"Ah." His friend briefly pointed his gaze to the heavens. "Have you kissed her?"

"Bite your tongue, man. I barely know her!" He had only selected her because she had blonde hair, and he had a weakness for women of such coloring. "A true English rose, you could say. Strawberries-and-cream complexion."

"Does she have goals or aspirations?"

"Beyond marrying well and being a wife and mother?" Peregrine shrugged. "I couldn't say. Most of the time she is guarded by a sister or mother when I see her in public. I haven't asked her out driving or for an outing yet."

"Then why do you wish to court her?" Concern once again lined the other man's face as he glanced at Peregrine. "Seems a rather bad prison to leg-shackle yourself to her merely to stave off boredom or loneliness."

God, it was frightening how well Charles knew him. He forced moisture into his dry throat. "While it's true that being back on land permanently hasn't always been to my taste, I would like to see if we get on. If she adores the sea, perhaps we could relocate to somewhere I can at least have a glimpse of it."

Charles snorted. "And what? Become a fisherman and live off the uncertainty of that? You are better than such an idea." He shook his head. "Hell, if you miss it that much, spend time at my country estate in Kent. The sea isn't far from there."

"Trust me, I have thought of that, but eventually you would tire of a perpetual house guest." And he didn't wish to disrupt the viscount's life simply because Peregrine yearned to hear the crash of the waves again. "When the craving becomes too bad, I go to Hyde Park and watch the water of the Serpentine. Yes, it is a river and a lake—bodies of water really—but if there is a breeze, the ripples along the surface remind me of the sea. It is better than nothing."

"Perhaps you do need a woman in your life and in your bed." Charles drained the contents of this glass, and once again regarded him. "How long has it been since you've bedded a woman?"

"For an empty liaison merely to release the needs of the body?" Peregrine shrugged. "Just after I came back to London in January. It meant nothing, of course, and she is part of the demimonde but favors military men." When he'd been away in the navy, occasionally he had patronized various courtesans in the bigger ports, but beyond that? There had only been one singular woman whose memory he tended to recall when the nights were long and dark. That summer afternoon when he had taken his fiancée's innocence and pledged his life to hers two months ahead of their nuptial ceremony.

Where he'd left her standing outside the church.

"If Miss Beaufort is who you want, are you prepared to marry the chit in exchange for one night of pleasure? That is, if she won't go into hysterics the moment you take off your clothes." He made a distasteful face. "It's why I won't go near innocents."

There was much truth in that statement. "I believe I am ready for marriage now that my commitment to the navy is over. However, the woman in question would need to accept me as I am now, scars and all."

"Does Miss Beaufort do that?"

Peregrine hesitated in his answer. "She hasn't said anything, for she's too well-bred, I think, but I've noticed she won't stand to my left." It was quite worrisome.

"Then perhaps you should continue searching. Settling will do you no favors." Companionable silence sprang between them. "What are your plans for the future beyond taking a wife?"

"Honestly, I haven't thought that far ahead, which is odd for me. Usually, I like to have my life charted out with no surprises." It had always been thus for him since he was a youth. So when he'd fallen hard for Cora Hasting, had asked for her hand after a mere three months of courting, he had been absolutely terrified on the morning they were to be married. There were far too many unknowns in the offing.

Still were, perhaps, but he had matured since then.

Did he harbor regrets for breaking the engagement, for turning tail and running as fast as he could away from that sort of commitment? Yes and no. The love of the sea had won out over what he'd felt for Cora, and though that wasn't an excuse, it was the truth.

"No doubt I won't muck a second time up as I did the first," he said in a matter-of-fact voice while he finished his brandy.

"God, Cora Hasting. Haven't heard you speak about her in an age." Charles rubbed a hand along the side of his face. "Have you given her thought over the years?"

"Every now and again, but captaining a ship took most of my time, though when I first returned to London, I wished to see how she fared."

"And?"

He shrugged. "Eventually I decided it was better to move forward with a fresh slate. Let sleeping dogs lie, as it were." Not that he tried hard to track her to earth. Their paths wouldn't have crossed anyway, for she was of the *beau monde*, and while he was a gentleman and a captain, they didn't move in the same circles, but perhaps merely overlapped at times.

"Well, since the conversation has come 'round to Cora, I should tell you that I saw her about Town recently. Ordinarily, I wouldn't have brought her up to spare you the pain of memories."

Shock plowed through Peregrine's chest like a blow. "Where did you see her? Has she married?"

"Walking about the shops behind an older woman, and I rather doubt she's wed."

"Why?" Not wishing to seem too eager for word, he buffed his nails on his breeches.

Amusement danced in Charles' eyes. "There have been rumors through the *ton* that her father is in dun territory. Taxes haven't been paid on the country manor and all that." With a sigh, the viscount struggled to his feet then moved in the direction of the sideboard. "The older Hasting girls took paid positions."

"Truly?" He couldn't imagine how devasting such an occurrence had been for the whole family. Baron Landover was a proud man and never wanted assistance.

"Indeed. Cora's older sister Amelia was recently a companion to some *nouveau riche* chit, who then went off to marry a banker, while the sister wed Viscount Wycliffe."

Peregrine couldn't help a gasp. "That bounder?" How did any of that come about?

"I guess he's changed his ways for the love of her." Charles grinned as he selected a bottle of red wine. "It must be true that it's a love match, for when they wed last month, his pockets were still to let."

"And Cora?" He could hardly force out the words.

"I believe she is the companion to the recalcitrant and pain in the arse Mrs. Bromington. The woman's a widow. Her husband made a couple of fortunes in shipping, but she's a real scare. Has already run off several companions in the last year and a half."

If Peregrine's chest tightened further, it would snap his ribs. "Cora is a companion? She was forced to find a living?" A sick feeling circled through the pit of his stomach, for he might not have been the whole problem, but his defection certainly had added to the family's troubles.

"Miss Hasting has been in Town for four months. So far, the old woman hasn't tossed her out, so they must get on." Charles brought the bottle of wine back to his chair, but he didn't sit. Instead, he wrenched out the cork with his teeth, spit it out, and then took a deep draught. "Misfortune is what it is. Anyone who can stand that miserable crow must be made of stern stuff."

"Or else Cora has let herself be cowed for the sake of coin," he said in a hushed voice. When he'd known her, she had a refreshing personality and a stubborn streak, which is what initially attracted her to him, but it was always kept fettered by her mother and the need to be a proper young lady, the need to always do what the *ton* dictated. Cora's mother had preached endlessly that she hoped all her girls married well.

God, what a waste.

"I can see from your expression you haven't forgotten about her as successfully as you want me to believe, even if you never spoke of her onboard ship." Charles snickered. "You could always pay a call on her. Mrs. Bromington resides in Manchester Square. You know, should you wish to catch up… or apologize to Miss Hasting."

Heat went up the back of Peregrine's neck. Did he even wish to see Cora after what he did? So much time had passed. She had her life, and he had his. Plus, there was Miss Beaufort to consider. Realizing his friend waited on a reply, he blew out a breath. "Perhaps, but there is no reason to open old wounds. She is better off without me. Especially now."

"Ah." Charles shook his head. "Because you're scarred, forced to retire with no anchor so to speak, are renting rooms with no permanent source of income?"

When his life was so summarily itemized out like that, it was even more depressing. "Partially, yes, but also because I should never have jilted her to begin with. I can't imagine life has been easy for her since then. What would I even say?" Of course, he'd had plenty of time to think about his actions the three years he'd been at sea. If he hadn't been injured, he would still be aboard his ship, but fate had decreed that life over.

"You could be honest. No matter what happened, being honest now would be more appreciated than anything else."

"It's a tall order, but life has moved on, I have moved on."

"Have you? I seem to recall a year and a half into our orders, you procured a tattoo on your back that bears her name."

"Oh, God, I'd forgotten about that." The heat on his neck blazed hotter than ever. "Such a mistake."

"I wonder." Charles narrowed his gaze. "I rather suspect you have been lying to yourself. At the very least, there should be some sort of closure for both you and Cora."

"How can that be possible when there is Miss Beaufort underfoot?"

"Indeed. It is a conundrum." The viscount frowned. "However, we have come full circle." A swath of silence brewed between them. "Do you believe after spending more time in her company you'll offer for the chit?"

"I don't know." At least it was honest. "Unless there happens to be a spark between us soon, I can't imagine I should, even though it is probably the natural progression."

"Not a good basis to build a life together." After taking another swig from the wine bottle, Charles rested it on a table. "Don't do anything stupid."

"Have I recently?"

The look his friend shot him was questionable at best. "You forget, I have known you for far more years than the navy."

"Yes, well, that also works the other way." For a moment, Peregrine grinned. It was good to have such a loyal friend. "Where are you going?" he asked as the viscount headed toward the door, provoking Peregrine to stand up from his chair.

"To the club. It is nearly teatime, and you are in danger of becoming poor company if you slip into a maudlin mood." He gestured to Peregrine. "Afterward, we'll play cards, perhaps make a few wagers, and then hopefully someone will talk sense into you."

Sense according to who? "To an extent, I suppose, unless you are trying to push me back into the past, where I absolutely don't belong." There was only the future to think of.

"We shall see. Then I'm going to force you to accept some invitations later. You need to mingle within society more than you do. Otherwise, you and Matey will just be a lost cause."

Peregrine didn't like the way that ominous statement sounded, but there was nothing for it. "Matey is a good dog," he said on the way out of his rooms.

"Yes, but he's not a woman, and I'm trying to make you more attractive to eligible women." Amusement rang in his voice. "If you won't change the trajectory of your life, I'll have to guide the helm a bit."

"What of you?" He adored the camaraderie between him and the viscount, and truth be told, he appreciated the prodding.

"Let us sort you first, then we'll see."

They both shared a chuckle, the past and its mistakes forgotten.

CHAPTER THREE

May 19, 1817
Somewhere in Mayfair

CORA STIFLED THE urge to groan, for a megrim was working its way to the surface at her temples, and that wasn't ideal, since the rout had started thirty minutes ago. It had taken that long for Mrs. Bromington to make her way from the front door to the staircase due to her being quite the social butterfly.

"I don't know why you are already pouting, girl," her charge said with a smirk as she slowly climbed the treads. The candle-light winked off the necklace of round sapphires about her neck and her wrist. Her navy taffeta skirting rustled with each movement. "We will no doubt be here until midnight. I want to be sure and have my dinner before leaving. Best come to terms with that."

"I don't begrudge you the meal nor seeing your friends, Mrs. Bromington, but I will warn you I have a megrim lurking, so I might need to find a quiet place." And they often plagued her when she was under pressure or anxious about something. So had it been since she'd come into the widow's employ.

"Mind over matter, Miss Hasting." Mrs. Bromington tsked her tongue as she gained the second floor with Cora in tow. The lace lining her widow's cap ruffled slightly in the breeze brought on by the force of her hand fan. Tight gray curls beneath gleamed, for the hair had been washed earlier that morning. "Strong women don't let things like that dictate their mood."

My dear heaven, please give me patience to not pitch her down the stairs.

"Ah, then I shall try to learn from your more *substantial* experience," she muttered while they moved out of the way of foot traffic.

Not that she was given a choice about whether she'd wished to come tonight to this house across Mayfair, for Mrs. Bromington wanted to visit with her friends. One of which was the mother of the host. The rub there was the fact that her employer thought Cora not good enough to attend the rout as a guest, which would mean rubbing elbows of women like her. Since the widow had quite a fortune left to her by her husband, she considered herself better than Cora, whose family was in reduced circumstances, regardless of class position or her being the daughter of a baron. Apparently, according to her charge, women who are in such dire straits and forced to take paying positions didn't deserve to speak with their betters or enjoy entertainments.

As if I am not alive or breathing. To say nothing of being impressed upon to wear a decent gown so I won't embarrass her while walking the corridors.

In essence, while Mrs. Bromington enjoyed herself tonight, she expected Cora to go belowstairs with the staff and wait until she was called, as if she were a dog. Or, if she couldn't manage that, then to keep herself away from the core of the society event and out of sight. After all, she was a companion, *not* a guest.

According to her whim. It largely depended on who the widow wished to impress.

"Watch your tongue, Miss Hasting," Mrs. Bromington warned with a slight curve to her lips as if she found their exchange amusing. "I won't tolerate sass."

"As if you have tolerated *anything* since I came into your employ. Probably ages before that, too," Cora shot back before she could recall the words. With a gasp, she met the older woman's gaze. "I apologize. That was unkind."

The widow rapped Cora's shins with the tip of her cane. "That'll be enough, girl. You have no reason to be so ungrateful. At least in this position, I'm keeping you from making a living on your back."

Oh, dear lord. The heat of embarrassment went through Cora's cheeks. "Of course I am grateful to you." *But that doesn't mean I don't wish you at least a tiny bit of misfortune for your acerbic tongue.* At the last second, she stopped herself from rolling her eyes and tamped down the wild urge to say exactly what was on her mind. Being nine and twenty was hardly *girl* status any longer, and neither did her current circumstances dictate a certain treatment. "Do you see your friends?" she asked instead, as they both peered inside the crowded drawing room.

"Yes, I do." The widow waved a gloved hand to someone across the room. "I shall require your assistance promptly at midnight."

"I will wait for you at these doors." After sweeping her notice about the area, her gaze alighted on a grouping of two delicate chairs with light blue velvet cushions waiting at the end of the short corridor. "In fact, I will be there should you need me later in the evening." A longcase clock struck the nine o'clock hour, and she stifled another groan. "I hope you have a delightful time tonight."

Three hours until I can go home. The megrim worsened slightly. *Let us hope I don't need to retch before the night is over.*

"Thank you for your regard." The widow's expression softened. "Be certain you eat something tonight." Just when Cora thought the woman actually cared, Mrs. Bromington went on to say, "It simply won't do to have you drop from weakness or hunger when I need you to escort me downstairs later."

Of course. She pasted a smile onto her stiff lips. "I certainly won't fail at my position. Perhaps I will pop into the library downstairs and hope the quiet will help with the megrim."

"Good girl. It's a difficult time to be sacked, what with the wealthy in Town leaving for their summer estates soon." Then the widow moved into the drawing room to mingle with the guests already milling about.

Cora fumed for a few seconds while she watched her charge talk and laugh with acquaintances. Why did the woman treat her with such contempt? Though, to be fair, perhaps she was still grieving over losing her husband not so long ago, or perhaps the fact she didn't see her children that much caused her to be maudlin and lash out. She snorted and turned away, moving back into the corridor. Truth be told, Mrs. Bromington was just a vile, unhappy, bitter woman and that was why her family didn't wish to gather round her much.

Truly, it was a wonder she retained any friends at all.

Her parents had known—and were currently battling— various hardships, but neither of them treated the people about them with anything less than respect. Perhaps it depended on the temperament of the person; no doubt Alice Bromington had been born sour. Not that it mattered. Surely, this position and the need to make a living wouldn't prove permanent. Soon enough she could be away from the widow, but right now, it was her lot, and she had to make the best of it. Because the admission of a megrim hadn't been a lie, Cora slowly traversed the staircase, holding the skirting of her jonquil satin gown away from her feet lest she accidentally trip and take a tumble. The widow wouldn't like that, would she?

By the time she gained the lower floor, many of the guests had already migrated to the second floor and the drawing room, which left her the freedom to explore where she would in peace. The townhouse was significantly larger than the widow's, but was what wealth would bring a person, yet locating the library was easier than she'd anticipated. With one last glance about the immediate area to make certain she was alone, Cora pressed the polished brass door latch, pushed the wooden panel open, and then slipped inside the room.

Immediately, the scents of leather, ink, and old paper assailed her nose. Quickly and quietly, she closed the door behind her. The farther she moved into the room, the more relaxed she became. This was what Papa's library at Landover Hall used to feel like before he'd been forced to sell off some of the more expensive volumes. Those had been sad days, for each loss of a published work had stabbed Cora in the soul.

But this room! Oh, it was glorious, and with only a couple candles lit in tall silver candlesticks, shadows swallowed most of the room. Groupings of leather furniture rested throughout the room, and the sofas, chairs, and footrests were all quite inviting. Small, round tables inlaid with both rose and ivory were scattered through, some containing short stacks of books, some decorated with bric-a-brac, while other lower tables waited to be in service. Easily she could envision the owner of the space taking tea in this room or even enjoying snifters of brandy or glasses of other spirits while reading to his heart's content.

If only she had that luxury as well.

For the moment, it was enough that she'd been able to slip into the room. The silence was a stark contrast to the noise and merriment throughout the rest of the house. At the side, French, paned doors opened to a side garden that would no doubt lead to the rear garden behind the house. Moving across the room, her slippers made no sound on the luxuriously thick carpeting. Once at the doors, she turned the latch and easily pushed one of them open. Immediately, a cooling breeze came into the room, and she gladly lifted her face to it, breathed in that fresh air. It reminded her so much of being in the countryside that another wave of homesickness came over her.

I hope Papa is doing better now that some of the burden is being lifted from his shoulders.

For long moments, she stood at the garden door while peering out into the darkening night, but before she could move away and settle into one of the inviting sofas, the soft snick of the corridor door opening and closing seemed to echo in the silent space.

She frowned. Who the devil could that be? Mrs. Bromington come to harangue her again? Truth be told, she didn't much care, for this was her time, so she continued to focus her attention on the shadow-filled garden, briefly contemplated fleeing from the townhouse and never returning to the widow's employ.

Cologne betrayed the intruder as a male. The subtle hints of clean freshness tickled her nose, accompanied by the smell of sea and salt. It was one of her favorite things about living in the countryside, but she frowned, for the cologne was quite familiar, both comforting and arousing.

"There you are. I had been searching for you since the rout began."

Oh, no!

Now she knew why the scent made her feel that way, and the sound of *his* voice reinforced that knowledge. Gooseflesh popped along her skin, but she still didn't turn around; she couldn't, not while his very presence here had immediately thrown her into a storm of confusion, rage, and need. Deciding to play along in order to determine what exactly he wanted, she said, "Oh? Why is that?"

"You are beyond tempting in that yellow gown, so I followed you, wishing to have you alone."

The whisper of his voice, the resurrection of his scent in her memories, the way his presence filled the space, all left her at sixes and sevens. "Did you believe *I* wished to be alone with *you?*" Already, they were flirting with scandal, and if Mrs. Bromington discovered her with this man, there would be hell to pay, and loads of it, yet it was somewhat flattering to know he'd deliberately sought her out after the horrid history between them.

"I had hoped, of course." He came up behind her, and when he placed his hands on her upper arms, pulled her back against the hard wall of his chest, sensations threatened to swamp her.

"Though I realize we have only seen each other socially, I wondered if you would be amiable to me paying my addresses to you."

Wondering what had become of his gloves flew right out her head as she was presented with this riddle. What was this, then? The odd string of words yanked her out of the warm cocoon she'd temporarily fallen into. Cora frowned. Obviously, he had mistaken her for someone else. Her emotions went crashing into the pit of her belly. Keeping her voice low so he wouldn't be able to identify her, she said, "Well, Mr. Wetherford, that is quite an offer…"

Obviously, he harbored no feelings of guilt or regret. The thought sent a stab of annoyance through her chest.

"If you must use a title, I am Captain Wetherford, but I would prefer you to call me Peregrine when we are alone." When he nuzzled the crook of her shoulder, Cora froze.

Dear heavens! He used to always do that to her, and the fact he did so now had butterflies waking in her lower belly that she thought long dead. "A captain." That *was* surprising, for when she'd known him, he had only recently joined the navy. No buying a commission for him. That integrity had been one thing she'd adored about him… until he'd erased that by abandoning her. "How exciting. Are you in London on leave?" One of her fears at the time had been he'd choose the sea over her.

"I am retired now." The barely there glide of his lips over her skin had tingles playing down her spine. "And I believe I am ready to settle into the next phase of my life."

"How lovely." The megrim all but forgotten, Cora leaned slightly back against him, letting herself sink into the warmth of him, and as his arms came around her and he continued to place feather weighted kisses along the side of her neck, she softly moaned. Yes, this was beyond wrong, but it had been such a long time since she'd seen him. If she were honest with herself, buried under the hurt and resentment and anger, she had truly missed him, for he had been the first and only man she'd given her heart to. "The stories you must have to tell." Though he obviously thought her another, part of her was curious to know how far this charade would go.

"Aye, and I would like to share them with you if you wish to enter into a courtship." When he gave her earlobe a light bite, Cora nearly melted into a puddle at his feet.

Drat him! He would give such attention to another woman, intend to marry said woman where he had fled from her, but had hardly given her a thought? Pushing the musings from her mind, she hoped she had misunderstood him and that he knew who she was this whole time, that he had deliberately sought her out. *Cora, girl, you are a ninny. Stop that at once!*

"Mmm," was all she could manage, for he'd moved his hands up to cup her breasts, and she teetered on the edge of being lost. How well she remembered how he'd made her feel years ago, how lovely that madness had been when they'd coupled. This was exactly the distraction she needed to wash the bitterness of her employer away.

"Ah, I do adore a responsive woman," he whispered against the shell of her ear. The captain continued with his caresses, and the moment he applied the slightest pressure, Cora shook with need. "Let us discover if we are compatible carnally, for that will make everything else much easier."

"True." She hoped he hadn't recognized the sound of her voice, and if he hadn't, damn him. Did he not remember how her body had felt against his, in his hands? Then flutters of pleasure swamped her, for as he continued to tease her breasts through the thin satin of her gown, her nipples hardened, and need for him intensified. How she wanted to feel his hands, his fingers, his lips all over her body! At least once more, to remember and perhaps in an effort to forget as well. As she made a sound of encouragement at the back of her throat, he chuckled, brushed his lips along her nape and then slowly slipped the fingers of one hand beneath her bodice, beneath the shift and stays to rub along that pebbled tip. "Mmm, yes." Of their own accord, her hips bumped into his, and there was no mistaking the rampant evidence of his desire.

"Ah, sweet Cecily, you feel all too wonderful." He followed the erroneous identification by a teasing pinch to the nipple and a light nip at the crook of her neck.

Dear heavens, the man hasn't lost his potency.

"I could say the same of you," she said in a barely audible whisper, for despite her annoyance with him and his apparent inability to remember her, she wanted him, wanted this, for it was as her maid had said. With the right man, it was truly remarkable.

"Will you allow me to discover that sweet nectar only you possess?" As he spoke, Peregrine slipped his free hand down the front of her gown, past her abdomen to rest briefly as her mons, but when he drew up her skirting, Cora trembled.

"I… I suppose…"

"I shall take that as permission."

This is wrong, this is wrong! But why did it feel so incredibly right? Perhaps she was naught but a desperate woman, for she nestled her body closer to his, and when his fingers wandered through the curls between her thighs, she widened her stance slightly to give him greater access. "Touch me, Peregrine." Would that soft utterance be what gave her away?

"So silky, so lovely, so wet," he crooned into her ear. The warmth of his breath, the rhythmic circling of the swelling button at her center had the power to sweep her away into a world she hadn't visited in far too long. Regardless of the consequences such a thing might bring if she allowed him to go much further. "Do you want me that much, then?"

"I have always wanted you." Perhaps had never stopped, and that was the crux of her problems. He had already made his choice, and she hadn't been it. She needed to move forward in her life; so did he. Though she shook with lust and need, Cora found her backbone and her self-respect. "Enough. This is wrong." Shoving away from him, when their connection was severed, she turned about with a half-sob half-cry of regret. "I am not who you apparently think I am, Captain Wetherford."

"Shit!" Shock reflected in his eyes and lined his face as he stared at her. "Cora?" He shook his head. "I thought you were Miss Beaufort; you are wearing the same color gown as she, have similar hair."

Truly, the man was a nodcock if he couldn't figure out at least subtle differences, yet shock slammed into her all the same, for she'd almost let him do unspeakable things to her out of need and memories. "I never thought to see you again, and now I discover you are back in London, wishing to not only court another—marry her—but also fall into scandal with her. Willingly, this time, apparently." Why hadn't he wished to do that with her?

"I... I..." He held up a hand, palm outward. "I don't know what to say except to apologize profusely."

Cora shook her head. Heat burned through her cheeks. "I assumed you had sailed away—ran away—like a coward because you couldn't bear the thought of marrying me, of marrying anyone. Yet that has just been proved untrue." She bit her bottom lip as she took a step backward, and then another until she was nearly through the French doors and into the garden. "After what you did to me, after how my reputation was shredded, I don't wish to see you again."

So saying, she fled into the garden as tears filled her eyes. *I am naught but a fool, and I do not need that man.*

CHAPTER FOUR

Peregrine barely had time to acknowledge what had happened before Cora charged back into the library, marched straight up to him, raised her right hand, and then delivered a hard slap to his right cheek. Obviously, when she said she didn't wish to see him again, that was a lie.

Almost as much as the absence of her former meek and mild disposition when he'd known her. "I suppose I deserved that." He put a hand to his stinging, hot cheek. "Hallo, Cora."

God, could he prove more of a nodcock?

"Of course you deserved it, you scoundrel!" Though she kept her voice low, there was no mistaking the animosity, the feeling, in her voice. She raised her hand as if she would slap him again, but appeared to think the better of it, for she retreated a few steps, her chest heaving. Then, a frown tugged at the corners of her mouth as her gaze roved over his face.

Standing near one of the candles, he no doubt appeared grotesque in the play of light and shadows. "What?" Part of him steeled, for she must have noticed the wreck of his face. Though he wanted nothing more than to hide, Peregrine stood his ground.

I'm tired of hiding.

"Dear heavens, Peregrine, what happened to you in the years

since I last saw you?" The utterance was said in a horrified whisper as she peered more intently at him. Her eyes rounded, the blue irises darkened slightly, and she pressed her lips together. This time when she closed the distance between them and lifted her hand, she didn't slap him. Instead, she drew her gloved fingertips along his cheek, the side of his head, let them drift over the curve of his ear and she sucked in a breath. "What you must have suffered…"

"Stop." Even though their close proximity and her fleeting touch left him confused, he detested the emotions bordering on sadness in her eyes. He grabbed her hand, held it away from his face. "I don't need or want your pity." If there was annoyance or perhaps disappointment in his voice, he couldn't help that fact.

"I wasn't giving it." Cora wrenched her hand away, took a few steps backward while she bounced her gaze between his scars and his eyes. "I simply wished to understand, to know what happened, but since you apparently know best, I'll leave you to that misery."

Shock plowed through Peregrine's chest. "I might be many things, but I am *not* miserable." The woman had no right to say he was such.

"Ah, so then that assumes you attend social events with regularity. Is that correct?" One of her finely feathered blonde eyebrows went up in challenge.

Dear God. She had matured since he'd last seen her. At some point, she'd developed womanly curves that would drive vicars to drink in excess or monks to flirt, and the turbulent emotions in her blue eyes spoke of secrets and sadness that oddly enough tugged at his chest. "I… Well, I…" Quite possibly, he didn't know her any longer. "That is to say…" The words flew out of his mind and refused to jump off his tongue. Why was he so flustered around her?

Slowly, she shook her head. An expression of confusion lined her face. "Why did you have to come back, Perry? I was perfectly fine thinking you didn't exist, that you had perished in some heroic death far away. At least it would have explained many things. Perhaps it would have put an end to the cycle of anger and fear and guilt and regret I keep putting myself through."

"I had no idea." Cora was the only person in the world who used a shortened version of his name, usually when she was aggravated or exasperated by him.

"Of course not. How could you?" She threw up a hand. "You destroyed my life!"

"I'll admit, I didn't give thought to any of that when I left…" That was perhaps the wrong thing to say, and never had he been at such a loss for words as he was now. Not knowing how to respond in the face of her anger, he studied her instead. The jonquil hue of the gown suited her pale complexion, but it was the square bodice that allowed the upper slopes of her breasts to peek out that captured his attention. The remembered feel of how her pebbled nipple had felt or of how her honeyed heat had dampened his fingers sent a shiver of need down his shaft.

"Have you *nothing* to say?" When she propped her hands on her rounded hips and glared, he gave his head a slight shake to clear his thoughts. "Standing there after violating me when you assumed I was another woman? And now nothing is apparently in your head except broken sentences?"

Bloody hell, when did she learn how to dress down a man?

Where had the woman he'd pledged his life to gone, and why had this near-shrew of a woman replaced her? Though he wasn't nodcock enough to think he'd hadn't a hand in that change, he refused to dwell on it now. "I apologize." What the devil was there to say? How had he not been able to ascertain the difference between women? In the dim candlelight, golden and caramel strands of her hair almost glimmered within the blonde mass. Emotions shadowed her cornflower eyes, too many for him to discern just one. "That wasn't well done of me." To be fair, he hadn't known what Miss Beaufort felt like in his arms, and he hadn't noticed perfume at the time.

"What wasn't?" Clearly, she wouldn't allow him a reprieve.

He huffed with frustration. "For daring to put my hands on you, even if you *did* give permission," he couldn't help but add, and when her eyes narrowed, he instantly regretted that decision. Heat went up the back of his neck, for the whole thing was quite embarrassing. "Also, for thinking you were Miss Beaufort. It was an egregious error."

"Yes, it was." Cora crossed her arms beneath her breasts, which only pushed those rather full charms closer to the edge of the bodice. "Yet now you stand here before me, as big as you please, and there is no regret or claims to responsibility for what you did to me three years ago? Instead, you are more concerned about courting someone new."

"It *has* been over three years." Of course she hadn't forgotten. Why would she? When she nearly sprang at him, he took a step backward. Yes, he'd broken their engagement without an explanation, and yes, that action had no doubt ruined her reputation, and yes, he'd returned to London without a word, but couldn't the past remain just that? "I assumed we had both moved on from that time."

"That is exactly what I'd expect a man to say. No one ever looks askance at a man in such situations." To his mortification, her chin trembled. *That* he remembered about her. When she was upset, it always manifested with her chin first, but to her credit, she stared him down and shot daggers from her eyes. "I was forced to pick up the pieces of my life, thanks to you! And also, because of what you did, my family and I had to flee to Bedfordshire in shame." Apparently agitated, she drifted through the open door to the garden beyond.

One broken engagement had the power to do all that? Intrigued yet beleaguered by the hot guilt stuck in his chest, Peregrine trailed after her. Miss Beaufort was temporarily forgotten, for though he had been shocked to his core when he discovered the woman he'd dared to semi-compromise had been Cora, he was somewhat cheered to find out it *had* been her.

The woman he'd never thought to see again, or at least do his best to avoid.

"I don't know what to say that can make any of this better." Truly, he was at a loss, and to be honest, he'd never been gifted in conversing with ladies. It had been a minor miracle he'd courted and secured her hand to begin with. Or perhaps she'd gently led him through the motions, and he'd gladly agreed.

Immediately, the sounds of the night met his ears as he joined her. In many ways, he reveled in the songs of the insects and the soft calls of nocturnal birds. Even the rustle of the breeze in the leaves, for he had missed that while at sea.

"What do you want me to say, Cora?" Perhaps it was best to go straight for the heart of the issue. He wasn't adept at veiled hints.

"Are you daft?" Seconds later, she rounded on him, which had him retreating toward the library doors. "How do you think I felt when you met me on the steps of the church, gave me some rushed and confusing speech about how you'd changed your mind, and then you ran away?" With every accusation, she jabbed her forefinger into his chest. "Who does that to a woman, and one you said you loved?"

She had him over a barrel. "All good questions." As much as he'd hoped this day would never come, here it was, and looking like a tempest in yellow. Peregrine cleared his throat. "There were very specific reasons I had no choice but to leave you that morning," he said in a lowered voice. "But that didn't mean my love for you was false."

An unladylike snort escaped her. "If you truly loved me, you wouldn't have run."

"What makes you think I didn't?" A trace of annoyance stabbed through his chest in a hot wave. "I was going into the navy, Cora! It was an uncertain time when England was bedeviled by the American naval forces. If I perished, I didn't wish for you to mourn me."

Well, damn. That was the first time he'd spoken such things aloud.

"Then why couldn't you have told me that at the time?" Hurt shadowed her eyes, visible in the shadows and the play of moonlight. "I would have understood to a point."

"Would you?" Shaking his head, he frowned. "You were *quite* adamant that we marry, but you never said why. I assumed you wished to be away from your family, that you wanted to immediately start a life together, and that wouldn't have been possible with me receiving my orders that very morning."

Yes, mistakes had been made on both of their parts. There was no going back to correct them now, but perhaps airing the grievances would help.

For long moments, she stared at him while a myriad of emotions danced over her face: anger, longing, sadness, but since he didn't know her private thoughts, he was at a loss of how to help soothe them.

He cleared his throat, for the silence between them was quite deafening, and every second that ticked by, he grew more uncomfortable. "Beyond that, I was terrified."

"Of the navy? At being away from England? The sea?" Only then did he see the thin vermeil chain around her neck and the delicate band of carved ivory that rested on said chain. He'd given her that ring on the afternoon they'd gotten engaged.

Why had she kept it?

"All those things, except for perhaps the sea. God, I miss it so," he added in a barely audible voice. "I was also afraid of what sort of husband I would be, for my father was horrid in that regard." Why he hadn't told her that during their courtship, he couldn't say. "If your father wishes, I shall pay back the dowry he gave to me." That had also been a source of acute embarrassment for Peregrine, for the baron had put one hundred pounds upon her head as dowry. Not a king's ransom by any means, but it was nothing to sneeze at.

"No doubt that would help financially, but it won't solve all the problems... except perhaps make difficulties for you." Cora waved a hand, dismissing the subject. "Mia confided in me that she convinced Papa to waive her dowry, for she never hoped to marry. I suppose that was why he had the funding for mine."

Vaguely, he remembered her sisters, and often had them confused. "She's the one who recently married that scoundrel of a viscount." Thank goodness for gossip.

"Yes, and though he did wreck his reputation and his coffers are bare, Mia maintains she loves him. Perhaps that is all one needs in this life to be happy." The sound of a stifled sob escaped her, and once more a wave of hot guilt swept through his chest. "Unfortunately, what you and I shared wasn't that, neither was it strong enough to survive the challenges we would have faced."

"Cora, I—"

"It doesn't matter now," Cora finally said in a choked whisper, saving him from once more making a cake of himself without the proper words. "You left me in a precarious position, socially and otherwise. The *ton* considered me tainted; the rumors decreed you must have found severe fault with my character if you broke off the engagement on our wedding day." The space of a few heartbeats went by while she battled with her emotions. "I almost wish you would have perished at sea." The tears that welled in her eyes made the blue luminous. "Then you wouldn't be here, taunting me with your courtship of another lady, reminding me of what was taken away from me because you changed your mind."

Damn, he vastly preferred when she railed and ranted at him. That he understood and could counter, but this defeated version of herself tore at his heart, proving that the feelings he'd once had for her hadn't exactly faded. "I didn't change my mind, yet I couldn't bear the thought of leaving you a potential widow before we'd even had a honeymoon period." His throat tightened. "I wanted to ensure you wouldn't be trapped in a mourning period, that you could marry someone else quickly if that was your preference."

"I was in love with you!" The cry she uttered had been propelled by high emotion. Spots of color blazed in her cheeks as she advanced in the face of his retreat. Once more they were back in the library. "What sort of a nodcock were you? Love encompasses everything, Perry. Good or bad, richer or poorer, sickness and health. Everything in between, but we would have had the thought of each other. We could have written letters giving hope and keeping that love alive. There could have been that one splendid night together that might have changed everything." Her voice broke. "But you were selfish and a coward."

"I am not denying that." The urge to take her into his arms for comfort was dashed when she charged past him. She didn't stop until she'd reached the middle of the room. With a sigh, he followed. Always following this woman, yet there was a rightness that was far too disturbing.

Before he could respond, things went from bad to worse when Miss Beaufort appeared at the still open corridor door. "Captain Wetherford? Are you in here? I only just was given the note you left for me."

Bloody, bloody hell.

"Uh, hallo Miss Beaufort." What the devil was he supposed to do now? The thought to get her alone tonight and introduce her to kissing, see how far she might have let him take a passionate embrace to gauge their compatibility seemed gauche in the moment, especially with Cora still staring daggers at him. "I was merely talking to an old… friend."

A swift inhalation of breath from Cora immediately told him that had been the absolute worst thing he could have said.

Why the devil am I not gifted with words or flattery?

"I see." Though from the chit's tone, it was clear she did not as she bounced her gaze between him and Cora, confusion clear in the light blue depths of her eyes.

Eyes that were not deep enough blue at all. Then he frowned. The younger woman did indeed wear the same-colored gown as Cora. She possessed almost the same blonde hair, yet upon second glance, hers didn't glimmer as much as Cora's. *Oh, good God!* The realization smacked into his chest so hard that he stumbled backward a step. He'd chosen Miss Beaufort as a possible candidate for marriage for one reason only—she'd reminded him of Cora at least in looks, but not temperament… or anything else that made his former fiancée unique.

"Uh, could you please wait for me in the corridor, Miss Beaufort? This conversation is nearly concluded." How the devil could he continue a courtship of the young lady now? Certainly not after Cora had come back into his life accidentally.

"Very well, but I am missing the best parts of the rout by taking the chance at scandal with you," she said and there was most definitely a pout in her voice, but she took her leave.

Peregrine relaxed, but only slightly. He could walk away from Cora. Their paths would need never cross again, but… It was so damned confusing. Once Miss Beaufort exited the room, he rested his gaze on Cora. If she were open to resuming their relationship, he would tell the chit they wouldn't suit after all. "I apologize for the interruption."

"Yes, it seems as if you are *very* busy indeed." Sarcasm dripped from her rejoinder.

He ignored that as well as the heat creeping up the back of his neck. "We are both different people, don't you think? Too much has happened in the years apart for us to jump right into a relationship as if nothing happened." It was a large assumption on his part, but he guessed that was what she wanted.

Wasn't it? Surely that was why she was so angry at him.

"Ha! I cannot believe you said that to me."

"I don't understand." Truly, he didn't. "That is why you're angry, correct? Because I might be courting another?" He lowered his voice. "Especially after your responses when I—"

"Stop." She held up a hand, cutting off his flow of unfortunate words. "You have much to learn about women. Especially women still annoyed after being jilted by you." A bitter laugh fell from her lips. "Thinking that I want you now is laughable. After everything you caused to happen?" She laughed again, but there was no mirth in the sound. It scraped across his consciousness like fingernails against a slate. "I wouldn't have you, Peregrine Wetherford, if you were the last man on God's green earth. You have already proven you cannot be trusted."

Shock ricocheted through his tight chest, and his insecurities intensified. "Is it because of my disfigurement?"

"I beg your pardon?" A frown tugged down the corners of her lips. Her gaze flew to the left side of his face. *Something* flickered deep in her eyes, but it was too shadowy in the room to read the emotion. "Of course not. You cannot help what happened to you."

"Then why would you say such a thing?"

"Don't be an arse. Your word means nothing; you promised me a lifetime and gave me naught but scandal and grief instead." For emphasis, she shook her head. A strand of gold fell from its pins to frame her face.

"Miss Hasting!" The annoyed call from what sounded like an older woman echoed in the corridor beyond. "Where the devil have you gotten off to, girl? I'm tired and want to go home."

Ah, Cora's charge.

Her attention darted to the door. "Coming, Mrs. Bromington!" Then she glanced at him. "As I said earlier tonight, I never wish to see you again." Then she marched from the room with her chin at a stubborn tilt and the swish of her skirting about her ankles that put an odd finality to the scene.

"Cora, wait!" Peregrine trotted quickly after her, and when he gained the door, she had slipped an arm about an older woman's waist. "Good evening, ma'am."

The widow—or rather Cora's dragon—gave him a withering look up and down his person. "Best leave Miss Hasting alone. She's not one to linger in the company of men. Got too much responsibility as it is."

There was nothing he could say, especially since Miss Beaufort stared, round-eyed, at everyone suddenly in the corridor. How had life suddenly become more complicated? With a sigh, he approached the younger woman as Cora led her charge around the corner. "I apologize for such an interruption to the evening. Perhaps you would enjoy a lemonade and dancing?" He no longer wished to be alone with her. Much of the daring had faded from it.

"All right." The chit frowned, and an hour ago, he would have found the gesture charming and slightly arousing. "Who was the lady in yellow?"

"Someone I used to know a long time ago." The girl didn't need to know about their prior engagement or how it had ended. Neither did she need to be told that being in Cora's company—regardless of his reception—was cozy and familiar. "Needless to say, she wasn't happy to see me." He offered her his arm, but sighed when her gaze crept to the scars and marks on the left side of his face. Quietly, he moved to her other side and then offered his other arm.

"I think the lemonade would suffice for now, but perhaps you could introduce me to some of your friends if they are in attendance."

Of course, because he was only good enough to be a steppingstone to better offers. The cloying scent of honeysuckle wafted to his nose, making him breathe through his mouth. It wasn't nearly as pleasant as Cora's orange blossom and vanilla perfume.

As he escorted the younger lady to the staircase, there was no doubt in his mind what he needed to do—end the relationship with Miss Beaufort gracefully before it even started. It might make him the biggest dunce London had ever seen, but he wanted to repair things with Cora. The hurt in her eyes had wounded him more deeply than he'd anticipated, and above all, he was a gentleman, even if she didn't think so. To say nothing of the fact that the ring around her neck gave him an odd sense of hope.

If fate were kind, perhaps they could remain friends. After that, only God knew, but he refused to rush his fences.

CHAPTER FIVE

May 21, 1817
Bromington House
Manchester Square
London

THOUGH IT HAD been two days since seeing Peregrine had upset the dullness that her life had become as a companion, she hadn't been successful in evicting him from her mind.

Not that she'd had much time for herself. Since the rout, Mrs. Bromington had been annoyingly demanding, even more than usual. Yet the fact he was in London and a captain to boot kept sending heated anger into her cheeks. How dare he show his face in society as a celebrated sea captain, courting women as if he hadn't a care in the world, while the only way she could attend routs or balls was as a companion.

And, quite frankly, she didn't need the tabbies of the *ton* remembering her name or the old engagement. The complication came because she couldn't forget how those fleeting kisses to her neck had made her feel, and she rather missed that intimacy with him, but on the heels of that came another wave of sadness and grief from the consequences of the last time she'd given herself to him prior to what should have been their wedding day.

"Girl, the game only works if you keep your focus on the cards instead of woolgathering." The censure in her charge's voice yanked her from her thoughts.

"I apologize. Just stewing, I suppose." If she were honest with herself, she tried not to let jealousy eat her alive. Miss Beaufort hadn't been all that beautiful, but she *was* exceedingly young. Perhaps that was what he wanted now in his life.

"You forget, young woman, I have been at this business of living much longer than you. I know when a girl is distracted by a man." Mrs. Bromington shook her head, and the lace edging her widow's cap fluttered. She rapped the knuckles of one hand on the table where they were playing cribbage, or at least her charge was playing while Cora was pretending due to distraction.

"It won't happen again. He is not worth the tears." She frowned at the several cards in her hand. They were a mess, with none of them matching. "In fact, he isn't worth the thoughts, but yet he is there regardless."

"Then you are already defeated, and I won't have that." Mrs. Bromington huffed. She set down her cards, face up, on the table. Of course she had a whole suite. It was rare she ever lost at any card games they played. "By the by, your mind is never on our games. I know you aren't stupid, but you need to apply yourself, or at the very least, square with your life as it is now." After a huff of breath, she held Cora's gaze with hers. "It might not be ideal or the dream you once had for yourself, but you are not on the street nor on your back. That is something."

Perhaps she needed to show more gratitude in her life, even if her charge constantly worked her nerves. "I appreciate this position." She frowned at her cards, then with a sigh, she dropped them upon the table. "I never thought I would be nine and twenty, unmarried and unwanted." It was no doubt a mistake to share that with the widow for it would make her that much more vulnerable, but she couldn't help it. Since she'd arrived in London, she'd been isolated and with no one to talk to except for the maid.

"Some women take immediately in society; some do not. Marriage is no guarantee you will be happy." The older woman shrugged. The jeweled rings on her fingers sparkled in the sunlight streaming into the drawing room from the open windows. "Look at me, for example. I married at eighteen. Gave my husband forty years and four living children, three dead ones, while he spent that time at his clubs or at his textile business. Next thing I know, his heart attacks him three years ago, leaving me a widow and barely knowing the man he was."

"I'm sorry to hear that." It was the first time her charge had ever shared anything of a personal nature, and she was loath to interrupt. The puzzling thing about the widow was the fact that none of her children ever came to visit and she never visited them. Why?

"I can also tell when people lie to me." Mrs. Bromington winked. "Which you are doing now. You have no interest in me beyond the wages I pay."

"That isn't true." Cora frowned at the lady across the table from her. The steel gray curls, the droopy lace cap, the deep lines framing her mouth and her eyes, the wall she built about herself to keep from being hurt, all spoke to someone who had been disappointed in life and was largely dissatisfied. "I always hope you'll find a bit of happiness in this season you are living."

It would make her position a bit easier, anyway.

"Ha. I suppose it is a good thing you don't dissemble well." The widow shook a finger at her. "I also like how you don't let me cow you into submission."

Cora pointed her gaze briefly to the ceiling, but she couldn't help a small smile. "Perhaps your personality stirs my own." Yet she didn't want to become that bitter person later in her own life. "If fate intends to match me with a man, it will."

It was the widow's turn to huff. "Men are only men, and pinning your hopes onto them is a horrible decision."

"So say you, who have a fortune at your disposal. That isn't the experience of most of us." Cora gathered the cards from the tabletop. "My father's health is failing. The taxes on his country estate haven't been paid for more years than I can fathom. The paltry amount of coin I manage to send him monthly, I think, barely helps, and I rather doubt I'll catch the eye of a titled, rich man. Not here at least."

"You have my respect by wishing to help your father, but it is his mess, not yours." Mrs. Bromington shook her head. Truth shone in her faded green eyes. "A word of advice from one who has witnessed the comings and goings of the *beau monde* all her life. Most of those men drink to excess, bed anything in skirts, have the pox or other diseases, and are only loyal to those in power at the moment. Not a brain between them." She tsked her tongue. "You are better than that."

Cora stared as shock moved through her chest at the tiny compliment. "I am trying my best to survive at this point," she admitted. Though it was unlikely she would confide her secrets to her employer, this interlude was lovely and out of character for the widow. "If I could manage to release that dream of romance I've carried around with me since a young girl, I would be much more content."

"That's the spirit, and once you pass the six-month mark with me, perhaps I'll think about traveling the world with you." The widow gave her head an energetic nod. "Nothing worse than traveling with a mopey, moonstruck, or surly companion."

Yes, because surliness or bitterness is quite rare in this household.

The arrival of the butler spared Cora from making a verbal comment.

"Excuse me, Mrs. Bromington, but there is a Captain Wetherford here to see Miss Hasting." One of the man's graying red eyebrows rose as if it was the height of scandalous for a member of the staff to receive a social call. "Should I send him away?"

The heat of embarrassment went through Cora's cheeks as she darted her gaze to her employer. "I am so sorry. I never invited him to call," she said in a whisper.

"Oh, of that I have no doubt, but your eyes say otherwise."

With a cackle of laughter, the widow rose to her feet. She smoothed her hands along the front of her rust-colored dress, took up her ivory-headed cane, and then moved across the room to occupy her favorite chair near the cold fireplace. From that vantage point, she could see the bulk of the drawing room, and nothing ever escaped her eagle-eyed gaze. "I need entertainment for the afternoon since Miss Hasting has proved a lousy card player. Send the captain up, Mr. Riley."

Oh, dear heavens. Panic rose in Cora's throat. She shot to her feet. "I don't wish to see him, Mrs. Bromington."

"I wonder if that is true, but we shall soon see." The widow's grin was this side of disturbing. "Since this is my house and I am bored as well as nosy, I'm going to allow his visit, merely so I can give him a dressing down and make it so he'll never wish to do something as daring as call again."

"Please don't." Cora's hands shook, so she fisted her fingers in her skirting. Today, the pink muslin stamped with tiny green vines didn't lend her confidence.

Mrs. Bromington waved her into the matching chair near hers. "Come now, girl. This will be so awkward and juicy that it will be a lovely interlude." She gestured at the butler. "Go ahead and send him up. Then order a tea service for us."

"At once, Mrs. Bromington." Then the butler departed the room, his tall form slightly bowed at the back.

"If you wish to receive him so badly, at least let me retire to my room," Cora begged as she perched on the edge of the chair. Knots of worry pulled in the pit of her belly, for after the charged words she'd hurtled at Peregrine, there was nothing else to say.

One side of the widow's mouth quirked in a grin. There was a predatory light in her eyes Cora didn't trust. "Hush, girl. I'll do what I please. Since you are my companion, you will remain by my side."

"Why do you delight in making those around you miserable?" Cora asked in a barely audible voice as she pleated a section of her skirting. Perhaps the preliminary bonding from earlier was an abnormality.

"When you reach my age of two and sixty, and widowhood, you'll find you need entertainment. Making people squirm and do my bidding is how I gain amusement." Then her attention pivoted to the door as Peregrine came into the room.

Drat the man's eyes! He was even more handsome in the daylight than he'd been in the shadows of the library the other day. Clad in buff-colored breeches and shiny Hessian boots, the lean and muscled firmness of his legs were unmistakable. Did he regularly ride, or did he prefer to walk in order to take exercise? She didn't know, but she couldn't stop staring at him. The sky-blue waistcoat embroidered with green vines and white birds drew the eye to his flat abdomen, and in the lawn shirt, a navy superfine jacket that emphasized the breadth of his shoulders as well as his wide chest, he was every inch a gentleman about Town. He held a beaver felt-top hat tucked beneath his left arm, and his chestnut hair had been arranged in a popular style without the aid of pomade.

There was no doubt his presence commanded attention from everyone he met, and in that moment, it didn't matter he apparently was tongued-tied. Cora shifted in her chair as their gazes briefly locked, and he slowly moved to the middle of the room. The closer he drew, subtle hints of his cologne or shaving soap teased her nose. As unobtrusively as she could, she took a deep breath and reveled in the scents of salt, the sea, and a hint of perhaps oak. Obviously, she couldn't be clear, but it didn't stop the desire to go over there and sniff his skin until she could identify the notes.

"Good afternoon, Mrs. Bromington. Miss Hasting." The captain executed a slight bow from the waist, but his expression was one of unease as he bounced her gaze between them. "Thank you for allowing me to come up when you had every right to decline my entry."

Well, at least his manners were impeccable. Cora offered a slight nod but gave away no other clue as to how she felt.

Her charge, on the other hand, was much more animated. "Good afternoon, Captain Wetherford." The widow glanced at him as if he were horseflesh at Tattersalls. "Not exactly a looker, are you, with those horrible scars and burn marks."

"Life is sometimes harsh, Mrs. Bromington. Only the strong survive." He brought his free hand to the crisp folds of his cravat, checked the knot, and then dropped the hand to his side where his gloved fingers slowly curled into a fist then relaxed. "However, I appreciate your candor. Far too many people ignore my injuries, when we both know they exist."

Remarkably, the widow smirked. "Best test your mettle straightaway, hmm? What do you want with Miss Hasting?"

There was something to be said for her charge's direct attitude, for Cora was quite curious too. If Peregrine wasn't up to the task, she would destroy him with her acerbic tongue.

"No games with you, eh, Mrs. Bromington? I appreciate that as well. A man knows where he stands in your estimation without games."

She nodded. "I don't believe in playing at such things, and my time is valuable as well."

"Excellent way to live, for life is indeed short." With a slight grin, Peregrine widened his stance, and he was every inch the sea captain. Easily, she could see him standing on the deck of a schooner with the wind riffling through his hair, and the spray of the seafoam dampening his shirt. "As for Miss Hasting, she and I have history together; we were engaged."

"Ah, so that is the secret you've been keeping from me," the widow said as she swung her notice to Cora. She tsked her tongue. "Should have been honest, girl."

"It was an embarrassing time for me," she said in a whisper, desperately trying to ignore Peregrine, but his big presence filled the room. "I had no choice but to put the past behind me when I came to work for you."

The widow thumped the floor with the tip of her cane and once more focused on the captain. "Can I assume you cocked up the relationship in some way?"

Mottled color rose up his neck above his collar. "In hindsight, I could have taken care of things much differently." He glanced at Cora. "As I said the other night, I apologize for the broken engagement as well as other… liberties." After clearing his throat, he spoke again. "Since that accidental meeting at the rout, I haven't done a bang-up job of explaining myself."

For long moments, silence brewed throughout the room. Then Mrs. Bromington poked Cora's shoulder with a forefinger. "What have you to tell him?"

Obviously, the widow wanted her to tell him off, but suddenly, the perverse side of her wished to see the two of them argue. "Perhaps we should give him the opportunity to explain." Would his story change in a new day?

Peregrine shifted his stance, tucked his hat beneath his other arm, and let the fingertips of his left hand drift over his scars. "As I told you two nights ago, I had just received my orders to report and ship out the next day, and I didn't want to leave you a widow should I perish. Above everything, I was frightened of the responsibilities facing me." Honestly shone in his eyes.

"But if you truly loved me to begin with, none of that would have mattered." Tears rose in Cora's throat. She didn't want any of this to play out in front of her employer, didn't want to revisit the whys or wherefores. Not now, not when she was withholding a secret from him that she absolutely didn't want to speak in from of the widow. The truth of the matter was love could have met the challenges. "I meant what I said, Peregrine. I don't wish to see you again."

Pain shadowed his face, gone with his next breath. "While I can understand why you would say that, fate has decreed our paths should cross once more. Can you not put the mistakes of the past behind us to explore a friendship or at the very least so I can explain in my own words and not in front of an audience or a rushed conversation?"

She straightened her spine, for he sounded quite endearing. Part of her resolve crumbled. "That is—"

"No." Mrs. Bromington again thumped the tip of her cane against the floor. "I'm sorry, Captain, but if you think to worm your way back into Miss Hasting's good graces, that won't be allowed." Her frown was fierce as she glared at Peregrine. "She is *my* companion and the best of the lot I've had, so I'm not keen in releasing her. Especially not for a man."

While the captain's eyes widened with shock, Cora snorted. "I am not a prisoner here, Mrs. Bromington."

Although it felt like it sometimes.

"I never said you were, girl, but if you leave this position, I'll make it very uncomfortable for you to find another." The not-so-innocent statement was accompanied by a smile that was just as fierce and frightening as her stare.

A stab of annoyance went through Cora's chest, she blew out a breath. "Why would you do that? You said I was the best of the lot." Did no one appreciate her for merely… her?

The widow shrugged. "I'm old and my family has turned their backs on me despite my money." She chuckled as if that were the funniest joke she'd ever told. "Well, that and the fact I told them the coin would never be theirs because they're far too grasping. Fortunately, I need entertainment more than I require family connection." Yet there was a flicker of pain in her eyes that tugged at Cora's heart.

It seemed everyone was a little broken in this life, and that more compassion was required to keep them all grounded.

Even a widow whom she would like to toss out the window.

"I'm sorry you have such difficult relationships, Mrs. Bromington," Peregrine said in a voice modulated to soothe and placate. "That must rankle at times."

What was the dratted man about now?

"Don't trouble yourself, Captain. They made their decisions. So did I." She waved at him in dismissal. When the butler brought in tea service on a silver tray, she refrained from continuing until the repast was laid on a low table in front of her chair and Cora's. Once Mr. Riley left the room, she blew out a breath. "I am old enough that I have seen everything, outlived my husband and most of my siblings, bore children." She gestured at Cora to start pouring out. "When you reach this age, your days can grow stale and dull, so I like to make people do my bidding because I can."

"Do hush, Mrs. Bromington." Cora handed the widow a teacup. "We are not marionettes, and you are not a puppet master."

"I wouldn't be so certain, girl, though perhaps one of these days I'll compel you to dance." A cackle escaped her before she took a sip of tea. "So, Captain, now you know why I can't release my companion. The girl is my responsibility, and from what I can manage to piece together from everything the two of you *haven't* said, you wounded her greatly."

Cora paused with her hand outstretched as she offered him a cup of tea. What would he say? What did she expect him to?

"I can see you'll be stubborn about this. For the time being, I will retreat, but don't think you have won the war, Mrs. Bromington. I've never been one to run from a fight." Then he dismissed the older woman in favor of glancing at Cora. "I thank you for consenting to see me this afternoon, but know this. I shall call again, for I refuse to leave things at odds between us, regardless of what your dragon has to say."

Slowly, Cora pulled her hand and the teacup back. Without thinking, she took a sip then made a sound of disgust; Peregrine took his tea straight whereas she preferred it sweetened. "Have a lovely afternoon, Captain Wetherford. I wish you luck in your endeavors."

Did that mean she wished to encourage his efforts? It was too early in the conversation to say with any conviction.

After putting his top hat on his head, Peregrine touched the brim, nodded at them both, then took his leave.

"Mark my words, that man has nothing but trouble on his mind," Mrs. Bromington said with a shake of her head.

"I wonder." For long moments, Cora stared at the empty doorway and sipped at the unsweetened tea.

CHAPTER SIX

May 22, 1817
The Albany
London, England

PEREGRINE FROWNED AT his beagle, Matey, then transferred that frown to Charles. The viscount had come to inquire as to plans for the evening.

"Supper at the club, of course, but I have an errand before then—to call on Cora. Except the widow is maddening. There is no way to garner a few minutes with Cora while she's on guard," he complained to them both while scratching the beagle's ears. "And I rather doubt she truly cares about Cora. She merely doesn't wish for Cora to have a life beyond serving her."

His best friend shook his head. "Why do you care? I thought you'd decided to court Miss Beaufort and that Miss Hasting was firmly in your past."

Heat rose up the back of his neck and into his ears. "Yes, I did say that. However, unexpectedly meeting Cora the other night and seeing that I'd only chosen Miss Beaufort due to her being a watered-down version shook me to my core." That had really driven home the fact perhaps he hadn't truly forgotten what she'd once meant to him before he'd destroyed everything.

Viscount Maubrey looked at him with a hefty dose of skepticism. "Interesting how I can see it now that you've mentioned it." When he tsked his tongue, Matey bounded over to Charles' location by one of the windows in the drawing room. After ruffling the dog's fur and playing a mock-chase game, his friend undid the latch on the window and pushed open the glass. "Do you mean to pursue Miss Hasting again, or is what you are after merely closure?"

"Interesting question." Peregrine rubbed his fingers over his eyes. What exactly did he want from Cora? "When I accidentally misidentified her the other night, there had been an undeniable connection between us, which made sense since it was her."

"Then she dressed you down properly and ordered you from her life." The viscount meandered over to the sideboard and selected a cut-crystal glass. "Yet you made the decision to pay a call on her yesterday knowing full well the dragon she plays companion to wouldn't let you past the entrance to her den. Why?"

"I don't know." Yes, confusion currently swirled through his mind. "I'm days away from opening my shop, and that should excite me, but ever since I've returned to London permanently, I have felt there is something missing from my life." He moved over to the window, took deep lungfuls of semi-fresh air as the sounds of pedestrian and carriage traffic drifted to his location from outside. "I miss the excitement and adventure and mystery of the sea, and the only thing that ever came close to that was being in Cora's company."

"All of that is well and good, but you haven't answered my question." One of Charles' eyebrows rose in inquiry. "What do you want from Miss Hasting?"

God, why was this so difficult to ascertain? He kept his gaze on two young ladies on the pavement walking an exuberant Corgi. "At the moment, I want to make amends."

"Why?" Crystal clinked against crystal while the viscount poured out a measure of brandy.

"After she left the rout that night, and after I gave a mangled mess of an explanation of what had occurred to Miss Beaufort, a few people started conversations and a couple of them asked if I was the same man who'd been engaged to Miss Hasting years before." He turned away from the window to regard his best friend. "When I confirmed it, attitudes shifted and changed. In some corners, I was hailed a hero, but in others, I was a scoundrel."

"And?" Charles watched him from over the rim of his brandy glass.

"It made me feel more of a heel than I already do." He despised knowing he'd destroyed Cora's life and her chances for a future. Perhaps she could have been married by now if it hadn't been his careless actions that had caused her family to flee London. "I want to make amends, perhaps find redemption in her eyes."

"Why do you care so much? There is no need for you to ever see Miss Hasting again; you said it yourself. She is a companion. Your paths will never cross, yet you are driven to seek her out regardless that a handful of days ago, you were hellbent on courting Miss Beaufort." Charles sipped from his glass. "Does it go deeper than just redemption and forgiveness?"

Fragments of that night at the rout came back to him. The scent of her, the satiny warmth of her skin beneath his lips, the soft sounds she'd made in encouragement or pleasure with barely exploring her all worked to send a shiver of interest along his shaft.

"Honestly, Charles, I think I may still harbor feelings for her. Walking away from her on the morning of our wedding day was the biggest mistake of my life, and I didn't realize it until I saw her again."

Perhaps that made him a nodcock or a scoundrel, for he'd been away at sea for three years, and though thoughts of Cora had haunted him during that time, he'd been skilled in either ignoring those musings or shoving them to the back of his mind and keeping them in a box. He'd had a job to do while in the navy, and he'd climbed the ranks quickly due to his determination and focus. Distractions would have meant his downfall. When his injuries had sent him back to England, the urge to seek her out had nearly overwhelmed him at times, but he'd been too much of a coward, and now with his disfigurement, he suspected he wasn't good enough for her.

"Ah, now we're digging to the heart of the matter. You love her?"

"It is… complicated. Let us just say there is the possibility of that."

"I see." Charles came across the floor and then dropped into a leather chair. Immediately, Matey bounded over the carpet to plant himself on the toes of the viscount's boots. "Do you believe Miss Hasting will return your feelings?"

"Ha." Peregrine's chuckle was a bitter affair. "There is a good possibility she hates me to the end of time, but there are secrets and longing in her eyes that give me pause. Because of that, I believe there is a chance, a tiny hope, and what is more, she didn't shrink in revulsion when she saw the wreck of my face, only seemed concerned. I mean to pick at that until something gives." He shrugged. "If, at that time, she is adamant that she wants nothing else to do with me, I shall wish her well and go on my way."

"You mean bury yourself in your watch repair shop until the constant ticking drives you into insanity." Charles tempered the statement with a grin. "Listen, my friend. I didn't save your arse on that ship only for you to toss it away on an impossible endeavor that will ultimately cause you renewed pain."

"I appreciate that." Peregrine dropped into the matching chair. "Without you, I wouldn't be here, and I haven't forgotten my roots, but I can't help but feel there is something else for my destiny, and it in some way includes Cora." He tapped his chest with his fingertips. "That intuition is what I relied on throughout my time in the navy, and it has never steered me wrong."

"Very well." The viscount nodded. "Then I will do what I can to support you."

"Excellent. Now if only Cora will come 'round that easily." His grin felt entirely too cheeky. "But I do enjoy a challenge, and I've never had the opportunity to slay a dragon."

"Go carefully. I'd rather not see you further broken." Once more, Charles frowned. "Women come and go, but friendship and the love therein will endure long past everything else. I've heard tales that Mrs. Bromington has destroyed stronger men and women than you."

Peregrine leaned over and grasped his best friend's shoulder. "Fear not, Maubrey. I look forward to the fight. My sword has sat rusting for far too long. At least it will give me a purpose."

And that had been sorely lacking since his naval career ended.

Bromington House
Manchester Square
London

WITH HIS HEAD full of determination and a heart full of courage, around midday, Peregrine put Matey on a leather lead, and since it was a rare fair day, he decided to walk the mile and a half from his rooms in Piccadilly to Manchester Square. The dog needed to exercise his legs, and truth be told, so did he. The walk was pleasant and refreshing, and as he passed Berkley Square, Grosvenor Square and then further up, Bond Street, he couldn't help but whistle a jaunty tune as he went.

By the time he arrived at Manchester Square, his confidence was quite high.

"Ahoy, Matey, there is Number 12. Put on your most charming face," he said to the dog as he pushed open the wrought iron gate and urged the beagle up the short walkway to the red-painted door. Seconds later, his rap on the panel was answered by the same grim scare of a tall butler he'd met yesterday.

"Good afternoon, Mr. Riley. I am here to call on Miss Hasting."

The man peered down his long nose at him. "I am sorry, Captain Wetherford, but Mrs. Bromington is not seeing visitors at this time."

He tamped down on the urge to curse. "I didn't ask to see her. I would like to talk with Miss Hasting."

Matey whined at the delay. He pulled at his lead, clearly anxious to go inside.

"I have my orders, Captain. When Mrs. Bromington isn't receiving, no one else is either." Then the door swung closed with a finality that stuck in Peregrine's craw.

Unable to loiter on the step, he turned away and retreated with Matey up the walkway. When they gained the pavement beyond, he frowned up at the brick façade of the house. At the second-floor window which was the drawing room, movement at the glass indicated someone watched him. Was it the dragon or Cora?

With no way to tell for certain, he began the walk back to the building where his set was located.

"This is but one battle, Matey, and though we were defeated, I am quite tenacious and refuse to be routed by a crotchety widow."

Half an hour later saw him try again. Once more he'd walked to Manchester Square, and on this trip, Matey was more interested in sniffing every bush, tree, and gatepost along the way. Peregrine didn't mind, for he had restless energy crawling through his veins as well.

The second attempt at the door was met with defeat the same as the first. He held up a gloved hand, preventing the door from closing in his face. "When will the widow be open to receiving this afternoon?"

To his credit, the butler's lips twitched, but a grin or a laugh never materialized. "I couldn't begin to say, Captain Wetherford.

She is quite unpredictable."

Or rather she is all too predictable.

"Inform your employer this will not deter me." With a definite growl in his voice, he turned Matey around and retreated.

The door closed soundly in his wake.

"Well, now the dragon has stoked my ire," he told his beagle as both stared at the wooden panel that had barred them entry. As soon as he cleared the gate and began his journey along the pavement back the way he'd come, an object came hurtling onto the pavement not three feet in front of him. "What the devil?"

With a joyful bark, Matey gladly retrieved the item and brought it back to Peregrine with a proud trot with a lady's slipper firmly wedged in his mouth.

"What have you got there?" He knelt on one knee in front of his dog in order to extract the slipper from the mouth before it was completely destroyed. As it was, there was only a slight scratch to the navy satin, and the sole was thoroughly used. Tied to the footwear with a length of twine was a folded piece of paper. "How exceedingly odd."

Matey barked, nudged the slipper with his nose. Clearly, he expected his treat to be returned.

As he stood, Peregrine unfolded the half sheet of stationery.

Captain,

I'm sorry Mrs. Bromington is being a stubborn arse today, as per usual. She is unusually agitated. However, she regularly takes a nap at three o'clock, so please return then, and I will make certain I was conveniently taking a walk at the same time.

With respect,
Cora

When he glanced upward, a window on the third floor was open and Cora herself stood at the window. She gave him a quick wave, put a finger to her lips signifying silence, and then just as quickly vanished. No doubt she was summoned by the dragon.

"It seems our luck is about to turn," he told the dog as he tucked both the note and the slipper into the pocket of his jacket. He tugged on the lead, prompting the dog to once more head back to where they'd started. "If the widow thinks she'll come out the victor, she can think again, for I am as stubborn as she. And now I have proof it isn't Cora who is asking her to send me away."

After clearing his head with a repast of tea and honey cakes while Matey wolfed down bits of chopped chicken and copious amounts of water, he rang for the curricle he owned but made payments on. The pair of carefully matched bay mares had been hand-selected by him, and after he'd secured the set at The Albany, he'd bought the horses, which also meant he had to pay to house them in the mews at the back of the building.

The one saving grace was the fact that Charles had already gone home, so he didn't bear witness to Peregrine's two defeats.

When he entered his curricle with Matey sitting on the seat beside him, he guided the mares along the street, and this time the short jaunt across Mayfair took no time at all. Three houses down from the one in which the dragon resided, he spied Cora strolling along the pavement.

"Good afternoon, Miss Hasting!" If his call was more excitable than normal, he couldn't help it, for his confidence level had rebounded after the first two rebuffs. "Fancy a ride through Mayfair?"

To her credit, she made a big show of glancing up and down the street, but there was hardly any pedestrian traffic. "What a lovely surprise to see you, Captain Wetherford," she said as she stood on the pavement, her face shaded by the brim of her straw bonnet. The violet hue of her dress made her seem like a summer flower, yet the color suited her petite frame. A matching satin ribbon was the only frippery that decorated the headgear. A touch of lace that lined the modest bodice drew his notice to her décolletage that was more tempting than he remembered. "It is indeed a wonderful day for a drive."

He couldn't help his grin while at the same time he exited the vehicle and came around to her side of it. "Does that mean you'll consent to go 'round Mayfair with me?"

Matey added his encouragement by giving an excited series of barks.

"Well, it *is* one of my days off." Cora came slowly toward the curricle. "Will we return within the hour? Mrs. Bromington only sleeps for an hour, possibly ninety minutes, and then she orders tea. That is when I read aloud to her from the book of her choice, so I can't come up missing."

"But you just said it was your day off." Truly, the dynamics between the two were confusing.

She shrugged. A trace of hopelessness skated over her face before she banished it beneath annoyance. "The widow only sometimes honors it."

Shock rolled through his gut and brought hot guilt on its heels. It was his fault she held this position and experienced very nearly the same treatment as a poor relation. "I promise I'll have you back before the dragon awakens." He tightened his fingers on the reins when the horses became antsy. "I also promise not to make an arse of *myself*."

For long moments, she held his gaze. Finally, she nodded. "You had better pray that Mrs. Bromington doesn't hear about this."

"She is *not* your keeper, and you are allowed to have a life of your own," Peregrine said as he assisted her into the curricle. A whiff of orange blossom and vanilla went into his nose, but she said nothing in response. "You are a member of the *beau monde*, Cora. You needn't act as if you are from the laboring class."

"I have responsibilities that determine otherwise." Then the whole of her attention landed on Matey as Peregrine resumed his spot on the bench inside the curricle. "Who is this charming fellow?" A giggle escaped her when the beagle immediately climbed into her lap and gave an enthusiastic lick to her chin.

His chest squeezed from the sound. For far too long, it had only haunted his memories. "His name is Matey, and ever since I got out of hospital and finally found a home on land, he's been my constant companion." It was a tight fit inside the vehicle, and his shoulder brushed hers. Awareness went through his body in a quick wave. "My first mate, as it were."

"How delightful!" She busied herself with giving the dog all the pets he wanted, and he responded as if he'd never had attention paid to him before. When she turned her head and glanced at Peregrine, he was temporarily at a loss for words. "Why have you been so insistent about calling on me? Wouldn't most men leave well enough alone?"

"I am not most people." The depths of her blue eyes beckoned like a lake in the summertime. "I wished to give you my sincere apologies for the wrongs and scandal I inadvertently thrust you into when I abandoned you on our wedding day." There was no use in delaying the mission.

Though his left side was to her right and there was no hiding his scars and burn marks, never once did she act as if he disgusted her.

"I appreciate the honesty. You and I were far too emotionally compromised the other night." Cora transferred her attention ahead of them on the road. The swish of the bay mare's tails punctuated the silence that had sprung between them. The delicate tendons in her throat worked with a hard swallow. "For so long I hated you, Perry. Hated what you did to me, hated that you were able to go on and have a life that you apparently enjoyed, without me and without consequence."

"Understandable." He could hardly force the word from a tight throat. "However, I am beginning to see what you went through, and how people perceive each of us separately following the engagement. And..." This was one of the most difficult things he'd ever done in his life. "Facing peril on the sea I could do, stare down danger without a flinch, but knowing you are forced to be companion to a dragon, feeling the crushing weight of guilt every day that goes by I simply don't know how to fight."

Matey, ever attuned to his moods, whined. He left Cora's lap to climb into his. The swipe of his warm tongue to Peregrine's chin made him feel a modicum better.

Silence roiled between them for long moments. He couldn't see the emotions in her eyes or on her face due to the shallow brim of her bonnet, but her gloved fingers, clasped tightly in her lap, spoke to her internal torment.

"Then you wished to speak with me, to make things right between us merely so that *you* will feel better." It wasn't a question.

"What? No, of course not." He huffed, prepared to take umbrage, but then another whine from his beagle and a thump of his tail tempered the reaction. "Well, yes, I would like to not feel tortured all the time. However, I wanted to make amends to you. I… I miss at least the friendship we used to enjoy." On the verge of babbling, he guided the horses down Bond Street. "I understand that I might not be your favorite person any longer, and I deserve your ire if you still wish to churn it, but at least know that I'm dreadfully sorry for what happened, and that I wish I could turn back the time and make it right."

"If that were to happen, would you follow your orders, or would you have married me, let us have that one night before you left?" The inquiry was couched in a choked whisper, and she stiffened on the bench beside him.

"Definitely I would have married you, given you a wedding night you wouldn't have soon forgotten, but the lure of the sea will always be part of me."

"You will go back?" This time she turned her head and sought out his gaze once more and there was a blush in her cheeks. Had she thought about said wedding night?

"I don't believe so, though I do miss the sound of the waves at times." He gathered the reins into one hand so he could pat Matey with the other. "Viscount Maubrey has invited me to his country property that has a view of the sea if the craving grows too acute."

"It must have been difficult for you, giving up something you loved through no fault of your own."

Did she refer to her or captaining his ship? He was far too much a coward to ask. "Indeed."

She frowned as she glanced about the narrowed, cobblestone streets lined with shops where people milled about on the pavement. "Why are we in this portion of Mayfair?"

"I wish to show you something." With his nerves fairly humming with nervous energy, Peregrine guided the horses into the cul-de-sac and then tugged on the reins in front of the still empty shop. "Do you see that space there? The one with the brown paper covering the window?"

"Yes, why?"

"I'm renting that shop. This time next week, I will be repairing pocket watches and selling nautical instruments." When he shrugged, his shoulder brushed hers, and another wave of heated awareness danced over his skin. He grinned when she looked at him. "On longer voyages, I learned how to take apart pocket watches and some smaller clocks, find out how they worked, and then put them back together. It's a talent I honed, that cleaning and repairing. Oddly enough, I enjoy it and it keeps my mind from spitting back anxiety or fear."

Compassion jumped into her eyes. "Do you often suffer from such?"

"Sometimes. More now that I look like this." He gestured to the side of his face.

"Please don't think less of yourself." When Cora lifted a gloved hand and lightly rested it against that side of his face, he stifled a gasp. "Has it made you stronger? I wouldn't doubt it, but you have also weathered that particular storm and now stand as a testament to that strength and a beckon of encouragement for other victims of war and military service."

"You don't believe I'm a monster?" The question was asked in a low voice as he leaned toward her.

"I do not." Her gaze briefly dropped to his mouth. "You are still the handsome man I used to know, and perhaps you've grown even more so. Don't let small-minded people demean your confidence." As she talked, she moved slowly toward him, and in the crowded space, it didn't take long for that distance to be closed.

"Thank you for that. I am quite conscious of how I appear to others, which is probably another reason I've avoided society events." With each word, his lips nearly brushed hers. It wouldn't take much to steal a kiss.

"Everyone has opinions, and most don't matter," she whispered. The heat of her breath warmed his cheek, his lips, and her fingers slipped from his cheek to his nape.

Dear God, he wanted—needed—to kiss her, to remind himself there might still be a sliver of a chance. Maneuvering around the beagle in his lap, he snaked his free hand to the side of her neck. Barely had his lips met hers when Matey, apparently miffed because no one paid attention to him, surged up between them, and he found himself with dog hair stuck to his lips and inside his mouth. "Bloody hell, Matey!"

A string of giggles came from Cora, but she also discreetly wiped at her mouth with the back of a gloved hand. "Oh, come here, you jealous little doggie." She pulled the beagle into her lap, uncaring about the dog hairs the animal shed upon her. When she met Peregrine's gaze, she offered him a small grin. "Though I cannot forget what you did to me years ago, after the past few days and seeing you work so hard to call on me, I forgive you."

The wave of relief that surged down his spine had his shoulders finally relaxing. "Thank you. I have long waited to hear those words." Perhaps it was just as well he hadn't kissed her, for that had the potential to become a disaster.

"Well, I should get you home." Clicking his tongue, he set his horses into motion.

"No doubt you have plans to see Miss Beaufort tonight, hmm?"

When he glanced at her, she'd turned her head to examine the shop facades they passed. "Uh, actually I'm taking dinner with Maubrey tonight. I have told Miss Beaufort there was no substance to our relationship and that she should cast her net again."

"Ah." She buried her face into Matey's fur. "You'd best hope it holds. A young lady like that might consider a bird in the hand too valuable to just release on a word."

"I have every confidence she will move on." He hoped, for being beside Cora again, listening to her voice and laughter, seeing how she interacted with his dog, dragged the old feelings for her out of storage.

Oh, he still wanted a courtship, but now he wanted it with Cora. Just as fate had decreed years ago.

CHAPTER SEVEN

May 22, 1817
Bromington House
Manchester Square
London

"COME, MRS. BROMINGTON. We must take advantage of the sunshine while we have it," Cora reminded the widow, for she had indicated an interest in taking the air at Hyde Park for a couple of hours. "You know you don't enjoy the trip if it's crowded."

And there was every possibility that Peregrine might just "happen" to run into them this afternoon as he'd hinted at when he drove her home yesterday.

"Don't rush me, girl." Her charge had done nothing but grouse since she awoke that morning. Most of it was ignored by the staff, yet it was still annoying at times. "The old bones don't move as fast as they used to," she continued as she made her way down the stairs to where Cora waited.

"You are quite gifted in dissembling, Mrs. Bromington. There is nothing wrong with you that a little fresh air and a stroll around the Serpentine can't cure." In fact, the woman was still quite spry in her movements as well as how her mind worked. It was a constant choice to prove recalcitrant.

"Just wait until you are my age, young woman. Perhaps then you'll be gifted with compassion, or hope someone shows you the same." If possible, the widow descended even slower than she had before. "We shouldn't go out today at all. My bones ache."

"No, you don't wish to go because *I* might enjoy myself," Cora countered, determined not to let the woman burrow beneath her skin.

During the brief ride with Peregrine, she had come to a greater understanding of the man. Truly, he had been all too honest in his apology, and since it wasn't in her nature to hold a grudge or continue to show anger toward another person, she had forgiven him. Perhaps she should have held her ground; what he'd done to her reputation and her future had been terrible enough, but acting in such a manner would eventually make her like Mrs. Bromington, and that was something she actively wished to avoid.

"I don't pay you to enjoy yourself," the widow said as she finally gained the ground floor. She thumped the tip of her cane against the floor. "I pay you to follow my dictates."

Reminding herself that her charge was forever in a foul mood because she'd pushed everyone in her life away for whatever reason, Cora offered her employer her crooked arm. "You pay me begrudgingly regardless, so I may as well find some joy in my position." As quickly as she could convince the other woman to go, she moved them both into the short entryway where Mr. Riley assisted the widow into her spencer of a moss green brocade. Cora merely had a light wrap about her shoulders, for the day was quite fine for late May, and she wished to soak up every bit of the sun.

"Ungrateful young woman." Mrs. Bromington sniffed. "I assume you took your customary walk yesterday while I napped."

Not for worlds would she let on that she'd done anything other than walk. "I did, for it *was* one of my days off." And thank goodness for that. The drive through Mayfair next to Peregrine had brought back not only memories but had also awakened old feelings she'd thought long dead.

Not that she was interested in having him back in her life for anything other than perhaps friendship.

The widow sniffed. She allowed Cora to lead her out of the house. "Mr. Riley told me Captain Wetherford called a couple of times, but that he wasn't allowed entry."

"Oh, did he?" If her charge insisted on playing games, she would do the same. The widow had previously instructed her butler not to show the captain up regardless. "I hadn't been aware."

"The man isn't good for you; none of them are, in fact."

Cora kept her own counsel as she and the driver assisted the older woman into the open carriage. It had belonged to Mr. Bromington, and since it had been paid for, she kept the vehicle and paid for its upkeep for the few times she might like to leave the house. Errands she had were never run by herself. Usually, she coerced a maid or the butler to do them for her.

"I never said I wanted one," she said as she joined her employer in the carriage. After exchanging a speaking glance with the driver, she told him to take them to Hyde Park, for the widow wished to take in the air.

"Of course, Miss Hasting."

Mrs. Bromington frowned as the carriage lurched into motion. "I can take in the air perfectly well from the vehicle. No need for me to get out."

With the last vestiges of her willpower, Cora stopped herself from saying exactly what was on her mind. "Exercise is good for you. It keeps you young."

"Why the devil would I want to extend my life when it's already horrid?"

Why indeed?

"No doubt that is largely due to your decisions." So much for not saying what was on her mind. She stared the other woman down. "If you want love, put that out into the world. If you want friendship, do the same. People aren't willing to gravitate toward someone who is full of vinegar." Her smile felt all too false, but she did it anyway. "I, for one, look forward to a few hours in the park, watching the ducks and geese on the water. There is more to life than hiding away inside one's house."

At least she hoped so, for there had to be more than being the widow's companion.

A grudging respect reflected in the older woman's eyes. "You are quite something, Miss Hasting." She brushed a speck of dust from her green skirting. "I read in the paper the other day that your sister married a viscount. Something about him being one of London's biggest scoundrels. I assume that was the reason you needed a holiday last month. How does your family feel about her choice in husband?"

That was a valid question, and one Cora herself had pondered since Mia wed the love of her life. "Mama is thrilled, of course, but I think Papa is more reserved about it. However, it was Mia's choice indeed, and love is a very powerful force." She shrugged. "My sister is the practical one, so if she found something redeemable in her husband, I don't doubt her."

Mrs. Bromington sniffed. "You young girls and your adherence to love being a forever sort of thing." The widow waved a hand in dismissal. "It only lasts as long as the other person wishes it to."

That was a truth Cora was only too familiar with. "On this I will agree with you. However, it doesn't mean we should lose hope or let ourselves turn sour." Once more she offered a smile. "Besides, there are many different sorts of love. Perhaps you should concentrate on some of them to reignite the beauty of the world around you."

"Surely, you aren't thinking about letting that stubborn captain back in your life, are you, girl? You can do better than him, and he's disfigured besides."

Hot anger lanced through Cora's chest. "A person's looks

have nothing to do with the state of their heart or soul." How dare the woman demean Peregrine for something he'd had no control over!

"Then from your own words, the captain's heart was in the right place when he allowed your reputation to be shredded the morning he begged off from marrying you?" One of her thin, gray eyebrows rose in challenge. "Was his soul clear when he left you drowning in scandal so he could sail the seas and no doubt bed anything in skirts at whatever port he pulled into?"

Cora sputtered, but deep down, she'd had the same worries as Mrs. Bromington had just expressed. Had he given her empty words yesterday when all along he'd been out sowing wild oats while in the navy? "I cannot speak to that. We met at a society event four years ago. He was on extended leave to help his mother when his father died." Prior to that, he'd already served in the navy for two years.

"Cling to your morals, my girl. Men like him are nothing but trouble. His mistress will always prove the sea. If he left you once, he'll do it again."

If there was one thing the widow excelled in, it was preying upon Cora's insecurities. "We are not together, Mrs. Bromington, so please don't worry yourself." It wouldn't do to make the woman aware of the almost-kiss of yesterday afternoon. If it hadn't been for that sweet beagle, she would have kissed the man who'd ruined her life.

Forgiveness was good for the soul, but taking steps to open the door to let a man make the same mistakes? That was quite another.

Some of the joy and anticipation had faded from the outing.

"Men are lovely in their place, but they only ever want a quick tup. Don't give them access to your heart or emotions, for you will come away hurt every time. Trust me on that." Mrs. Bromington leaned forward and patted Cora's knee. "I'll keep you from such a fate; you and I will get on just fine, I think. Perhaps we shall spend Christmas in Rome. The sun and warmth will be most welcome during that time, and it will get you away from London and *him*."

She said nothing except gave a tight nod. Had the widow said the truth of it? Was Peregrine that type of man? Certainly, they had anticipated their wedding night years ago, which had led to disaster and heartbreak, yet they were both different people now. It was too confusing to think about, for his return had her at sixes and sevens, but that longing—that hope—she kept hidden deep in her soul refused to fade.

Only time would tell.

Eventually, the carriage arrived at the main arch of Hyde Park.

"I am looking forward to our stroll, Miss Hasting." She slipped a hand about the upper portion of Cora's arm, and it was almost as if a shackle had gone around her. "You were correct when you said I should go outside."

Of course she was pleased, for with a few strategically placed words, she'd stolen Cora's positive outlook. "It is indeed a fine day. Many people are out strolling and riding. Quite fashionable, really." But there was no enthusiasm in those words. Even she heard it in her tone.

A half hour later saw them at the narrow portion of the Serpentine where it was more river than lake. Sunlight sparkled on the constantly moving water like thousands of diamonds. The faint quacks of ducks and honks of geese blended with calls and laughter from people picnicking on the lawn. Shrieks of delighted children echoed through the air as governesses and parents chased energic little ones, while even more splashed at the edges of the water.

"I'm told my grandchildren adore the park," Mrs. Bromington said, and the wistful note in her voice caused Cora to frown.

"Why do you not call upon them? I'm certain the children would adore seeing their grandmother." She remembered how lovely it had been to spend time with her own grandmama. Her chest tightened to think her charge's stubbornness was putting up walls between everyone in her life.

"Bah." The widow tsked her tongue. "If my children wanted me to see theirs, they would have treated me better after their father died. They are aware of how to contact me."

"That is quite sad, Mrs. Bromington." Cora had no idea what she would do without her tightly knit family to support her or bring comfort. "My family is everything to me." She nearly dissolved into tears, for she thought, hoped, dreamed she might have had her own family by this time before fate yanked that from her.

"Don't think to lecture me, Miss Hasting. I have far too much experience and I know my reasons why I am alone." Then her eyes brightened beneath the brim of her bonnet. "Oh, look! There is Lady Heretsford and Mrs. Stapleton. I haven't seen them since Christmas." She released Cora's arm to wave at two matronly ladies sitting not far from their location. A maid and a footman stood by a grouping of boulders, clearly at the ready while tea was served. "Can you entertain yourself for an hour while I visit with them?"

"I will certainly try." A weight seemed lifted off Cora's shoulders, for she'd been given a reprieve. "You don't wish for me to stay near?"

The widow snorted. "I should say not. Some gossip shouldn't reach the staff's ears."

Ah, then that whole bit about being concerned for her wellbeing while in the carriage had been naught but an act. *When will I learn?* "Enjoy yourself, then."

Mrs. Bromington left Cora's side, and remarkably, the stiff joints and aching muscles the old woman complained of before seemed healed.

Dear heavens, why do I very much wish to toss her into the water?

Truly, her charge was the most impossible person she had ever interacted with. After watching the widow greet her friends, Cora took a few deep breaths and let them out, then she gained the bridle path with the intent to lose herself in the less populated portions of the park merely to have time to herself.

And think.

The more distance she put between herself and her charge, the less beaten down she felt. Cora lifted her face to the sunshine, and then when she moved beneath the canopy of trees, she smiled in wonder at the light as it filtered through the leaves.

"Is there more of a lovely sight than seeing a beautiful woman in such a setting?"

At the sound of Peregrine's voice, her heartbeat tripped then accelerated. She put a hand to her throat as he approached her from the other direction on the path. "Perry." The word was quite a breathless affair. "I wasn't certain you would be in the park today."

"I told you that I would yesterday." When he grinned, she suddenly felt like tittering as if she were a girl at her Come Out. "I might not have kept my word years ago, but since we were last together, I have made it a point to do so."

Not knowing what to say or how to order her muddled thoughts after what Mrs. Bromington had said, Cora nodded. "I have an hour free. My charge is with friends at the moment, and knowing her penchant for gossip, she'll be occupied for some time." Quite frankly, she wasn't keen on returning to the woman just now.

He nodded. "Then we will make the best use of this boon." When he offered her a crooked arm, Cora sighed as she slipped her fingers onto the sleeve of his jacket of bottle-green superfine. "You seem discomfited today. Has something occurred? Is all well?"

Well, he was attuned to her moods. It was rather… lovely. "Mrs. Bromington has been a trial today. She cautioned me against getting involved with you, for you would only break my heart again."

The muscles in his arm went taut beneath her gloved fingers. "Pay her no mind. She is alone for a reason, and she means to drag you with her for as long as she can."

"I realize that, but I cannot help but think some of what she's said makes sense."

"Meaning?"

"I suspect it hurt her deeply when she lost her husband."

"Which was what I tried to spare you from when I broke our engagement."

"Yes, so you have said, and I can appreciate that now, yet I fear my ability to make my own decisions is faulty. If I say I want romance in my life again, Mrs. Bromington will call me a fool, but if I decide to become a spinster, will I hate myself?"

"These are the things only you can answer, but I will say I have struggled with the same. In the end, when I returned to London, I wanted to toss my loneliness into the sea, which resulted in seeking out a suitable lady to possibly court."

"Miss Beaufort might not be a good match," she said, and with horror heard the same disparaging tone in her voice that Mrs. Bromington had used on her.

"I have since come to realize that for myself." His deep chuckle resonated in her chest. Tiny flutters moved through her lower belly. "Truth be told, she is a poor replacement for you."

How interesting. A frown tugged at the corners of her mouth as she turned her head and peered up at him. "What exactly do you want from me? Is it only friendship?" Due to their history and the already mercurial emotions they'd both displayed since his return, she didn't feel the need to dance about the issue.

Or more to the point, what did *she* want from *him*?

"Before I answer that question, we should come to know each other a bit better. I suspect we have both changed in a myriad of ways since that morning at the church." When he grinned, the gesture didn't send light dancing in his eyes, but it did pull the scars at the side of his face.

"Very well. I had a mind to get lost in the more remote portions of the park. Perhaps even more so now." The scent of him wafted to her nostrils and she unobtrusively breathed it in. That heady smell combined with the summertime world around them set her at ease. What was more, having someone she used to know with her in London eased the solitude a tiny bit.

"Then you are in luck, for I know just the place you might remember. I hope you still think of it fondly."

When they came to a spot where the path branched, he took the lesser fork. A set of stone stairs cut into the side of a soft hill led them downward. The lower path winded about through groupings of trees, and by the time they came to a small wooden footbridge over a babbling brook, awareness and memories crashed over her.

"This is where you proposed to me," she said in a low voice, for that had been at least four years before. They'd enjoyed an engagement of a couple of months before wishing to marry; he'd been concerned he'd be recalled to service regardless of him being in mourning.

War didn't make concessions for life's foibles.

"Yes." Except he didn't lead her to the bridge as she assumed. Instead, he continued farther down the path until he came to a stone bench that rested near a moss-covered statue of Athena. Vines and shrubbery had nearly reclaimed the statue. "I don't wish for that unforgettable moment to color what might become a new one."

"I don't understand." Why did he need to speak in riddles? When he gestured at the bench, she frowned, for that had also been claimed by moss, and though she wasn't vain, she didn't want green stains on her ivory dress.

"Pardon my lapse." Quickly, Peregrine divested himself of his jacket. Once he'd draped it over the bench, he encouraged her to settle. "During my second stint in the navy, it was every bit as exciting and full of adventure as I could have hoped."

She frowned at her lap, pleated her skirting until the maroon stripes disappeared into the ivory. "You had more fun at sea than you would have in being a husband." It wasn't a question.

"I rather doubt that, for any man worth his salt that would take you on would never find himself bored." It was a lovely compliment whether he knew it or not. "Especially the woman you have grown into in my absence."

Heat slapped at her cheeks. "I have had to be strong in more ways than one."

"Again, I am sorry for the part I played in that." Peregrine paced back and forth in front of the bench where she sat. "My point in bringing up those years was in the quiet of the nights, when it was just me and the star-strewn endless night skies, when the wind blew over my face and I watched the moon traverse the heavens, I wondered if you were looking up into those same stars, conversing with that same moon. I hoped you might give me a kind thought as I did you."

"That's lovely." Cora's throat constricted from his admission. She owed him one of her own, and this conversation was long overdue. "I couldn't help but think of you, and there were a few reasons for that. In the beginning, I missed you fiercely, where I could alternately carve out your heart for your defection or hope to bring you back to me merely by calling you forth from my thoughts."

Briefly, he put a hand over that organ. The pain that shadowed his eyes tugged at her compassion. "And after that?"

She shrugged. "I taught myself to forget you, forbid myself from thinking about you at all, especially after…"

Oh, dear heavens, how could she tell him this next bit?

"After what?" Peregrine paused in front of her, worry in his expression, the scars and burn marks that marred the side of his face stark in the dappled sunlight.

"Ah…" Perhaps she was a ninny, but she couldn't bear to watch his eyes, so she focused on her hands in her lap. "Shortly after our engagement broke and you left, it became evident that I was with child." The words were barely audible, prompting him to draw nearer. "Two months along, a product of that wonderful night we'd come together."

"In that field on your father's country property," he said in a whisper.

"Yes." She nodded but kept her attention on her hands. It had been so long since she'd thought about that day. The memories overwhelmed her, and as they crashed into the secret hope that had been dashed for her, tears welled in her eyes. "No one in my family knew except Nora. She suspected, so I confided in her, swore her to secrecy, for bearing a child out of wedlock would have broken our parents' hearts." A teardrop fell to her hand, then another that stained her skirting. "I wanted that child, Perry. It would have been a part of us both, someone I could have loved of my very own, a reminder of you, who I didn't have any longer."

"What happened?" He sat on the bench next to her, a close fit to be sure because he was a rather large man.

"Fate? My body not quite ready? The stress of the broken engagement?" She shrugged and finally raised her gaze to his. Shock and sadness warred for dominance there. "I lost the babe three months into the pregnancy. Thank goodness no one else suspected. Nora told the family at large I was abed with a stomach ailment that was quite nasty. That explanation kept most of them away, and eventually I recovered. Physically, I mean." She sniffed and wiped at her tears. "I don't suppose I will ever forget that child, will always remember when it should have been born, wonder what it might have looked like."

"Ah, Cora. I don't know what to say." Before she could respond, he gathered her into his arms and held her.

That simple touch, the familiar comfort, was so unexpected and soothing that she melted into him. "I was devastated for a long time after that."

"I can just imagine." The warmth of his breath skated across her cheek while the strength of his arms around her invited her to fall apart, if only for a few moments. "If I had but known, if you had written, I would have done everything in my power to come home, to marry you, enjoy being a father..." A choked sound interrupted his words.

"I didn't know where to write or even how I would have told

you. It seemed crass to break that news in a letter." When a trace of moisture came away on her cheek, Cora marveled over the fact he cried along with her. "You wanted a family?"

"At the time? It terrified me, that responsibility and wondering if I would fail."

"And now?"

He wiped at his eyes with the back of his gloved hands. "I rather think I'd be a good father, or at least that is the hope." The crooked grin sent flutters tumbling once more through her lower belly. "It is time to begin the next phase of my life, don't you think?"

Did he mean to do that with her?

"Yes, I actually do." Her gaze dropped to his mouth. "And I hope you *are* that someday. You are too good a man to remain by yourself."

"Which brings us 'round to your original question: what do I want from you." Yet he didn't continue with words. Instead, he cupped her cheek, drew his kid-covered thumb along her bottom lip while his eyes bore into hers. "I would like a second chance, to correct the mistakes I made before, to show you how wrong I was."

Did it make her a ninny as Mrs. Bromington assumed that the statement had some of the bricks around her heart crumbling? In this moment, she didn't care, for she and Peregrine had bonded in grief, had admitted to truths they probably would have kept hidden if a meeting hadn't come about accidentally.

"I wouldn't say no, but I'm not certain I'm strong enough to survive potential heartbreak again."

"There are times in life when we must trust that faith will put wind in our sails to carry us to safety." Then he crushed his mouth to hers, drew her close against his chest as he kissed her with every ounce of tenderness and gentle caring she'd kept in her memories of him. And she encouraged him at every step. With a sound of acceptance or surrender, Cora slipped her arms about his shoulders, reveled at their breadth and the feel of him in her arms, and she returned each overture. His lips were firm but yielding as they moved over hers. When he licked and nibbled at the corners of her mouth, she wanted to melt into a puddle at his feet.

Dear heavens, how she'd missed him!

Eventually, they parted and had no choice but to stroll back toward the path where they'd met while talking of nothing in particular. Things had subtly shifted between them to a point where she couldn't wait to explore the new direction, regardless of whether Mrs. Bromington sponsored it or not.

Then the bottom fell out of her stomach when Peregrine was hailed, and what was more, she recognized that voice.

"Captain!"

They both halted and turned toward the young woman running in their direction with a maid trotting along behind her.

A groan issued from him. "Bloody hell."

"I'm so glad to glimpse you, Captain, for I wished to speak with you since the night at the rout." Miss Beaufort's explanation was slightly breathless as she closed the distance. "I know you told me to chase after someone else, but I'm not about to give up on you."

"You haven't." It wasn't a question.

"Yes!" She smiled, and showed entirely too many teeth. "We *will* suit, I just know it." The whole time, she studiously ignored Cora. "I can even learn to overlook those scars, for you are quite a handsome catch."

Cheeky girl.

The scars were as unique to Peregrine as his grin or the way his eyes sparkled when he was particularly amused. Still, jealousy stabbed through Cora's chest. Would the flattery manage to convince him? She glanced between them, only somewhat mollified that he looked quite perturbed. "What are you waiting for, Captain? The girl obviously wishes to talk with you most desperately. I need to check on my charge, besides."

"But..." The look he gave Cora brimmed with annoyance

and indecision. "We are not finished with our conversation."

The hint of command in that sentence sent shivers of awareness zipping down her spine. "If you manage to puzzle things out, you know where to find me."

In some aggravation, Cora left him to his fate. If he wanted to gain back her good graces, he would put a period to whatever was between him and Miss Beaufort. She wouldn't tolerate shared allegiances or distractions, nor would she have him keep an easier mark to fall back on if they couldn't get along.

Best to have the truth out now before her heart was engaged a second time.

CHAPTER EIGHT

May 23, 1817
Bromington House
Manchester Square
London

NOTHING WOULD CHANGE in life if he didn't make different decisions.

"It's perfectly acceptable to call on the lady after a kiss," he said with certain defensiveness in his voice as he stared at Matey, who lay on the bench beside him. Around noon, he had parked his curricle at the curb in front of Mrs. Bromington's townhouse, but as of yet, he hadn't gathered enough courage to alight.

Was wishing to pursue Cora a different enough decision, though?

One of the beagle's eyebrows went up as if he questioned the thin logic.

"No, I'm not desperate at all."

The dog whined and covered his eyes with a paw.

"I simply wish to see Cora, to show her that I choose her above Miss Beaufort." To be fair, he had already told the younger woman there was nothing between them—twice—so it wasn't strictly his fault she hadn't moved on with grace.

Matey huffed, clearly either unimpressed or in disbelief.

Peregrine frowned as he stared at the brick façade of the building. His thoughts drifted to Hyde Park yesterday where Cora had revealed the remainder of the reason why she'd been forced to flee to the country after he'd broken their engagement. She had been with child—his child—but had ultimately lost the babe.

We could have been a family.

It had nearly shredded his heart when he'd heard that she'd gone through something so devastating alone, and that she'd hated him during that period in her life. Yes, he had shipped out for the navy, but he could have found a way to come back to her, even if it had meant certain court martial for desertion. And yes, he hadn't been ready to be a husband or father when he'd left her on the steps of the church, but that didn't mean those things frightened him now.

Yet he'd never known, had never suspected the grief Cora had been plunged into, and she'd kept the secret from everyone except for her twin. That time had passed as had the support he could have given, and the urge to court her all over again, armed with this new knowledge and greater life experience, grew ever stronger with each passing day.

He wanted what he'd taken for granted before, what he'd stupidly tossed away over three years before, and he wanted it with a ferocity that surprised him. If there was any chance at all he could win Cora's heart, he had to try, and none of that would happen by sitting in his vehicle, pondering like a coward, because he didn't wish to face the dragon guarding her.

Get off your arse, Captain, and remember the man you fought to be.

"It's time, Matey. We are going up to that door and demanding to talk with Cora, and we aren't taking 'no' for an answer." He tugged on the lapels of his jacket. Made of gray superfine, it was subdued enough not to draw much notice but fine enough that he felt as if he could compete with much of the *ton* and wouldn't give Mrs. Bromington an excuse to pick him apart. His waistcoat was of sky-blue satin and a favorite, while the breeches of a lighter gray completed the aesthetic. The fact he'd dressed with care this afternoon served as testament to the fact his confidence didn't wane. "Let us not waste more time."

Now that his mind was clear regarding the subject of Cora, he wished to usher in the next part of his life with alacrity.

Gathering his daring and his courage, Peregrine brought his vehicle around to the back alley and parked it in the mews. After tossing the reins to a groom, he exited the curricle, took Matey's leather lead in hand, then he came back around the building, walked up the short pavement to the front door, and rapped with authority on that panel with his gloved knuckles.

Seconds later, the butler opened the door and frowned. "Mrs. Bromington isn't receiving visitors today."

"That is her prerogative, of course, but I am here to see Miss Hasting, and this time, I won't hear your objections or the widow's."

Matey gave a low bark of support.

One corner of Mr. Riley's mouth quirked but a grin never fully emerged. "Very well, Captain Wetherford. Follow me. I'll show you up to the drawing room."

"Thank you." Peregrine glanced at his dog, and it seemed to him the beagle grinned back.

It took next to no time to traverse the house, and soon enough, Mr. Riley announced him at the drawing room door.

"Captain Wetherford to see Miss Hasting. He was rather insistent."

Before Peregrine ever set foot in the room, he heard the grousing in the widow's voice.

"Since I'm in the mood to dress someone down, he'll do."

Peregrine exchanged a look with the butler, whose expression more or less wished him luck. Adjusting his hold on Matey's lead, he entered the room, and immediately his gaze landed on Cora, who sat on a chair with a book in her hand near to where Mrs. Bromington lounged on a sofa, a mess of crochet in her lap.

"Good afternoon, ladies. Thank you for seeing me."

"As if you've given me the choice?" The older woman wore a fierce frown. "I'll tell you what I did the other day. Miss Hasting isn't for you, and she has responsibilities to me besides. Today is not one of her days off."

"Then let me talk with her for a mere half hour." Again, his notice jogged to Cora, and in a day dress of robin's egg blue, she was truly a summer vision.

Those expressive eyes of hers first registered pleasure but then quickly shuttered to reflect mild annoyance. No doubt she took exception to the interruption from Miss Beaufort yesterday. Before she could respond, the widow rushed into the silence.

"You have managed to surprise me with your tenacity, Captain." She dropped her handiwork into a basket at her side, turned on the sofa cushion so she could face him directly. Then her scowl landed on Matey, who uttered a weak growl before hiding behind Peregrine's boots. "A man who relies on a canine for his interactions in life usually doesn't have confidence to speak of."

When Cora tsked her tongue and lowered a hand, Matey shot across the room. The leather lead slipped from his fingers before he could grasp it, and seconds later, the traitorous beagle skittered to a stop at her feet, madly thumping his tail against her legs as she gave him much needed pets.

Of course, the jab from her employer was expected, so he ignored it. "I dislike leaving him at home, for he gets restless and tears into pillows and things."

"I see." Another frown, this one directed at Cora. "Don't be too used to that mongrel, girl. I won't tolerate animals in this house. My children constantly begged for a pet, but I maintained my ground. No need to invite filth."

He clenched his jaw so tightly he feared he might crack a tooth. "Matey is quite tidy." When she didn't answer, he cleared his throat. "Would you give your permission to Miss Hasting to walk with me for a bit?"

"I wonder at your motives, Captain. Oh, yes, I saw you walking with her in the park yesterday." The widow swept a victorious glance between them. "You always assume I don't know what is going on around me while I'm otherwise engaged, but I do. Besides, Miss Hasting was far too uplifted when we rode home." She shook her head. "I won't tolerate sneaking about beneath my nose."

Cora snorted. "We wouldn't need to sneak if you would let him have his way."

The widow huffed. "When you allow a man his way, you have already lost the battle, then they will proceed to ruin your life."

He resisted the urge to tug at his suddenly too tight cravat, for her words *did* have some validity; he'd done exactly that to Cora already. "Be that as it may, I truly mean no harm to Miss Hasting. I am trying my best to call and perhaps pay my serious addresses to her if she'll allow it."

"*I* don't allow it," Miss Bromington said with the thump of her cane tip on the floor.

"You are *not* her keeper." He couldn't keep the annoyance from his voice. The woman was most vexing. "And neither are you her parents, so begging your pardon, ma'am, but neither of us need your permission."

A show of respect went through the older woman's expression, gone at the next blink. "You think you are so sly with your pretty words and bold actions." She shook her head. "Since I'm not likely to rid myself of you easily, I'll let Miss Hasting have an hour to herself."

"Thank—"

She held up a hand, interrupting him. "On one condition."

Cora pressed her lips together, but amusement danced in her eyes as she continued to lavish his dog with attention.

"What?" he practically spit out.

"I have a handful of errands that need running. Since one of Miss Hasting's duties is just that, if you were to take the responsibility off her hands so she can spend that time with me, you will be allowed to speak with her or stroll in the square behind the townhouses."

Bloody hell. Indeed, the woman was a dragon, and a worthy opponent.

"Fine. Procure me a list of places. I'll leave Matey with Miss Hasting so you'll know I'm in earnest and will come back."

"Excellent! It seems you can be trained after all, Captain." A chuckle escaped the older woman while Cora frowned.

"You are deliberately being mean, Mrs. Bromington."

"Am I? I thought it a perfectly fine arrangement." The widow rooted about the basket, and once she tugged out a small leatherbound notebook and a pencil, she opened it to a blank page and then jotted down a few lines. "Don't dawdle. If you cannot show some efficiency in this errand, the window of time to talk with Miss Hasting will close."

"You have my word." Not about to further antagonize her, Peregrine crossed the floor and took the page she'd torn from the notebook. "And if some of these shop owners require payment?"

Mrs. Bromington shrugged. "How badly do you wish to speak privately to Miss Hasting, Captain?" Victory sparkled in her faded green eyes. She waved in dismissal. "Off you pop."

With a glance at Cora, who mouthed the words "I'm sorry" at him, he crushed the list in his fist and nodded. "I'll return in an hour."

Damn, but the woman was maddening. If this was what he had to do in order to win time with Cora, so be it, but sooner or later she would need to find her backbone and fight back against the dragon.

As he left the room, he peered at the list.

A box of candlesticks from Andressen's.
Specially ordered ladies' handkerchiefs from Furrows' Linens.
A box of French chocolates from Rogert's Confections.
Pick up a pair of half-boots that have been re-soled at Elbert's
   Cobbler Services.

If she assumed that he would fail, she had another thing coming. Thank goodness all the shops were within close proximity in Mayfair.

TRUE TO HIS word, Peregrine stopped at each and every shop on Mrs. Bromington's list. At two of the shops, the widow didn't have a credit account, so he paid for the items out of his own pocket, for the goal wasn't to please the widow but to win Cora. Like Odysseus, he would happily go through a series of challenges if it would put her back in his life.

Once he arrived at the widow's townhouse, it was his turn to claim victory, for the surprise on her face to see that he'd done everything she'd asked was priceless.

"Very well." Mrs. Bromington sighed. "It seems you are more stubborn than I've given you credit for, Captain." She gestured at Cora, who was writing out a letter, apparently at the widow's dictation. "You have earned an hour of Miss Hasting's time, uninterrupted, as long as you stay close by in the event I need her."

Matey, who lay curled on a cushion on another sofa, completely ignored him.

"Do you wish to finish the letter, Mrs. Bromington?" Cora asked as she put the stopper on her inkwell.

"We can do it later. I'd much rather have the captain out of my hair." When Peregrine moved toward Matey, she shook her head. "Leave the dog. I want assurance you'll return my companion."

"You drive a hard bargain, ma'am." He tamped down on the urge to grin. The woman was a fright and a formidable opponent, but he *would* win this game. "Do you wish to walk a bit, or would you prefer a different activity?"

"I need to stretch my legs, and it's such a fine day, I'd hate to waste this weather." After setting down her pen, she stood, shook the wrinkles from her skirting, and then crossed the carpet to where he stood. "The square is quite lovely and lush with vegetation and trees. Truly, it's one of the best places to live in Mayfair."

The widow nodded. "My husband had an inkling when he bought this house. Best thing he ever did." Then she narrowed her gaze on him. "Don't think to seduce the girl while you're away. I'll be watching from my window upstairs with my opera glasses."

Of course she would.

By the time Cora gathered her bonnet and gloves, and they left the house through the library doors, some of the tension left Peregrine's shoulders. When he led her through that rear garden and into the square beyond, the annoyance he'd felt from the dragon's machinations faded.

"I apologize for Mrs. Bromington. She has her quirks, but I can't believe you let her manipulate you like that," Cora said as she laid a hand on his arm. "It was impressive, if stupid."

The gentle breeze brought with it the scent of growing things and a whiff of her perfume. "I'd hoped it would show I was in earnest."

Her grin was evident around the shallow brim of her bonnet. "You were that."

"Good, because I am." The parkland was indeed as lush as described. Few people strolled the area, for it was too early to be fashionable, and most people preferred to be seen on Rotten Row anyway. If members of the *ton*, they had no doubt only awakened for the day having been out late last night for society functions. "However, if your dragon refuses to allow you freedom, I am only too happy to fight for that."

"Why? I assumed you would have your hands full with Miss Beaufort. She has shown a remarkable penchant for clinging to you."

He couldn't determine if that was sarcasm in her voice or

amusement. "I told her more firmly this time that she and I will not suit, that my interest was on someone else."

"Oh?" When she glanced at him, surprise reflected in her eyes. "What did she say?"

"She was hurt, but I believe she finally took the hint." He blew out a breath. "If I were a devious man, I would send her in the direction of Viscount Maubrey, but not even he deserves her. Perhaps there is a man closer to her age that will appreciate her... enthusiasm."

"Why did you ever show interest in her to begin with?"

"As I said, I was tired of being by myself, and I was ready to marry, thought choosing someone young would be more apt to accept me and my flaws." Clearly, that had been flawed thinking.

"Yet she didn't. I wanted to pitch her into the brook yesterday for the slight she uttered about your looks." Her fingers tightened on his arm. "Don't accept anything less than the best for yourself."

"I'm not, which is why I would like to court you again." It was better to be forthright and tell her the truth. "If you would allow it, and hopefully get you away from that horrible widow turned dragon."

She uttered an unladylike snort. "That largely depends."

"On?" Anticipation buzzed at the base of his spine.

"On whether you can improve upon the kiss you stole yesterday. If I'm to allow you back into my life on any sort of regular basis, I want to know you will be able to meet *all* my needs."

"Oh?" Why had he suddenly been reduced to one-word replies?

"Neither of us are growing any younger, and beyond wishing to feel pleasure, I don't know that I have the strength to see you leave again if something better comes along." Her eyes bored into his. "If I agree to a courtship, I want your unerring promise." Then she pulled him behind a grouping of trees and shrubberies that would keep them halfway hidden. "What have you to say to that?"

"I will not hurt you again. That was a mistake of my past, and I have changed as a man." When she didn't appear convinced, he offered a grin. "Perhaps this will help." He cupped her cheek while wishing fervently he wasn't wearing gloves so he could feel her skin. "Believe me when I say I missed you while I was away."

"Show me, then. Words are useless, as you've already demonstrated."

Bloody hell, had it been his fault she'd grown into this practical, slightly mistrustful woman who spoke her mind? "Gladly." Peregrine dipped his head and kissed one corner of her mouth, for it simply wouldn't do to kiss her in a frenzy when he wished to be a gentleman. When she murmured a sound of acceptance, he did the same to the other corner.

For long moments, Cora rested her hands on his chest. "Lovely, of course, but I need something more exciting before I decide." She held his gaze, searching for God only knew what, then she lifted onto her toes and pressed her mouth to his.

The sensation of falling assailed him, for it was as if the angels themselves had granted permission for him to proceed. With a growl, he took her more firmly into his embrace and set out to rediscover every secret of her lips. Over and over, he drank from her as if she held the last drink of water, and it was as if someone had dropped a match to dry tender. As he sought to deepen the embrace, one of her hands curled about his nape while she looped her other arm about his shoulders in an effort to apparently hold him close. He didn't mind, for that only pressed her body into his, and her breasts felt all too lovely crushed against his chest.

It had been quite some time since he'd let passion carry him away, but kissing this woman, knowing they shared history together, had lost something precious together, tangling his tongue with hers with nothing but raw heat and desire behind it, was beyond amazing.

And he couldn't have enough of her.

"Ah, Cora..." When he pulled slightly away, she offered a protest, he tugged her deeper into the lush foliage, turned them about, and then pushed her back against the wide trunk of an oak tree. "Would that we could erase the past few years." The whisper blended in with the bird song and other animal sounds coming from the trees.

"But we can't, and we are both changed besides. Going into this with our eyes wide open." She grazed her teeth beneath his jaw, and that exploration, that teasing sent heat licking through his blood as if she'd set fire to it.

"Perhaps the second time 'round will be better." Again, he claimed her mouth and this time it was with a series of insistent, hard kisses that would tell her in no uncertain terms how much he wanted her, wanted that new chance. As she returned those kisses, he explored her body, slid his hands up and down her sides, traced her ribcage, eased one down to squeeze one soft arse cheek. A squeal sounded against his lips, and he grinned. "I adore these curves." Pulling slightly away, he took precious seconds to yank off his gloves, toss them to the ground, but he quickly returned to kissing her and this time, he cupped one of her breasts. The thin muslin of her dress was a mere wisp of a barrier, and he was a man determined to give her the pleasure she'd alluded to. As her nipple hardened when he brushed the pad of his thumbs over it, a moan escaped her.

"Oh!" She broke the kiss to peer up into his face. "I have missed that feeling…" Those words trailed off as he urged down the plain bodice and freed her breasts from the dress. Today, she hadn't worn stays, no doubt thinking she wouldn't see anyone, and it took very little time to ease the lawn of her chemise away from those quivering mounds.

"As have I." With memories of the one time he'd seen her naked years ago dancing through his mind, Peregrine took her breasts in his hands, and they filled his palms perfectly. Needing to taste them, he lowered his head and took a pebbled tip into his mouth.

"Perry, yes!" She hissed in a breath, but when he manipulated that bud with his tongue and lips, another moan escaped her throat. "More." Her responses were much different now than they'd been when he'd stolen her innocence, and they fired his imagination as well as his desire.

With need shuddering along his stiffening shaft, her fingers dug into his shoulders. She moved her body, brushed her breasts against his jacket, so he moved his attention to her other one. When that elicited the same response, he grinned against her skin and started the cycle all over again while his length pulsed with anticipation.

"I want you." While he caressed her breast, he kissed her and let the other hand wander. Digging through layers of fabric, he encouraged one of her legs upward until it rested at his hip, and holding her between his chest and the tree, he put his hand between her silky thighs. "God help me, I want you so damned much." As soon as he glided his fingers along the soft, heated skin at her center, she trembled.

"Touch me, send me flying." The fingers of one hand curled into his lapel. "I need that release."

"That is my current endeavor." Dear God, she was heat and fire. He dipped his head, suckled one of her turgid nipples while rubbing his fingers over the swollen bud, daring to dip a finger into the honeyed heat of her. "I dreamed of this those years at sea, of you."

A blush stained her cheeks while her dark blonde lashes formed perfect arcs against that skin as her eyes shuddered closed. "I forgot how freeing this is, how empowering."

"A pox on your dragon. Let her watch as I claim you, for we were meant to be together, Cora. I firmly believe that." And he thrust another finger into her passage, priming her while he worried her button with his thumb.

"Oh, God." She groaned, and it didn't sound pleasurable at all. "I'd forgotten about her and her dratted lorgnette." With a light nip to his bottom lip, she planted her palms against his chest and pushed him away. Immediately their connection broke and her skirting fell back into place. "Trust me when I tell you she is no doubt watching. She spies on everyone in this square, knows exactly what they're doing and where they're going." As she spoke, Cora tugged her bodice back into place. "I must go. She'll need me to settle her for her nap, besides."

"Damn." His shaft pulsed with need against the front of his breeches. "You will sacrifice our hard-won time together in the face of her ire? She's a sour puss about everything." If he was more annoyed than usual, he had ever right.

"I know." Regret shadowed her eyes. "I know! But I still have a living to get, and I can't jeopardize that, not even for you."

When she would have pushed past him, he caught her hand. "I'll escort you back, for I need to retrieve Matey, but does this mean you agree to a courtship?"

Pain lined her face, which quickly changed into sadness. "I don't know. It will cause far too much friction between you and Mrs. Bromington."

"I shall handle the dragon, especially if it means winning you." He wasn't about to let the matter rest, for there had been far too much attraction and desire crackling between them to forget it altogether, and until he'd cleared her from his blood, something needed to be done. "I want to see you again, and soon."

Her nod was curt. "My next day off is Sunday, in two days. Come then. Mrs. Bromington attends church and then spends the remainder of the day visiting friends or entertaining them at home. We can go… somewhere if the day is fine."

It was better than nothing. "Do you promise to give me your answer at that time?"

"Yes." Her expression softened. "I'm sorry, Perry. I don't play games with men; there are many things in my life that I feel bound by, and if one goes bad, it's not just my life that is destroyed."

"I understand, but know this, I will prevail, and if I must continue to fight the dragon to show you my resolve, I will do it until my strength gives out or hers does."

She didn't answer, but there was a soft smile curving her lips as they slowly walked back to the house.

CHAPTER NINE

May 25, 1817

PEREGRINE COULDN'T IGNORE the fact that he was in a rotten mood.

He hadn't seen Cora in two days, not since she'd ignited fires in his blood, kissed him as if he'd been the only man in the world, and then she'd pushed him away, cutting the chances of a quick tryst short. It had resulted in him hovering in a state of semi-arousal and grumbling to the point that Charles had made jest of him last night at the club.

To top it off, it was raining.

"Are you going to stand at the window all day or will you actually go do something about your current obsession?" A hint of amusement went through the viscount's voice.

With a huff, Peregrine wrenched himself out of his thoughts. He and Charles had taken luncheon at the club, for his friend had duties to his parents later. Somewhere in another room, a longcase clock chimed the two o'clock hour. "You're right. It's Sunday. I need to stop stewing and call on Cora once more."

"More than that, you need to bed the woman, put her from your mind, and then concentrate on opening your shop." Charles clapped a hand to Peregrine's shoulder. "If you mean to court her, then do it, but if you don't, cut her loose. It's not fair to either of you."

"True." He turned about to regard his friend. "I'm nervous, though."

"Why? You aren't part of the navy any longer, so you won't chase after the sea, and you aren't given over to chasing skirts."

"Why?" Rubbing his eyes, Peregrine sighed. The problem wouldn't be easily solved. "I'm afraid I haven't adequately convinced the lady she can trust me. And she's skittish."

"I thought she was amenable to your suit."

"So did I. It matters not if we connect physically, she falls back on responsibilities to her family, as if she's their only damned savior." He shook his head. "While I appreciate that she wishes to help pay the back taxes and keep the hall's roof over her family's head, at some point, her parents need to accept their part in said responsibility. Otherwise, she is always going to be held hostage by them."

And in the process, she would sacrifice her life for theirs.

"To say nothing about the dragon she looks after."

"Somehow, I feel the dragon would be the lesser of two evils." Compassion reflected in Charles' eyes. "You have already gone out of your way merely to see her. However, if you can honestly see a future with her, you must find a way to persevere."

"I am beginning to realize that." As he blew out a breath, he readjusted the knot of his cravat.

"Yet you hesitate. Why?"

"I am afraid." It was difficult to admit, but his best friend would never steer him wrong.

"Of what?"

He shrugged. "Of failing. Of disappointing her again." It had the potential to beget nightmares.

"What of failing yourself, disappointing yourself if you don't create a life that you can be proud of, that you want deep down in your heart of hearts?" Charles frowned. "You didn't survive the incident that should have killed you to languish now."

"I know."

"And I didn't risk my life to pull your unconscious body out of the fire to see you humiliated. Perhaps if Miss Hasting isn't moving along those same lines, she is not the one you need regardless of what your prick thinks."

It was a hard conversation, and even harder truths to accept. "Thank you, my friend." He tugged on the bottom of his jacket, the same blue superfine he'd worn before. On a captain's pension, he wasn't afforded to keep a large wardrobe. "I suppose I should go discover if I'll meet my destiny today or if fate will hand me yet another obstacle."

"I'll come 'round tomorrow to hear the tale."

"Let us hope it's favorable."

THE RAIN HADN'T lessened by the time he pulled up in front of Bromington House. Thank goodness he hadn't brought Matey with him today, for the dog would have tried to jump out of the vehicle multiple times; he adored the rain… and the mud it made.

At the same time, the red-painted door opened, and the object of his quest came out of the house. Pale blue skirting stamped with tiny blue dots rippled in the breeze, while a plain ivory spencer and straw hat kept the rain from her person.

"Cora!" Would she hear the hail above the rhythmic drum of the rain?

Her head jerked upward. "Peregrine?" She lifted a gloved hand in greeting as she came toward the conveyance, and he climbed down from it. "I wasn't certain you would call, so since I had an errand, I decided to run it instead of foolishly waiting for you."

"I deserve that, but I'm here now." When she joined him on the pavement, he slipped a hand around the upper portion of her arm. "Come with me. I'd be delighted to drive you to wherever you need so you needn't walk in the rain."

"Then I accept. I do detest the rain." She let him assist her into the vehicle then smiled at him when he resumed his own seat. "Where is Matey?"

"At home, probably sleeping. He is rather exuberant in the rain and makes a disgrace of himself in the gutters." With a smirk, he set his horses into motion. "I didn't think you'd want your skirting muddied as well as covered in dog hair."

"Good heavens, Mrs. Bromington had much to say about the stray dog hairs on the furniture." She twisted the strings of her reticule around her gloved fingers. "The woman is intent to drive me to Bedlam."

"I won't argue the point, but I'm curious why you think so, beyond the obvious."

A sigh escaped her. "For the past two days, she has been hinting that my attention has been divided and that if it doesn't improve, she will be forced to sack me."

"Ah, let me guess, without references? Because she is that petty?"

"Yes." Cora nodded. "One of the maids confirmed to me that's what she did with all my predecessors."

"How outrageous. She is quite horrid." Perhaps he ought to act the gentleman and leave her alone. When Cora didn't comment, he continued. "Where does your errand take you? Surely not for more candles or handkerchiefs."

"No." Though she smiled, it wasn't reflected in her eyes. "To be honest, Mrs. Bromington didn't need any of those items urgently. She merely wanted you out of the house."

"Oh, I am quite aware, but I long ago learned the art of patience." He kept his gaze on the horses' ears. "She doesn't like me."

Cora snorted. "She doesn't like anyone. I think it's because deep down, she's hurting and lonely. She's been disappointed and disenchanted by life and is terrified of having that continue."

"That doesn't give her leave to act nasty toward others, especially those trying to help." Hot guilt rose in his chest. "Again, I apologize for putting you in the position of which you needed to take a paying position."

For long moments, Cora remained silent. Then, "It was unfair of me to blame all of this on you. Yes, my reputation was destroyed when you ran out on me, which meant decent men wouldn't take a chance on me. Beyond that, my reputation would have been shredded if my pregnancy had been made public. However, my father's negligence in not paying his bills was what prompted me to make a living."

Little by little, the tension faded from his shoulders. At least she could admit that. "In this life, men—and women—must take responsibility for their own mistakes. I have certainly learned that in recent months." Taking the reins in his right hand, he held one of hers in his left. "Mistakes help us course correct and find the path we should be walking. They are not there to shame us."

"I was never ashamed of being with child. It was something of you I could have with me always," she admitted in a barely audible voice that was snatched away by the sound of the rain.

A lump of emotion formed in his throat. "I don't know what to say."

"There is no need to say anything." She squeezed his fingers. "We needn't do the errand today. It can wait, for it's not important."

"Are you certain?"

"Yes."

Awareness danced over his skin. "What do you wish to do instead?"

"Surprise me, Perry. I have had precious little of that in my life for quite a while." But that look in her eyes practically begged him to take her to bed.

"Very well." The same need lanced through his shaft as he manipulated the reins. "We will go to my shop. It'll be out of the rain, and I do have the capability of making a kettle of tea." Perhaps she would think the shop quaint. "By the by, I've chosen a name for it."

"Oh? What is it?"

"Charts and Springs." He shrugged. "It's not much, but those in the know will appreciate it, and perhaps with time, it will prove successful."

"It has promise, to be sure. Will you live above the shop?"

"I could if I wished, but I'm rather content in my set now. Should my future circumstances shift, I will consider it." Yet was that any sort of life to offer a potential wife? He didn't want to rush his fences.

"Life certainly didn't turn out as we'd dreamed, did it?"

"No, but that doesn't mean it can't be even better than that."

There was a mews house not far from his shop's location, accessed through a series of turns and alleyways, but it would do for a few hours to have someone take care of his horseflesh. After tossing a few coins to the stable hand, he escorted Cora back 'round to the street side and they scurried along the pavement until they reached his shop.

Seconds later, he ushered her inside, then closed the door behind them.

"This is going to be lovely once you fully unpack." As she wandered about the cozy room, she removed her bonnet and her gloves, which she rested on a polished wooden counter. "Already I adore how you've stocked the shelves."

For the first time he saw the place through new eyes. Immediately to a potential customer's left and right, wooden shelves lined the walls. Books on nautical subjects, astronomical charts, star guides and such were contained there as well as navigational instruments sailors needed to way find, along with spyglasses, clocks and the like.

A round table graced the center of the room, also highly polished, and would eventually display pocket watches, both aged and the newest models. At one end of his counter was a glass display case where he would put the more valuable things such as jewelry, pistols, silver grooming sets, or instruments made of brass and silver.

"I believe I'll have some sort of success. The sign painter will be here in two days. Hopefully during that time, I'll have the remainder of the stock that is in the back room out on the floor." He shot her a grin. "I'll admit, I'm quite excited to start."

"You should be." Slowly, she manipulated the frog fastenings of her spencer. "Will you show me the upstairs space?"

"Of course, but be warned, there isn't much in the way of furniture or décor."

"That doesn't matter. I am proud of you, regardless."

The unexpected praise warmed him, and he didn't realize how much he'd missed that since leaving the navy. "Thank you." He gestured her around the counter. "Come. I'll give you a quick tour." When he led her into the back room, most of the room was lost in shadows, for there wasn't a window there. Crates and boxes had been crammed into the space to line the walls. A sturdy oak desk had been situated in a corner. "I expect I'll have to manage the books by myself until I turn enough profit to hire on a clerk."

"I can ask my sister if her husband can recommend someone. I seem to remember the girl she was a companion to married a banker earlier this month."

"That would be appreciated." A narrow wooden staircase was accessed at the back of the front room. Upstairs, the space was divided into a small, cramped sitting room and a bedroom. "Good for a bachelor quarters, but I can't envision raising a family here." Neither could he do the same at The Albany. A chuckle left his lips. "It reminds me much of being on my ship." He removed his gloves and rested them on the top of a box. His top hat followed.

"It is good for your needs at the moment." She touched his shoulder as she looked about the nearly empty rooms. "Don't rush your life or your accomplishments. You should enjoy them; you have worked hard for them."

"As long as you remember the same. Surviving Mrs. Bromington is quite the achievement."

"Yes, it is." With a glance about the empty rooms, she made her way back down the stairs. "When will you take the paper off the front window?"

"As soon as I'm ready to open. Should be the middle of next week, but I have a few speaking engagements on the schedule as well, so I should amend my statement to say when time allows."

"I would be more than happy to come by on my next day off. Perhaps my employer might need a spyglass." She winked as she removed her spencer. "It would be easier on her eyes than a lorgnette."

The sense of humor she'd nurtured was quite adorable, and it was as powerful as a siren song. "Would you like tea? There's a small stove in the back, and I can unearth a kettle from one of the boxes."

"No need. There is something else I would rather indulge in, I think." With a tug on his cravat, Cora pulled him into the other room he planned to use for storage and a makeshift office. "At least here, we won't be spied upon or interrupted."

Bloody hell. "That is only partially true, for there is a bookshop on one side. We shouldn't be too loud; I don't need the complaints as a new tenant." The woman was an enchantress; always had been where he was concerned, but now that she had experience behind her as well as confidence, she was even more so, and she was playing severe havoc with his peace of mind. "Before we go further, there should be no misapprehensions about what we both want from this moment."

"Agreed. Mrs. Bromington might cry foul, but *I* certainly will not." She swept her glance along the floor. "A rug would make this room quite tidy."

Perhaps he did need a woman's touch for the shop, but that would come with time… hopefully. That thought didn't quell the need mixed with anxiety in his gut. "Does that mean you trust me? Or are you merely desperate for release?" She wasn't the only one who indulged in plain speaking.

Cora blew out a breath as she drew her hands up and down

her arms. "I do to a point." She pressed her lips together, which called his attention to her mouth. Longing stabbed through him to taste her. Those quick kisses from two days ago hadn't been enough to satisfy; they had merely teased. "But I also crave your embrace, and if that brands me as desperate, then so be it." When she met his gaze, there wasn't a trace of shame or embarrassment there.

And that confidence worked to further arouse him.

"At least you no longer hate me." Though intercourse fueled by such an emotion would be nothing short of spectacular.

"I don't." She clasped her hands in front of her, and the innocent gesture had desire shivering down his shaft. "My world fell apart when you left, and then it kept falling with life's disappointments, but sometimes, luck and fortune are absent for a time."

"That is true, for I've suffered disappointments as well where I never thought I would see a way out of them." A stab of guilt went through his chest. "While there is comfort in taking refuge in self-pity, it only lasts so long."

"Yes! I came to that conclusion as well, especially when Amelia discovered the unpaid taxes on the estate and Papa's declining mental health was brought to light." She came toward him a few steps. "At first I felt powerless, but above everything, I wanted to help if I could."

Well, damn. He'd not known about her father's decline. There would be no fixing his own mistakes, then. "I'm sorry to hear about your father's health."

"So am I. Quite terrified if I let myself think too deeply on it. At least toiling for Mrs. Bromington occupies my mind most times."

"Yet, because your soul is kind and there are responsibilities pressing in on you not of your own making, you have trapped yourself into prisons. If you leave one, you will merely fall into another." He frowned and crossed his arms at his chest. "When will you give yourself permission to live life on your own terms, for your own happiness?"

When would he?

"I…" Confusion shadowed her expression in the dim illumination. "I am doing my best."

"So am I." What happened when that wasn't good enough? A trace of annoyance went through his chest. They were forever circling back to the past. "Again, I ask, what do you want of me?"

Because there's nothing I wouldn't do for you, to make you happy. As I should have done years ago.

To his horror and surprise, tears welled in her eyes. "I don't know, because I am far too broken to go forward with any man, let alone you." She gestured helplessly around the room. "There is much potential in your future. When you left me standing on the steps of the church as if I didn't matter on what was supposed to be the most important day of my life, I wondered what was wrong with me." Her voice broke and the sound slammed into his person. "I was alone and frightened with my dreams crumbling about my feet." Abruptly, she cut off her words and rushed at him. Emotions danced over her expression, the same ones that battered his own bruised heart. "I was devastated that I wouldn't be able to grow old with the man I'd fallen in love with… because he didn't love me enough, and that haunted me."

"I told you why, and it had nothing to do with the level of love." Peregrine caught her in his arms, but confusion warred with need. "I wanted the chance to begin again, to court you, yet you haven't agreed to my suit. How do you think that makes *me* feel?" He hadn't meant to share on an emotional level with her, but here they were.

"My life changed years ago, and those changes haven't stopped. It's dizzying and sad, and quite frankly, I'm tired of it. Tired of the struggle through all of it." With a curled fist, she beat her hand on his chest. Perhaps she needed that outlet. "Mama and Papa don't deserve that struggle either, not after they raised all of us and took the two youngest girls in when their family perished in a fire. In fact, one of them has injuries much like you, and I never realized that before." A half-stifled sob escaped. "What will become of them once Papa passes and we lose the hall?"

That was an interesting tidbit. "Ah, sweeting, none of those concerns should ever rest on your shoulders."

"Yet I can't help but worry! Amelia certainly didn't marry a rich man. The viscount's pockets are near to let, and he has monetary troubles of his own." Tears fell to her cheeks, and he held her, let her vent her anger, disappointment, and grief. "She's the oldest! She should have at least *tried* to help."

"Did she not send coin home?" he whispered and brushed her forehead with his lips.

"Yes, some of what she'd gotten when she was let go from her position, yet there are expenses, bills, servants to pay, food to buy…" Her voice was barely audible. "I'm so tired, Perry."

"I'll wager you are. You've kept all this inside for far too long." He held her closer. "Lean on me for a bit. Borrow from my strength. I'll keep you safe as the storm rages." It was the least he could do.

Cora nodded. "Why is everything so dratted difficult and exasperating?" Her fist lightly thudded against his chest. "I just want something to look forward to, to not be afraid or angry, and I have no time to fall to pieces. I want to be happy again, for I haven't been that in far too long, but I must think about my sisters."

"Let them come up to the mark. They might surprise you."

"Or they might make it worse!" She shook her head as another sob escaped. "Gigi is going to drag the family name through the mud, I think, and dear Nora. What will become of her?"

"I don't know." Barely did he remember Nora's troubles, but he suspected they were more than not being able to hear.

Tear tracks showed on her cheeks. "The Hasting family needs a miracle."

"Don't we all?" He held her closer, and she rested both fists on his chest, the fight apparently drained from her. "But until the angels align, we must make do the best we can under our own power while hoping for the best." Could she feel how much her proximity affected him? Though he wouldn't force the issue, he certainly hoped she would let him kiss her, and if she wanted that embrace merely for comfort, that's where he would leave it.

CHAPTER TEN

"Yet patience isn't where I shine. I need to know when and how things will happen..." Her words died as she stared at him with moisture-spiked lashes, her eyes dark blue pools that offered him a temporary respite from all he struggled with.

"That is understandable, but for the moment, take a breath, find a bit of peace, then you can start again with trying to save the world." That determination to help everyone endeared her to him even further.

Cora nodded. "Everything is a mess, Peregrine..." Her swallow was audible. "It's not fair."

"Life was never supposed to be fair, I think. Challenges are there to teach us, guide us, strengthen us." He cupped her cheek and wiped at the tears lingering there. "We must meet those challenges the best we can."

"Then what happens?" She nuzzled into his palm, and he rejoiced at the trust she showed.

"You must find a way to make it through until the storms clear and it's smooth sailing once more." Daring much, he drew the pad of his thumb along her lower lip. "That's what you're doing now in finally shedding those pent-up feelings."

"Who will catch me if I fail... in everything?"

It was a question he couldn't answer. He didn't have that right, but he desperately wished to. "Once the cleansing is done, you'll have a new outlook on life. Perhaps you'll finally find happiness and peace. That is something we all hope for. I am no exception."

"Perry…" She appeared so lost that his protective instincts welled. "I need *you* to catch me," she whispered, and another tear fell. "At least in this moment. Remind me I'll come out right if I let go, if I don't try so hard to save my family. I'm so weary…"

There was only so much willpower a man could tap into before he broke. "Shh, it will be all right." Peregrine crushed his lips to hers in a savage kiss that told her in no uncertain terms he wanted her. In that moment, they were more well-matched than they'd ever been. By the time he wrenched away, they were both breathless. He sought her gaze with his. "This afternoon, here with me, there is no right or wrong. You don't have to remain strong if you don't wish it."

"I want to pretend we're not at odds, to forget what our lives might have been like if we were never ripped apart." She tugged his shirttail from his trousers and then shoved her hands beneath his shirt. The heat of her seared his skin, ignited his blood. His body caught fire and was fueled by the stark want in the blue depths of her eyes. "I only need you."

It was folly to give in. Everything would change between them yet again, but if a quick coupling would help rid her of the residual anger, the confusion…

"Ah, Cora." He could never resist her. Would that this tryst brought them closer instead of putting them further at odds, and he hoped the trust she extended would continue. Peregrine embraced her, kissed her hard so there were no doubts of how much he desired her. Over and over, he devoured her mouth as if she'd evaporate into the air. She did the same, gave as good as she got, and soon they were panting, hands searching, fingers trailing over familiar skin, lost to the heat between them.

As desire overrode common sense, he carried her to the desk

and deposited her on it. "Are you certain this is what you want?" Shadows played over her face, hiding the emotions in her eyes, while the rain sounded rhythmically outside.

"Yes." She tugged him closer, her grip sure. "Tucked away here, no one will know so there will not be scandal, and with you, it'll be amazing."

The honesty in her words fed his ego as he settled between her already splayed legs. "I have waited long to reunite with you in this way." With a hand at her back, he pleasured her breasts, sucking the hardened nubs of her nipples through the fabric of her dress. Her soft cries of enjoyment spurred him onward, and when that wasn't enough, he manipulated the laces at the back of her dress. When the bodice gaped, he gladly tugged it down then spent a few seconds freeing her perfect breasts from the clothing.

"Touch me, Perry." The whispered plea near drove him to the brink of insanity. "Show me you still desire me instead of someone younger like Miss Beaufort."

He snorted. "She doesn't hold a candle to you." Then he availed himself of her charms. The warmth of her breasts in his hands was both familiar and erotic. While he kneaded that flesh, worried the nipples with the pads of his thumbs, Cora plucked at his cravat, doing her best to loosen it, tug it a bit free so she could access the skin behind it. The heat of her lips there, coupled with the feel of her in his hands, had hot need streaking through his shaft.

"I don't trust words any longer." She pulled him closer, dragged her lips beneath his jaw.

"Sooner or later, you will need to be brave, take the chance, and give someone the benefit of the doubt." But he understood her continuing reserve.

"If there was a guarantee I wouldn't be hurt…" Her words dissolved into a moan, for he'd taken one of her nipples into his mouth, worried that tip with his tongue before suckling it. "Mmm, yes." A shuddering sigh left her throat, and she slightly arched her back, which put her breasts more firmly into his care.

When he rolled her other nipple from root to tip, the sounds of pleasure she made went straight to his stones.

"The human condition practically means being hurt, but there is also the promise of unfettered joy, so I would say the risk is worth the reward." He returned to her lips, kissed her with such intent that he hoped it would relieve her immediate fears, and when he sought out her tongue with his, she returned the embrace with enthusiasm.

"Joy would be lovely…" Then she gave up the effort of talking in favor of kissing various portions of his face, neck, or chest.

For the next few moments, Peregrine lost himself in her body, her lips, her very being. She welcomed him and it was like coming home, as if being away in the navy had been worth it, for she was his prize.

By the time she reached for his frontfalls, his length was engorged to the point of pain. "I haven't been with any other man since you."

The confession both stoked his need but had another wave of protection welling for her. "Then I hope I won't disappoint you this time." As his member sprang from his breeches, he paused long enough to appreciate Cora in all her glory. Skin flushed, legs parted, skirting rucked up to her hips, eyes shining, she looked the part of a woman far gone in lust.

And his heart squeezed from the image.

"Why do you hesitate?" A frown turned her kiss swollen lips downward. "I've dreamed of this, ever since that one time in the meadow."

"Truth be told, I have kept the image of you in my mind. It kept me company, haunted my thoughts during those long nights at sea." Then her words sank into his passion-soaked brain. She dreamed of him, of them, doing *this*? Desire for her spiked. Circumstances weren't ideal but taking her on the desk would have to do. He couldn't very well carry her up the stairs, for he didn't even have a proper bed up there.

"At least there was that and I wasn't forgotten."

"Leaving you behind was the greatest mistake of my life; I *never* forgot you." There was no more time for preliminaries, for he needed her now. Peregrine shoved up yards of her skirting, and when she was bared to his gaze, he gripped her hips and brought her forward until she balanced on the edge of the desk. "Ah, Cora, I don't take this concession lightly." As passion drove his instincts, he kissed her, delved a hand between her thighs, and as the heat of her glided over his skin, he coaxed the button at her center out of hiding, and she gasped.

"It's been too long; I won't last." She wriggled from his ministrations, constantly clutched at his shoulders in an effort to hold him closer. "This is better than when I touch myself."

Bloody hell, she pleasures herself?

"What?"

On the heels of a strained giggle, she kissed him. "Can I help it if I needed a release, craved it at times, and you weren't there?"

The thought of that filled his mind, pushed him far too close to the edge. With his shaft pulsing, Peregrine rubbed his fingertips over that pearl with varying degrees of fiction, and true to her warning, Cora's breath shallowed. She threw back her head, levered herself on one arm while holding onto his nape with her other hand.

"Ah!" When she tumbled into bliss, twin spots of color blazed on her cheeks. A semi-stifled scream left her throat while she dug her nails into the fabric of his jacket.

It was incredibly erotic, and he couldn't wait any longer to claim her. Swift and hard, Peregrine kissed her, and at the same time found her center with the tip of his member, and then thrust with authority, penetrating her, and didn't stop until he was fully sheathed in her honeyed heat. "Oh, God," he whispered against her lips. "I have missed this—you."

"I know that feeling all too well." She clutched at his forearm. Need mirrored in her eyes. "Don't hold back."

He nodded. It had been a long time indeed since he'd been with a woman. Such a thing hadn't been a priority while in the navy, and when he'd returned to London, his time had been spent recovering from his injuries. But now, with Cora, it was raw, and real, and right, as if he'd been waiting for this exact moment.

As if fate was giving him a promise of sorts.

His thrusts were frantic, hard, and deep. At one point, he paused inside her merely to enjoy the blissful sensations of being that deeply connected to her. Cora held his head between her hands, brought his forehead to hers, and kissed him like a woman desperate for the very air he breathed. He kissed her back, of course, for how could he not? It was as if he'd never parted from her, as if that gulf had never been formed.

Then, he straightened as urgency compelled him to finish, for he had already passed the point of no return. He held her hips, the outside of her thighs in an effort to go as deep as he could, to claim her and tell her without words that everything would be right as rain, stroking over and over into this woman who'd managed to upend his life again.

All too soon his stones drew tight and hot pleasure rushed through his length. He ignored everything while he thrust quicker and faster. When she broke with a cry upon her lips and tears in her eyes, he kissed her, taking most of the sound into himself as he plunged into an intense release that left him shattered and sated. "Cora…" He ground his pelvis into hers to prolong the sensations, to continue feeling the fluttering of her body around his, but the act was over, even if he wasn't ready to let her go.

"Dear heavens, I had forgotten how potent you are," she said, and her lips brushed his. "So satisfying if quick."

His limbs shook as she clung to him. "My apologies. It has been an age since I coupled with a woman." Wanting to hold her, to prolong that cocoon around them, he picked her up, carried her to the other side of the small room where he fell into a sheet-covered leather winged-back chair. It would be where he relaxed between working hours, where he would enjoy a cuppa. Then he cradled her on his lap, her legs hanging over one side. In the aftermath, when his pulse pounded and the flutter of hers danced beneath his fingertips and their frantic breathing slowly calmed, the guilt snuck in once more.

I never should have left her.

One of her hands curled about his nape. Her ragged breathing steamed his ear, but the warmth of her against his chest, the smell of her in his nose lulled him into a state of complacency. Now, more than ever, Peregrine was convinced they belonged together, and what was more, the love he'd once had for her flew out of the box he'd tucked it into, and it blazed to life even stronger than it had been before.

For many moments, they remained in silence as he held her close, and in those precious seconds, he knew what perfection felt like. But at his core, he was a gentleman. "I suppose I should apologize. That wasn't well done of me even if I heartily enjoyed myself."

"There is no need. We both wanted this—needed it. For forgiveness, for closure perhaps."

He remained silent, for that sounded all too final.

Eventually, Cora roused. She caught his gaze as she tugged her bodice back into place. "For my sanity, we can't come together like this anymore, Perry."

"Why?" They were perfectly matched. "This was amazing. It reminded me of everything I ever wanted when I stupidly gave it up to keep you from grief, when I wasn't… ready."

"Yes, I agree it was a wonderful tryst." She sighed. "But you know why we can't continue in this vein."

He frowned even as part of him rejoiced that she felt that connection between them as well. "I *don't* understand. You wanted this coupling."

"I did." Shadows haunted her eyes. "I'm not strong enough to lose you again." Finality rang in her voice. "Where it angered me before, I fear it would break me this time."

His heart constricted. "I won't leave. This I promise you."

"You said that before."

"Now I mean it. I'm *not* going anywhere."

For long moments she peered into his eyes before dropping her gaze. "I fear that I'm not worthy enough of you, and I'm certainly not free. Not while my family is in dire straits. I should always have to take a paid position."

"I *will* take care of you. We *will* have enough." After everything, would he lose her?

"You know how impossible it will be to butt heads with Mrs. Bromington, and I don't wish to sneak around merely to see you. That seems wrong somehow."

"But—"

"Stop, Peregrine." Gently, she pressed her index finger over his lips. "I mustn't go home in defeat when Papa needs all the coin I can spare. Because of that, I have no time to invite a man into my life as a distraction."

"Though I can't help but think a distraction is a good thing, I will support you." He grabbed her hand and then kissed the back of it. "Give me a chance, Cora. We both can survive anything if we have each other. Let me give you a new courtship—a summertime courtship. Remember how lovely our last time courting was?"

"But, I—"

"And if, during that time, you adamantly find that deep down in your heart things simply won't work between us, I will bow out as a gentleman, leave you to your life while I go about mine, but don't shut me out merely because you're frightened and feeling trapped."

"Oh, why do you do such things to me, when I don't know my own mind?" She laid her head on his chest and sighed.

"Does that mean you give permission for me to pay my addresses to you?" He wasn't about to declare defeat. That wasn't who he was.

A tiny huff escaped her. "You will have a bad time of it with Mrs. Bromington."

"In the navy I'd been in tighter coils than this. It is only a matter of finding an appropriate weakness to wage my campaign." Placing a kiss on the top of her head, he wrapped his arms around her. "You deserve your own life, Cora, else you will be forever toiling for everyone else."

"I shall give you until mid-June. If I haven't fallen back into love with you by then, you'll need to square with the fact that fate doesn't want us together."

It was more than he had this morning. "Since you have obviously underestimated me, I can't wait to show you the second time 'round for us is better than the first, and I won't need that long. Mark my words."

He would fight any number of dragons and pockets-to-let parents to gain the life he had always wanted—with her.

Chapter Eleven

May 27, 1817
Waterstone Place
Mayfair, London

W*HY DID SHE insist that I attend tonight?*

Cora frowned as she navigated through the crush of people heading toward the smallish ballroom on the first floor. Since she only had three gowns in her possession, she'd worn the one of mint green that featured a gold satin sash around the waist, lace about the bodice, and gauzy, golden, short sleeves at the shoulder. It wasn't lavish or elaborate, but it suited her frame and complexion and made her blue eyes stand out.

"Come, girl. Stop dawdling," Mrs. Bromington demanded.

With a sigh, Cora left the relative safety of the base of the stairs where she'd paused and rushed to catch up to the older woman.

The last thing she wanted to do with her time was spend it with her stubborn and acerbic charge. It had been two days since she'd come together with Peregrine, two days since she'd suffered an emotional breakdown in his arms, two days since he'd comforted her and indulged her wish to couple.

And it had been beyond amazing.

To say nothing of her giving him permission to court her again. Why had she done it? Wasn't such a relationship between them far too complicated with too many obstacles littering the path? Part of her was flattered and excited, while another part of her was anxious and filled with dread, for any type of courtship would surely draw ire from her employer.

To his credit, Peregrine *had* come to call yesterday. But he was denied entry into the house, and after trying to gain access a few times, he'd apparently given up to fight another day, leaving a bouquet of wildflowers with Mr. Riley at the door.

She admired his tenacity, but he would face blatant opposition from her employer. Then she frowned at said woman. How did Mrs. Bromington know the Viscount and Viscountess of Waterstone? For that matter, why had her employer spent so much time on her toilette when usually she didn't care?

"I'm surprised you wished to attend with such crowds, Mrs. Bromington." Since she wasn't in charge of her employer's correspondence, she never knew which invitations had been issued or accepted.

"It isn't a crime to wish to mingle in society. My husband enjoyed it, certainly, and he had the knack of making connections regardless of class." She swept her gaze about the assemblage. "Ah, there. Since we arrived too late for the receiving line, let us greet our host and hostess."

Cora's frown deepened. "You are acquainted with them?"

"I should say so." But she didn't expand on the topic.

Without context and more than a little curiosity, Cora trailed after her employer, ever mindful of the cane. If someone was in her way, Mrs. Bromington simply rapped the end against shins and calves until a path was cleared.

The couple talked with a few others at the farthest point of the room, and when Mrs. Bromington approached, the viscountess broke off her conversation to rest the full of her attention on the older woman.

"Hello, Mother." Her smile was genuine. "I'd hoped you

might accept the invitation even though you ignore most of them I send."

Shock went through Cora's chest. Her lower jaw gaped slightly. "Lady Waterstone is your daughter?" she asked in a low voice from Mrs. Bromington's side.

"She is." As the older woman glanced back at her, a trace of pride went over her face. "The girl married well." To the viscountess, she said, "You ought to know by now I am quite choosy where I spend my time."

"So it matters not that your own flesh and blood wishes to have you about?" Hurt reflected in the woman's eyes, so much like Mrs. Bromington's, except the green wasn't yet faded. "Why must you continue to be so difficult?" She lowered her voice to a mere whisper as the viscount looked on in mild concern. "I don't care about your money; I only want you in my life, to see your grandchildren."

Without comment, Cora watched the drama unfold with undisguised curiosity. Perhaps in her early forties, the viscountess had looks near enough to her mother's to warrant worry. Those features would turn harsh if she didn't take care of her skin… or if she fell into bitterness.

"Or you could bring your children to see me. I don't know why it is my responsibility to visit with all my children. That would take up all my time, and I do maintain a schedule of my own." It wouldn't be true to Mrs. Bromington's nature if she proved amenable. More shocking still was the fact she'd deigned to attend this event if one of her family members was involved. She was forever disparaging their reputations to any of the servants or her friends that would listen. "Ever since you married, your time hasn't been your own and you've forgotten where you came from."

Exasperation lined the viscountess' face. "Yes, I know I've gained certain duties and responsibilities since I married, and I do have many charities that require my time, but your grandchildren are growing quickly. The oldest is fifteen. He'll go off to university soon. As for the girls, they would benefit from your wisdom."

That was debatable, but Cora held her tongue.

Mrs. Bromington sniffed. "Then bring them 'round. The only thing preventing your children from knowing me is you."

The absurdity of that statement, coupled with the confusion in Lady Waterstone's face tugged at Cora's heart. When she would have interjected, the viscountess spoke.

"We shall discuss such things later. This night is for celebrating your birthday, Mother, and it will be that much more enjoyable since you have decided to attend the festivities. My cook has made all your favorites for dinner, which will be presented at eleven o'clock after dancing."

Ah, so this is why Mrs. Bromington has come. The night centered around her, and all attention would be on her. The woman was naught but a notice sponge.

"That remains to be seen." But one corner of the older woman's mouth tipped in a smile. She nodded at Lord Waterstone, then at her daughter. "I thank you for remembering my special day. Now I'd like to visit with some friends." So saying, she moved away from the gathering.

"Of course. We will talk later." Lady Waterstone nodded. Finally, her gaze flicked to Cora. "Please, enjoy yourself this evening. Mother can sometimes be… difficult."

"That is perhaps a great understatement, my lady, but thank you."

"I try to please her, to placate her at times, but she is stubborn."

She nodded. "Thank you for your kindness this evening." Then she hurried after her charge. Once she caught up to Mrs. Bromington, she laid a hand on her arm. "Why did you not tell me it was your birthday?"

The older woman frowned. "There wasn't a need for you to know."

"But I would have given you a small token to mark the day."

"As I said, I don't require such. It would only add clutter to the house."

Annoyance streaked through Cora's chest. "Of course you didn't tell me, because now you can lord it over my head that I didn't even do that for you." Why did anything about the woman surprise her anymore?

"Don't be crass, girl." The widow waved a hand. "I wish to gossip with my friends. Find something to occupy yourself."

Cora briefly pointed her gaze to the ceiling before resting it on Mrs. Bromington. "Make certain you thank your daughter for the honor of the ball. It was a lovely gesture."

"Ha!" Mrs. Bromington snorted. "It is the least she can do for me. I gave her life, raised her with enough manners and properness and spirit that she caught the eye of a member of the *beau monde*. Then she left me."

What a skewed way of looking at things. "She is allowed to have her own life. That is what daughters do. Grow up and marry. Have their own families. Sons too." Yet she—Cora— wasn't even giving herself that same grace.

"They shouldn't forget their mothers."

"Then the mothers shouldn't deport themselves with such bitterness and angst that no one wishes to be around them." Cora frowned. "You consistently make yourself a terror so that you've shoved away your family. Why, I wonder?"

"You are quite cheeky tonight." The widow stared at her, no doubt shocked from Cora's audacity in speech, then she offered a half grin. "Make certain you don't involve yourself with a man tonight. You are here for me, and it would behoove you to remember your place."

"Of course, Mrs. Bromington." The woman was beyond aggravating, but for the moment, she was the reason for Cora's time in London, and sending a portion of that income back home to her parents was going toward paying the taxes on the country estate.

Finding a chair amidst the collection set up along one of the walls of the ballroom that housed an assortment of wallflowers, companions, and other unpopular women, Cora sighed as she sat. This certainly wasn't the life she'd wished to lead, but there was nothing for it. If she wished to help her family, she would endure, and seeing Mrs. Bromington interact with her daughter made her appreciate her own family even more.

A few murmurs went through the room as a country reel formed on the dance floor. A few of the young wallflowers turned to look toward the door at the top of the room. Cora glanced in that direction as well, and when Captain Wetherford entered the ballroom flushed with pleasure and victory, her heart fluttered, and the pulse accelerated.

Then she frowned. Had he trysted with Miss Beaufort or someone else to make him look so fresh and virile? Immediately, confusion gripped her. Wasn't he supposed to be courting her? Not having any answers, her gaze bounced to the man at his side, with the blond looks and form of a Grecian god. Perhaps he was a friend, for the two men talked quite animatedly to each other just inside the doorway while the country reel got underway.

As she watched, he ended the conversation, and when he made eye contact with her, he winked and slowly made his way around the perimeter of the room toward her location.

Oh, good heavens, he's coming this way!

Far too restless to remain seated, Cora rose to her feet. She hid her hands within the folds of her skirting to still their shaking. By the time he came to a stop in front of her, she harbored mixed feelings. Happiness warred with annoyance.

"Good evening, Miss Hasting. I trust you have been well?"

"Well enough, I suppose," she said in a low voice, conscious that the women around them watched with interest. "For a man who wishes to court me, where the devil have you been?" Especially after they'd come together like a summer storm two days before.

He huffed. "I did call yesterday but was denied entry. Did you receive the flowers?"

She blew out a breath. How could she remain out of sorts when he had tried? "Yes, they are lovely. I adore wildflowers. They remind me of—"

"That day on your father's estate," he finished in a whisper, and there was wicked promise in his hazel eyes that sent tingles down her spine.

"Yes." Drat him for being far too charming. It was impossible to maintain her annoyance toward him. "I'm sorry Mrs. Bromington has been less than a delight. I would have liked to see you yesterday when you called."

"It is nothing that I didn't expect, but I will try harder." He took one of her hands and brought it to his lips. "I am glad to see you tonight. That was an unexpected surprise."

"For me as well." She came toward him a tiny step. "The viscountess is Mrs. Bromington's daughter, if you can believe that."

"Oh?" Surprise went over his face. "Interesting. I was asked here by his son, to speak to a group of former military men before the ball officially opened." Pleasure lined his face, and it was one of the first times she'd seen him truly content. "My speech was appreciated, and if I do say so myself, my audience appreciated me as well." A waver entered his voice. "It makes such a difference when people accept me despite my scarred face."

"That is such a lovely sentiment." Daring much, she laid a hand on his arm. "I am glad you are finding an activity in society that gives you such confidence."

"As am I." With a half-grin that awoke the butterflies in her belly, he led her away from the grouping of chairs then pulled her behind a grouping of potted palms and ferns that acted as a partial barrier. There were a few such groupings throughout the room. "You are lovely in that color."

"Thank you." She couldn't have enough of him, but the only thing she could do was rove her gaze up and down his person. Clad in dark evening clothing with a silver satin waistcoat, he was far too handsome for her peace of mind. "Have you opened the shop yet?"

"Soon. Perhaps in a day or two. Everything is unpacked and the paper is down from the window." Excitement danced in his eyes. "Let us hope someone will find interest in what I have to offer, or merely come to see objects from my travels." He shrugged, which drew her attention to the breadth of his shoulders. "On that subject, I brought you something."

"Oh?" When he removed something from his waistcoat pocket and held it up, her heart skipped a beat. A hair comb rested on his gloved palm. The teeth were silver, but the top was decorated with stars and moons carved from ivory.

"I thought you might like this. To match your necklace." His gaze dropped to her décolletage.

An audible gasp escaped her, while one of her hands flew to her chest. "You noticed."

"I did." Emotions shadowed the depths of his eyes, but they were largely unreadable. "I gave you that ring to commemorate our engagement."

The thin silver band with the rounded top of ivory had graced her finger the whole of their engagement period. The morning he left her at the church, she'd taken the ring off, but couldn't part from it. Instead, she wore it on a chain most of the time. "I, uh… I wear it nearly every day. Couldn't bear to leave it lying around to be stolen. It's pretty and valuable."

"It is. I procured it in a tiny shop near the Horn of Africa while docked for supplies. At the time I didn't know why I'd bought it."

She nodded and blinked away the tears that sprang into her eyes. "It reminds me of you," she admitted in a soft voice, for that had been one of the sweetest days of her life, and they had made good use of that wildflower meadow afterward.

"Ah ha!" Peregrine winked. "The very fact you kept it and wear it often means you aren't as indifferent toward me as you want me to think."

"Perhaps." A blush warmed her cheeks.

"At least there is that." He moved behind her, and then he slipped the comb into her hair, just to the side of her upswept tresses. "Perfection." His fingertips lingered slightly longer at the crux of her shoulder. "I hope to always bestow such gifts upon you."

"It is sweet." She hoped that Mrs. Bromington wasn't watching them. "And I already adore it. Thank you."

As he came back in front of her, he trailed his fingers over her shoulder to brush the pad of his thumb along the side of her jaw. "If we were alone, I'd kiss you senseless. To remind you that I'm in earnest."

The blush in her cheeks continued to blaze, and suddenly she was tongue-tied. She touched a hand to his chest. "I—"

"Am I interrupting?"

Immediately, she sprang away from him. "No, I... We... Ah, we were merely talking," she said, as she recognized the man as the same who'd come into the ballroom with Peregrine.

The captain chuckled, and the sound tickled through her chest. "Miss Hasting and I were merely talking." He glanced at his friend. "Lord Maubrey, this is Miss Hasting, companion to Mrs. Bromington."

"Ah, the dragon's handler." His grin was wide as he availed himself of her hand and swiftly brought it to his lips. "A pleasure to meet you. I have heard much about you from Peregrine."

"Have you known him long?" Though he was quite charming, he didn't set her heartbeat to racing like the captain did.

He put a hand to his chest and assumed an expression of mock outrage as he stared at Peregrine. "You have told her nothing of me?" His blond hair glimmered golden in the candlelight. A few inches taller than Peregrine, he was slightly leaner but no less imposing.

"I'm afraid when we are together, there are other conversations to keep us occupied," Peregrine said as he bounced his gaze between them.

"I can well imagine." The viscount slipped a hand to the small of her back. "Come, Miss Hasting. A waltz is forming. Let me partner you in this set since my friend has such an appalling lack of manners that he hasn't asked you yet."

Peregrine glowered. "I was getting 'round to it."

"Oh, I don't… I couldn't. I'm not here as a guest." Mrs. Bromington would dress her down for certain.

"Nonsense. You are the daughter of a baron, are you not?"

"I am." Cora smiled. Clearly, Peregrine had told this man about her. It was a bit lovely to see the captain jealous. "Perhaps just one set, then. I would enjoy that, Lord Maubrey. Thank you." With a parting glance at Peregrine, she allowed the viscount to escort her to an empty portion of the dance floor. "I will no doubt be lectured by Mrs. Bromington once she sees me dancing."

"Tell her that a viscount insisted, and you really shouldn't deny a member of the *beau monde* a request." Then he winked as they waited for the opening notes.

"That will undoubtedly work. I hope I'll remember the steps. It has been rather a long time." Thank goodness this was a Viennese waltz. It was one she and her sisters learned early on in their lives.

"Fear not, Miss Hasting. I won't let you fall." For the next few moments, they concentrated on the steps and the intricate hand placements.

Soon enough, Cora remembered the patterns, and to her delight, she enjoyed the exercise. When she came back to partner the viscount, she smiled. "You have known Peregrine for years, yes?"

"Since school, and we served on the same ship in the navy. I was his navigator, the man who kept his crew in check and carried out his orders when the first mate was occupied." His eyes were kind as they circled around each other. "I was also the man who dragged his unconscious self from the fire onboard the ship, who saved him so he can vex me now."

"I wasn't aware." As questions whirled about her mind, she

switched partners, exchanged smiles with that man while she reeled internally. Once back with the viscount, she peered up into his face. "You rescued him." It wasn't a question.

"How could I not?" Shadows flitted through his eyes. "He is my best friend, sometimes my only friend, because of what the war has done to my mind, and he needed me in that moment. There was nothing else I could do; I want him to be happy and at peace now, but he is so damned stubborn."

"That is quite true." Her fingers glided over his palm in the movements of the dance.

"I am glad he's courting you, for he is often insecure due to his injuries."

"He needn't be. The man is as handsome as he's ever been, perhaps even more so now." Then the steps pulled her away and she had to wait to continue the conversation.

Lord Maubrey looked at her with speculation in his eyes when they came back together. "Obviously, I think Peregrine is one of the best people I know. He is having a difficult time transitioning to civilian life, and there is a certain anxiety regarding the success of his shop."

She frowned. "Why?"

"The man wants to be seen as a favorable catch, for he is adamant that he makes an impression on you." Nothing but earnestness lay stamped on his face. "It is no secret he still has feelings for you, Miss Hasting."

"I know." She dropped her gaze to the knot of his cravat. "Perhaps he already has made an impression." It both made her excited but worried.

"Go gently with him. He might appear confident, but deep down, he fears that he won't succeed. As a ship captain, he excelled, but being a civilian is a different beast." As the dance wound down, he looked at her with all soberness. "Above everything, he is trying to carve out a life for himself that can support a wife and perhaps a family, but he has a certain way of looking at things that might come off as too overbearing." He kept her on the dance floor for a few seconds after the other dancers disbursed. "Please don't hurt my friend, Miss Hasting. He was a broken man following your failed engagement. I hesitate to think of what will happen to him if you grind his heart beneath your heel."

A stab of guilt went through her chest. "I give you my word that I will be kind to him no matter what." That was the best promise she could give, for in this moment, she remained confused by him.

"I will hold you to that." Then he escorted her to the sidelines where Peregrine waited. "I am going to give my good wishes to the hosts."

An unexpected giggle escaped Cora. "The viscountess is Mrs. Bromington's mother. She threw this ball to celebrate her mother's birthday."

Lord Maubrey's eyebrows soared. "Then I shall wish the widow well, and it will perhaps give you a few moments of freedom, Miss Hasting."

"Thank you." She gave him a smile, and went he melted into the milling crowds, she looked at Peregrine. "He is quite lovely. I'm glad you have him in your life."

His throat worked as he battled with emotions. "Thank you." With a graveled voice, he offered his crooked arm to her. "Come with me for a glass of champagne while Charles does the pretty with your dragon."

"I would like that." The viscount's words still bounced through her mind as she put her fingers on his sleeve, and he escorted her from the room.

At the end of the corridor, a table was set up where a footman poured flutes of champagne and a maid handed them out.

"I must say, you seemed as if you enjoyed yourself while with Maubrey," Peregrine said as he gave her a flute of the bubbly wine.

"I did, actually. It's so refreshing to have fun at a society event instead of being told to make myself invisible because I am merely a companion." When she took a sip, the bubbles tickled her nose, and she sneezed.

The captain grinned. Flutters scudded through her lower belly. "Shall I call upon you tomorrow?"

"Yes, please, but I am on duty tomorrow. Thursday would be a more opportune time since it is my day off."

"Ah, but perhaps I wish to do battle with my biggest adversary." He winked as he took his own sip.

"Miss Hasting? Where the devil are you?"

Cora met Peregrine's eyes and laughed. Even to her own ears it was a genuine sound. Then she sighed. "Apparently, I need to go. Heaven forbid I enjoy myself." With a shrug, she handed him her flute. "It is my lot, but don't give up, Captain. We can't both of us let life defeat us, can we?"

Annoyance flashed quickly through his expression. "I'm still here, Miss Hasting, and I have no plans to let the dragon tramp all over me."

"Until tomorrow, then." As she blinked away tears of relief, Cora waved and then hurried to the ballroom door, where she was immediately set upon by the widow. "Let's see you settled comfortably, hmm? Dinner will be served soon, but I'll wager you wish to watch the dancing…"

CHAPTER TWELVE

May 28, 1817
Somewhere in Mayfair

CORA GLANCED ABOUT the drawing room with interest, for the usual furniture had been cleared away. In its place were delicate chairs with gilt-painted legs and light blue, velvet cushions arranged into four tidy rows of ten chairs each. At the front of the room, a pianoforte as well as a harp had been set up where musicians and singers would perform.

It had been Mrs. Bromington's desire to attend the musicale evening, and though Cora never voiced opposition, she did secretly wonder why. People milled about the room, talking quietly while some had already found seats.

"The recital will begin soon. We should find somewhere to sit."

The widow huffed. "What do you think I'm doing, girl?" She nudged two men out of her way by knocking her cane against their backsides before finally settling on a chair in the front row. "Sit." Gesturing with her cane, she indicated the chair next to hers. "This will allow us the best view and to hear the music without distortion."

"I had no idea you enjoyed such things."

"I am a regular patron to various causes like this about Town."

"Ah." Apparently, despite all the horrors that Mrs. Bromington was, she *did* support musicians. "What a lovely thing to discover."

"Yes, well, I feel that I should." A frown pulled the corners of her lips downward. "One of my children—a son—who perished before adulthood, was a gifted pianist. My husband and I thought that talent should be nurtured, so we hired tutors, but sadly, the boy contracted a horrid bout of pneumonia at the age of twelve. It continued to worsen despite all measures to thwart it, and eventually, he succumbed to the sickness."

"I am so sorry to hear it." Involuntarily, Cora reached out and put her hand over the widow's. "Then you support musicians in his honor?"

"Perhaps." Emotion shadowed her eyes before she hid it under her usual mask of disgruntlement. She moved her hand from Cora's. "Music is something I enjoy. Why shouldn't I become a patron to some of these young people?"

Despite her wish to remain decorous, Cora snorted. "Because you treat young people horribly. Well, you treat *all* people horribly, but I'm glad to know there is still a heart beating beneath all those layers of thorns and bitterness." It might have been over the line, but she couldn't help herself.

Remarkably, Mrs. Bromington chuckled—a wheezing sort of rusty sound as if she were unaccustomed to laughing—yet she didn't answer.

The first half of the musicale evening was quite mediocre with only a couple of excellent performers. Everyone else either had a bad case of nerves, or they hadn't cared to practice their craft all that much.

"I would enjoy a glass of punch, girl. Go fetch it for me. My old knees are aching, so I don't wish to get up."

"Very well." It would be lovely to have a few minutes away from her charge's company, regardless.

Of course, there was a bit of a queue at the refreshment table, which meant she had to wait. Finally, with a glass of punch in hand, Cora came back down the corridor toward the drawing room, and that was when the captain stepped into her path.

She gasped, and the hand holding the glass shook, the light pink liquid sloshing close to the rim. "Peregrine." Faint terror twisted down her spine, for if Mrs. Bromington caught sight of her lingering in his company, she wouldn't be best pleased, yet he was so handsome in his evening attire that she couldn't help but rove her hungry gaze over his person. "What are you doing here?"

A faint grin curved his sensuous lips. "I wished to speak to you, since I have been thwarted from doing just that with every call I make."

Truly, he *was* trying. She nodded while thoughts of stealing a kiss danced through her mind. "I'm afraid I can't spare the time to talk now. Mrs. Bromington is waiting for her punch."

"I thought as much." He glanced about then lowered his voice. "Meet me in the library ten minutes from now. I can't imagine you are enthralled about this evening's entertainment."

Excitement circled through her belly where it crashed into knots of worry. "But Mrs. Bromington—"

He shrugged. "Make an excuse." His gaze dropped to her mouth, and she trembled at the wicked promise in his eyes. "Tell her your stomach is upset. The ladies' retiring room is across the hall from the library on the first floor."

"Oh, I couldn't…" She *shouldn't* for she wasn't skilled in dissembling, but she wanted to see him. Finally, she nodded. "All right. Ten minutes." When she glanced about the immediate surroundings, she frowned when Miss Beaufort waved at her—or rather Peregrine—with a wide smile. "You should go since you are about to be set upon by quite a determined young woman." With her confidence slightly dented and annoyance firmly in her chest, Cora left him to return to the drawing room and Mrs. Bromington's side.

"You were gone far too long for such an errand," the older lady groused as she accepted the crystal glass from Cora's hand.

She bit back the less than ladylike reply she wished to utter aloud. Instead, she said, "There was a crush. I needed to wait my turn."

"Bah. Crowds. London is certainly being overrun these days. A pity my husband didn't buy property in the country. Surrey is lovely this time of year."

Cora had no response to that.

In short order, the second half of the musicale evening began with two sisters, one on the piano and one singing. They were quite lovely and received applause afterward, but the musician that followed was significantly less talented. Once, she glanced toward the rear of the room. Peregrine gave a slight nod with a raised eyebrow. Then he stood and exited the space.

Anticipation sent her heartbeat accelerating. While the third person—an older man this time—gained the performance area, Cora forced moisture into her suddenly tight throat. It was now or never. She put a hand to her belly and another to her mouth. Then she uttered what she hoped was a believable moan.

Mrs. Bromington huffed with apparent annoyance. "Are you ill, girl?"

"Uh…" *If you wish to see Peregrine, make this lie convincing!* Listening to the voice in her head, she nodded. "Yes. My stomach is upset. The monthly plague no doubt." Which, truly, such an event wasn't scheduled to come upon her for another couple of weeks. Since that wasn't a subject fit for any sort of company perhaps outside of with one's maid, the widow ordered her from the room to compose herself.

"I will come to the retiring room and find you after the evening has finished, once I visit with a few people."

"All right." On a rush of excitement mixed with relief, Cora fled the room with as much decorum as she could muster. She went downstairs still feigning sickness in the event someone watched her and would mention to her charge about seeing her, but there were hardly any guests milling about. Most were in the drawing room or going into the billiards room next to the library.

As soon as she went into the library, the door closed behind her, and Peregrine immediately tugged her into his arms. Shadows filled the room. Only two candles burned in silver holders on the mantel.

"Finally, we're alone!" The heat of his whisper brushed along her cheek just before he grazed his lips beneath her jaw.

As much as she wanted to give herself over to the feeling of familiarity of being in his arms, she gave him a shove until he released her. "Perhaps you should find Miss Beaufort. Clearly, she's desperate for your company." Why the devil did the young woman keep seeking him out?

"That would be quite impossible." As he prowled toward her, she retreated.

"Why?" There was an intense look in his eyes that awoke a flock of butterflies in her lower belly. Step by step, he matched hers, stalked her like a predatory jungle cat.

"I am courting you." In no time, he closed the distance between them, stalled her between a shelf and his body, planted a palm on the book spines near her head. "And right now, I'm of a mind to kiss you senseless due to Mrs. Bromington keeping you from me."

"Ah." Feeling much like teasing him, Cora ducked beneath his arm. She tried to flee, but he ended up trapping her between the hard wall of his chest and a triangular-shaped wooden ladder on wheels that tilted slightly toward the shelf. "This is hardly a private setting," she whispered and laid a hand on his chest.

"It is private enough, and quite frankly, I have thought about little else except being with you since that time in my shop." Before she could respond, Peregrine leaned into her, cupped her cheek, and then claimed her lips in a gentle yet intense kiss she wasn't strong enough to resist.

The heat of him, the fresh clean scent of him, the fleeting touch of his fingers sans gloves all worked at her undoing. Cora stared up at him as her heartbeat hummed. "What have you done to me? You are like a fever in the blood that won't stop burning until I'm reduced to dust." Then she gasped and her gaze darted to the mangled side of his face. "Oh, dear. That was a poor choice of words."

"I believe the description was apt. I take no offense, but I am grateful you have treated me no differently than any other man despite my looks." He slid his hand from her cheek and buried his fingers into her hair, kissed her again with more authority, and further words flew right out of her head.

And she was in danger of being lost.

Trapped between his arms and the ladder, she didn't want to move. "This is far too scandalous, Perry. We are tempting fate."

"No, we are chasing our own interests and dreams while perhaps escaping the prisons we keep ourselves in."

At least she would offer up a protest, feeble as it was, for each time his lips and fingers glanced over her skin, more of her willpower dissolved into dust. "We could be found out."

"We could, indeed, and if you decide we shouldn't indulge, by all means I will let you return to your dragon's side." Slowly, he drew up her satin skirting while nuzzling into the crook of her shoulder. "God, I adore it when you wear this yellow gown."

"Are you certain you haven't mistaken me tonight?" Not able to help teasing him, she grinned before an unexpected whimper left her throat the second his fingers feathered over her outer thigh.

"Never again, for I was naught but a nodcock that last time." Then he guided his lips down the column of her throat and followed the lace around her bodice. "Will you bid me nay, sweeting?"

The use of the endearment further had a cloud of passion scudding through her brain. "No, for I have hoped for more of your kisses since that day as well."

"Good." As he plied her with gentle kisses, he moved his fingers along the inside of her thigh. Shivers trailed in his wake, and when he did the same to the other thigh, a shuddering sigh escaped her, and she opened her legs slightly while balancing with her arse precariously perched on one of the wooden steps.

"Surely you don't intend to… play, like that, now…" It was pure folly. What if someone accidentally came upon them? But, dear heavens, she desperately wanted his touch!

"I do. The musicale will go on for at least thirty more minutes. Plenty of time to tease, don't you think?" Then he slipped his fingers between her thighs, dancing, exploring, caressing that sensitive flesh, back and forth in a mesmerizing rhythm, that made her nearly mad from needing him. "It seems you're all too ready. We must do something about that, hmm?" Before she could utter a response, he'd coaxed her swelling nubbin out of hiding, and then strummed those talented fingers over it.

"Oh!" Shivers of heated need fell over her, fracturing throughout her body and into every nerve ending. "You don't play fair."

"How so?" He followed the inquiry with feather weighted kisses to her lips, beneath her jaw, the crook of her shoulder, and all the while, he worked that tiny bundle of nerves, bringing her body into a frenzy of desire and plain lust.

"You could have merely kissed me, and I would have been ecstatic with that," she managed to gasp out. When she couldn't hold back a moan, he grinned, his lips sliding along the side of her neck.

"Perhaps, but you are a vixen, I think, and you should be shown how delicious you truly are." He licked the upper slopes of her breasts while continuing to caress her nubbin. "Especially since you are being kept from me by dear, selfish Mrs. Broming-ton."

"Ha! No one has ever likened me to such before," she managed to gasp out and curled her fingers around the side of the ladder merely to keep herself upright. The shivering tingles circling through her lower belly would make her dissolve into a boneless heap soon.

"I'll never stop berating myself for not choosing you that long ago morning."

Her heart squeezed. "The navy needed you more."

"Hardly. I was just one of many, I now know." When she thought she'd break from the exquisite torment, Peregrine withdrew his hand, and she whimpered a protest. "I'm not going anywhere."

"Then what…?" As she drew the next shuddering breath, he quickly eased down her bodice and encouraged her breasts from the nest of the remainder of her clothing. "Surely you've gone mad." A feeling of longing spiraled through her insides, for he hadn't sent her flying. No longer did she worry over the thought of being found.

Drat him.

"Not mad, at least not yet. Perhaps drunk on you." Peering into her eyes, he brushed the knuckles of one hand over a nipple until it tightened and pebbled. "Do I have your permission to do unspeakable things to you?"

"Will I enjoy it?"

"That is the hope, but only if you're quiet."

"Ah." Not knowing what he had in mind, she met his gaze, caught the knowing light in those hazel depths, and heat stung her cheeks. What he must think of her! Surely, she must be depraved if she wanted his continued attention. "I'm willing." Yet worry couldn't be entirely forgotten. This was improper and outrageously scandalous. *His* name and reputation wouldn't be ruined if they were discovered in highly compromising positions. Beyond that, she could fall pregnant, and then what would become of her or her family's name?

She'd have to run home in humiliation and scandal a second time.

"Stop thinking, Cora. I won't hurt you and neither will I leave." Once more he drew up her skirting and bunched it at her waist. As he dropped to his knees, he grinned up at her. "It is my hope you'll understand how much I care after this." Then he gripped her inner thighs and splayed her open. "So beautiful."

Why did he think so? Perhaps later she would ask. Anticipation battled with anxiety in her belly, for she didn't quite understand what he was about. She buried the fingers of one hand into his hair, upsetting his valet's carefully arranged style. "I may have changed my mind and—" A squeak cut off her words as he touched his mouth to her throbbing button.

He chuckled. The vibrations sent her into another level of delightful wonder. "Relax and concentrate on what I'm doing to you."

"Merciful heavens." From the moment he employed his lips and hot tongue to her most sensitive, private parts, Cora slowly lost the last vestiges of her sanity. "You..." She couldn't catch her breath, for with each nibble, every suckle, all the swipes and strokes of his tongue as he used the flat part as well as the tip, she was hurled higher and higher into pleasure where she'd ever gone before. This was all new to her, for she'd never been told a man could do such to a woman. How had he known? Did he think her woefully inexperienced?

Then it didn't matter, for the wild sensations dancing through her body left her heated and shaking with need.

"Perry... Oh, oh, oh!" Tears fell to her cheeks for the feelings were too big, too much, too overwhelming. Her breath came in short pants. Not once did Peregrine shy away from his work. He was a man bent on tossing her over the edge, and she hovered there, trapped, waiting with held breath and a hammering heart for him to release her into that dark void.

But he didn't. That blessed surcease didn't come.

At least not immediately.

The wicked man kept her poised on the razor's edge, pinning her there again and again with every penetrating stroke of his tongue, each calculated swipe, every new torment of suction on that swollen button until she openly cried out for him to stop but alternately plead for him to continue. She curled her hand into his hair to shove him away and cease the exquisite torment but also to hold him to her tighter exactly where she needed him.

This is like falling and flying combined.

Fearing she'd faint from the need tearing her apart, Cora squirmed, but he gripped her thighs that much tighter to keep her in place on the ladder. Her back arched, which put her deeper into his care, and still she made whimpering noises, because that was all she was capable of now. Laughter from the corridor beyond the library penetrated into her consciousness. The imminent threat of discovery merely enhanced the act.

"I can't quite grasp it, can't manage the fall..." The rushed whisper was filled with blatant pleading, but she didn't care. And oh, the sensations he'd already invoked inside her were glorious!

"It matters not. I only wanted to give you comfort, to show you I will always care. There will be more times to send you flying."

Despite the fact her body shook, the overwhelming feeling moving through her was peace and remarkably safety. Her thighs trembled in time to her racing pulse. "I wanted so much from you this night, but what you *have* given me is quite simply... lovely." She collapsed into the rungs of the ladder, uncaring that the hard wood dug into her skin or that she most likely resembled a broken marionette puppet. Even without that release, he'd managed to wring *everything* from her.

"I look forward to being with you thusly, to completing your fall." He stood, then, and leaning over her, brushed his lips over hers.

"So do I." Heat went through her cheeks, for his mouth had just been on the center of her being. "Will you, ah... Will you do *that* to me again?"

"Would you like me to?" Wicked promise gleamed in his eyes as he gave one of her nipples a light twist.

Pleasure streaked through her body, and she gasped. "I would very much enjoy that." When she didn't hear that laughter in the corridor again and, wanting him to feel at sixes and sevens as she did, Cora tumbled from the ladder to fall to her knees before him. "My turn, Captain."

"What?" Confusion lined his expression as he peered down at her. "Surely you don't mean what I think you are inferring to."

"Mmm, that largely depends on what happens next." Feeling uncommonly brave after he'd done such scandalous things to her, Cora cupped a hand about his equipage and massaged his length through the fabric of his evening breeches.

"Go gently." A hiss eased from his throat, but he laid a palm against the side of her head. "I don't wish to embarrass myself."

"If you fear me thinking differently about you, I won't." The more she caressed that part of him, the harder and longer it grew, and she knew a blatant need to see that erect manhood. Though she had no idea what she was doing, giving him pleasure became her new motivation. "To me, you have never been more handsome. Your scars only enhance that." Never had she been more honest.

His fingers in her hair tightened slightly in an effort to tilt back her head. "Do you truly mean that?" The wonder, the astonishment, in his voice made her eyes prickle with tears.

"I do, and I think I appreciate you more now." Suddenly shy, she dropped her gaze to his frontfalls as she quickly manipulated them with her trembling fingers. When his engorged length sprang free, she sucked in a quick breath. "Magnificent." She hadn't seen this part of him the other night at his shop when he'd claimed her on his desk. "To think you walk about all day with this… magical flesh, and then when you kiss me, it becomes as hard as iron."

Peregrine softly chuckled. "Not quite, but I thank you for the likeness." He laid a hand over hers. "Like this." Then he demonstrated, guided her hand, and taught her how to move her curled fingers along his shaft, how to caress him in a manner that would give him pleasure.

"Ah, I see." After batting away his hand, she scuttled even closer to him and then proceeded to work him over, hoping that her manipulation would bring him as much pleasure as he'd given to her. When she finally discovered how to twist her hand and massage his stones with the other, Cora glanced up at him. The ecstasy on his face made his visage that of an angel, and for the space of a heartbeat, she was transfixed.

Then she came closer, licked the head of his shaft. An unfamiliar earthiness came away on her palate, but it wasn't unpleasing, so she licked him again, and this time she swirled the tip of her tongue around and under the head, just below the crinkled skin.

"Bloody hell," he murmured, and he tightened his hand in her hair. "You are both my salvation and my destruction, I fear."

A sense of power enveloped her, and for the first time in her life, Cora felt as if someone appreciated her, not for what she could do for them, but for who she was—herself.

With a smokey bit of a chuckle, she licked his tip again, dared to wrap her lips around that velvety head, but then the sound of voices echoed just outside the library door. Peregrine's body stiffened. She slipped from his shaft and met his gaze. "Should I continue?"

"As much as I'd like for that to happen, we are in a more perilous position than we were at the first."

"True." Cold disappointment went through her belly. "Perhaps we can revisit this another time." A second bout of laughter prompted her to scramble to her feet. "I should go across the hall in case Mrs. Bromington comes looking for me." She tucked her breasts back into her bodice and arranged her clothing until the lines of the gown fell as they were supposed to.

"That might be best." With a faint frown, the captain righted his own clothing. "Oh, but there is this." After he delved his fingers into the pocket of his waistcoat, he removed a pink rose bud. "It's from the bouquet waiting for you at the widow's house. I had it delivered while you were out since I wasn't allowed to give it to you in person." When he tucked the bud behind her ear, he caressed the side of her face. "A lady should always have flowers."

"What a wonderful surprise." With a quick glance to the door, Cora closed the distance between them, lifted onto her toes, and then bussed his cheek. "I can't wait to see them. I'm so glad you remembered I adore flowers, roses especially. I must go." Then she scurried over the floor. "Thank you for tonight," she said in a lowered voice as she opened the panel enough to peer into the corridor. It was empty. Perhaps the men had moved into the billiards room next door. "Mrs. Bromington indicated an interest of walking in Hyde Park tomorrow near teatime, if you should wish to take in some exercise."

"I will," he said with a nod.

Seconds later, she slipped from the library and went across the hall into the ladies' retiring room, which was a parlor on other days. Since there was only one other woman there, who sat in a chair with her eyes closed, Cora walked as quietly as she could until she reached a rose brocade settee. Suddenly, the strength left her knees, and she hadn't the strength to sit properly, so she lounged with unladylike leisure against the decorative pillows to one side and let delicious lethargy moving through her blood to have at her.

"Good heavens, the man is potent," she whispered to herself as she closed her eyes. And it was becoming more difficult to resist him. Perhaps she wouldn't try any longer, for his unorthodox courtship was quite effective.

For the first time in a long while, she allowed herself to dream. In that vision there was a pretty little boy with blond hair and the captain's hazel eyes, squealing as a paper boat sailed upon the serpentine while she and Perry looked on...

CHAPTER THIRTEEN

May 29, 1817
Hyde Park

PEREGRINE HAD ALREADY walked a large loop through Hyde Park, but as of yet he hadn't spied either Cora or Mrs. Bromington, for with Cora's hint from last night, his plan was to definitely "meet" with them "accidentally."

With a rumbling stomach, for it was nearing teatime, he pressed on with his walk, following the bridle path toward the arch at the entrance to the park near Rotten Row. While he did so, memories from the night before trailed through his mind. He and Cora had been a bit scandalous. While he had only wished to kiss her and perhaps exchange caresses, she'd been a willing participant. To say nothing of how much she'd looked so delicious draped on that library ladder that he'd temporarily lost his sanity.

And that session had gotten out of hand all too quickly. Yes, it hadn't been well done of him to compromise her in such a way—again—but he couldn't help it. She was all too tempting. He could still feel the warmth of her on his hands, his lips, his tongue, and the images of her manipulating his shaft, nearly taking him into her mouth, left him straining even now. Through it all, his admiration and respect for her—truly, his feelings for her—had grown.

It was useless to deny it: he was more in love with Cora than he'd been the first time 'round. Truly, it would only be a matter of time before he asked for her hand again, and they could finally have the life they'd been denied over three years ago.

A hail in Cora's voice wrenched him from his musings. With a look around, his gaze finally settled on her and the widow as they moved away from an open carriage.

Schooling his expression into one of surprise, Peregrine met them beneath the arch where far more fashionable people milled about, talking with each other.

"Good afternoon, Mrs. Bromington, Miss Hasting." Nodding at each of them in turn, he dared much by taking the widow's hand and bringing it to his lips. "What a lovely boon to see you here." It was time to employ his charm on the dragon so she would let him spend time in Cora's company.

"Imagine that, Captain Wetherford." So much bitterness dripped from those words, he was shocked it didn't pool on the ground. "I wasn't aware you took regular exercise here."

"Why not? It is a lovely summer day, and rare enough that it isn't raining." He gave her a grin that he hoped would placate her. "One must take advantage of the weather when one can." Then he shifted his attention to Cora. "How do you fare, Miss Hasting?"

"Well enough, thank you." Though her smile was faint, it was there, and she was beautiful when she did so.

"That shade of blue is quite striking on you." Indeed, he might favor that periwinkle color, for it deepened the color of her eyes. When she blushed and murmured words of thanks, he moved his regard to her dragon. "Since we are all here together, perhaps I can escort you in a stroll, Mrs. Bromington."

"Don't think to employ flattery or flirting on me, young man." The frown she bestowed upon him was quite fierce. "I am far too old for you, and even if I weren't, I don't want another man besides."

"Well, while that is a bruise to my ego, I shall find a way to continue on." But he offered her his crooked arm anyway. "Come, Mrs. Bromington. The afternoon is wasting." He ignored Cora for the moment, for there was certain amusement dancing in her eyes, and he feared if he met her gaze, they would both burst into laughter.

"You might as well give into him, Mrs. Bromington. The captain can be quite persuasive," Cora said with a hint of laughter in her voice.

"Fine." There was a decided air of resignation as the widow bounced her attention between the two of them. "I suppose it couldn't hurt to have that stability, for I do wish to watch the activity on the Serpentine." She frowned at him. "But give me your other arm, Captain. I cannot take you seriously if I must gaze upon the wreck of your cheek."

As Cora gasped with outrage, Peregrine took the slight in stride.

"Of course, Mrs. Bromington." Once he'd shifted to her other side, he once more offered his arm. "There will be a crowd at the water this afternoon, for there is a bit of heat in the air."

The widow grunted but she laid the fingers of one gloved hand on his sleeve. "Far too many people in this world if you ask me."

Well, no one asks you about anything, for we already know what you'll say.

For the next several minutes, they strolled along the path that would eventually lead to the narrow portion of the Serpentine. Desultory conversation was held with the two women, but nothing of import came to light. The widow's posture remained stiff, and it might have been his imagination, but she relied more heavily on her cane. Otherwise, it was a partially pleasant way to spend the afternoon.

Eventually, the widow stirred. No doubt since she wasn't in control of the situation, she felt uncomfortable. "Don't think I don't know what's going on here, young man."

"Oh?" Refusing again to glance at Cora, he tamped down on the urge to chuckle. "What's that?"

"You are trying to get to Miss Hasting by flattering me."

This time he did chuckle. "I would never do such a thing." With a pat of her hand, he continued moving them along. "I merely thought you'd like to take in the air, and it's no doubt been an age since you were squired about by a man." He made a show of looking about, very much enjoying his role. "It's a good thing Miss Hasting is here as a companion, else I'd be tempted to kiss you."

"Good heavens, Captain, that is not well done of you," Cora managed to choke out amidst a poorly stifled giggle.

"I quite agree." Mrs. Bromington shook her head. She rapped his arm with her closed fan. "I am on to you, Captain. You won't defeat me that easily. Ah, there." With a gesture toward a grouping of trees near the banks of the Serpentine, there were a few wrought iron benches that rested beneath the wide boughs. "Leave me there. My legs are fatigued and are beginning to ache." Again, she rapped his arm with her fan's spine. "You have my permission to continue your exercise with Miss Hasting but keep her within my eyesight. I might wish to go home if my aches and pains grow worse."

It was a boon he wouldn't waste even if it wasn't quite being alone with her. "Ah. Very well. That is if Miss Hasting even wishes to continue her stroll." He dared to glance back over his shoulder at Cora, who flashed a quick grin at him with a nod.

"Don't play coy, Captain. We both know this is why you are here." The widow released his arm as she made her way toward one of the benches.

"She is, perhaps, not quite as uninformed as I would have liked to think, but that doesn't matter. I have what I wanted—time with you." Peregrine clasped his hands behind his back while Cora fell into step beside him.

"That was quite splendid of you trying to charm her." The

tinkle of her laughter went straight to his stones. "However, in the event you wondered, she is far too sour to let any such thing affect her."

"So I am coming to see." As they walked, he shoved all thoughts of Mrs. Bromington from his mind. "How are you today, after…. What we did last night?"

A blush stained her cheeks. "Quite well, actually. And I had the best sleep of my life. Well, since taking the position with Mrs. Bromington, that is."

His grin felt all too smug. "That is good to hear."

"I wanted to add that I hope Mrs. Bromington's careless words about your scarring doesn't make you think everyone feels the same." Cora laid the fingers of her right hand on his arm and peered up into his face past the shallow brim of her bonnet. Nothing but truth reflected in the blue depths of her eyes. "Some of us don't mind."

"Of course I know that." Briefly, he laid a gloved hand over hers. "Do you wish to know how I came by the injuries?"

"Only if you want to." She squeezed her fingers on his arm. "Lord Maubrey said he saved your life."

"He did." How much to tell her that wouldn't be completely shocking and off-putting? Perhaps it was best to just share from the heart. "It happened during a naval battle with a pirate vessel in the Eastern Caribbean Sea."

"Pirates? I thought they'd been eradicated already."

Ah, her intelligence was only one of the things he admired about her. "They largely were, but a few had managed to escape capture." He couldn't help but lean his head closer to hers. "I adore a woman with brains," he whispered against the shell of her ear.

"Perry, stop!" She urged him away. "Anyone could see, and Mrs. Bromington is no doubt watching like a hawk."

"It is no secret I am courting you." But he sobered. "My ship had been tasked with chasing down the last holdouts of sea criminals. For weeks we searched in vain before we finally found one." God, that time was seared into his memories so badly he still smelled the acrid smoke in the air, heard the crackling of the wood. "One of the cannons on my ship had been hit with enemy fire. When it exploded, I was standing far too close, which meant I took the brunt of the flying shrapnel. Some of the pieces were quite large." When he would have traced his cheek, Cora held onto his arm, preventing that movement. "Hot metal and burning bits embedded themselves into my skin. Some penetrated my uniform."

She gasped. "You have scars on your body that match your face?

"Unfortunately, yes."

"Is that why I have never seen you *sans* clothing?"

"Not fully. We simply haven't had the time." Knowing that she wished to gaze upon his form had interest shivering along his shaft. "Regardless, I never wanted to retire so early from the navy, but I was given no choice. My injuries made it impossible for me to continue."

"I'm sorry. You obviously were quite fond of your position as well as the sea."

"Yes." He nodded. "If Charles hadn't been there, I would have burned to death in the general confusion that followed the battle."

"Then I will be certain to thank him the next time I see him." She squeezed her fingers on his arm. "I am glad you *did* survive, though."

"Thank you." He pressed his lips together. "I won't lie and say it wasn't difficult to reintegrate into society upon returning." For the space of a few heartbeats, he thought over his next words. "The side of my face is ghastly, Cora. More people fear me than tolerate me. None of the accolades I accumulated during my service matter if the general populace can't bear to look at me."

"Then stop searching for acceptance by the wrong people, for the right people will always support you and welcome you with open arms." She brought him to a halt on the grass then turned to face him. "Never think less of yourself because some people are far too superficial for their own good. Perfection in society is largely unattainable, and why would you want that?"

"Agreed." Those handful of words humbled him, and he was more certain than ever he was rapidly falling for her again, deeper this time and from a greater height.

"Have you been happy, though, since returning to London? You seem fairly well adjusted."

Peregrine shrugged. Telling the truth would need a gentle hand, for he didn't want to lie but he didn't wish to spook her. "Largely, yes. I have been... content. There are pockets of society who do appreciate me and what I have to say. Doing the pretty with the ladies is sometimes wearing, but I have managed to overlook that—mostly." As he released a breath, he dared to take her hand. "As I have told you already, I want to marry, perhaps have a family, but be advised, it is expensive to live in London on a captain's pension. Even with the coin I take in from speaking engagements, I need additional income. That is why I'm opening the shop. I want my wife to be proud of me."

Perhaps that had been why he'd run from marriage the first time. He hadn't been proud of himself, had gone off to the navy to make a name for himself, to have something unique to his name that a woman might brag about to her friends.

Compassion warred with an emotion in her eyes he didn't dare to identify. "While I realize coin makes the world go 'round, please don't think that is all a woman wishes from the man she will marry." She lifted a gloved hand, brushed her fingertips over the scared side of his face, then let it fall again. "None of us have much to offer that is attractive."

"Ah, sweeting, you have no idea..." It was too damn bad he couldn't kiss her, for there were far too many people about.

"Come along, Captain. We are too exposed here." Cora led the way back around the Serpentine, and before too long, they made their way back to where the widow still sat upon her bench, scowling at everyone.

"You have been gone an eternity, girl," Mrs. Bromington groused as she stood and tugged Cora away from his side. He didn't quite trust the gleam that suddenly appeared in her faded green eyes. "I'm peckish. Captain Wetherford, why don't you come to the house with Miss Hasting and me? We can take tea together, since you were so charming earlier."

"Oh, I…" He shared a shocked glance with Cora, who shrugged. "I would enjoy that. Thank you." What was the old woman planning, for she must be plotting. The sad fact was Mrs. Bromington simply wasn't that kind.

⇥⤜⤜⤜

THOUGH IT WASN'T in Peregrine's nature to be mistrustful of people, he said very little while ensconced in Mrs. Bromington's drawing room, merely listened to the conversation between her and Cora. As he did so, he waited for the bad news to swoop down.

And it finally did.

"Argh!" The loud cry that issued from the widow's throat was enough to startle him. Before he could ascertain why she was in apparent distress, the woman dropped her teacup. "Oh, my legs!" She painted quite the dramatic picture as she clutched those extremities. "I don't think I can stand they hurt so badly." All the while, she implored Cora with her gaze as she listed to one side on her sofa cushion.

"Good heavens. Mrs. Bromington!" Because she was a good and caring person, Cora set her teacup down on the low table then swiftly moved to the widow's side. "Are you well? Does anything else hurt?"

Peregrine frowned as the Drury Lane production unfolded in front of him. He would wager the contents of his account at the Bank of London this was naught but an act, for the way she held her mouth told him she made jest of them all. Of course Cora didn't see it. When she pressed a palm to the widow's brow, then held her fingers to a pulse point to measure heartbeats, the widow acted as if she were two steps from an early demise.

"I cannot move my legs, girl!"

Very real horror etched over Cora's face. "Perry, help! We must do something for her!"

"This is true." In fact, the older woman needed a severe lecture, but that wasn't in his purview. Instead, he stood. "I'll call for the butler or any other staff that is close by." As he strode across the room toward the opened door, he shouted for Mr. Riley. When the butler hustled along the corridor, Peregrine bit back the urge to curse. "Mrs. Bromington is suffering from some mystery ailment. We need to take her upstairs."

Mr. Riley frowned, then peered around Peregrine into the drawing room. "I don't believe I can carry her. Shall I ring for a groomsman?"

The tears in Cora's voice as she questioned the widow pulled at his heart. "No need. I'll do it myself. Have the maids prepare her bed."

"Absolutely, Captain." Then the lanky butler shot off as if his heels were on fire.

Turning back into the room, Peregrine took command of the situation. "Cora, step aside. I'll bring Mrs. Bromington upstairs. Please order a warm water bottle for your charge's legs." Then, before either of the women could protest, he scooped the widow off the sofa where she'd been made comfortable, hauled her upward, and then set out across the room once more. No, she wasn't that cumbersome of a burden, but he would be damned if he'd let her continue the façade.

"Put me down, young man." Frost had formed in the widow's voice as her cane clattered to the floor.

"I can't do that, ma'am. Your legs are paining you, correct? And you said you doubted you could walk, so since you are ailing, I'm taking you abovestairs so your staff can see to your care." As Cora trailed behind them, he lowered his voice so only the widow could hear him while he narrowed his gaze. "For you and I both know you are lying. It's the why that escapes me at the moment."

Mrs. Bromington declined to answer, for she was too busy pretending to drift in and out of a faint.

To Cora's credit, she called for the housekeeper and maids. Once those people arrived in the widow's bedroom, Cora issued orders as if she were a seasoned admiral. Peregrine laid Mrs. Bromington on her wide four-poster bed, then was promptly shooed to the side so Cora could tuck her beneath the covers.

Knowing there was nothing more he could do for now, he waited just outside the room until the frantic activity ceased, and everyone left the older woman alone.

Finally, Cora came out, pulling the door closed behind her. Exhaustion shadowed her face and worry reflected in her eyes. "I have given Mrs. Bromington a drop of laudanum in water. She'll soon drift to sleep, but I don't know anything about her affliction. It came on so suddenly."

"Of course it did." Despite his willpower, he briefly pointed his gaze to the ceiling before resting it on her. "Mrs. Bromington is lying to you in an attempt to keep you with her. So you won't leave." He slipped a hand about her upper arm and led her toward the stairs. "The woman is insanely jealous of the time you're spending with me, and quite frankly, she is selfish to boot. You know this."

"I don't think so." She shook her head as tears welled in her eyes. "I believe she's truly in pain. I asked her to move her limbs and she couldn't."

He snorted. "Or wouldn't."

"Stop it! You can't be that cruel." Cora smacked his arm. She was very nearly in tears. "If she is truly paralyzed, perhaps she's suffered an apoplexy."

"Then one side of her body would be affected as well. I have seen that a time or two while in the service." When she didn't appear convinced and wrung her hands, he blew out a breath. "Come here." Gently, Peregrine took her into his arms despite the fact the staff was in a frenzy of activity. "Cora, sweeting, she is a cold-hearted serpent at best. She obviously doesn't care for the attraction between us, and she knows if our courtship deepens, I'll have a chance at winning you." While he spoke, he stroked a hand up and down her back in the hopes of soothing her. "Which means you *will* eventually leave her for your own life."

"Surely that isn't true." His Cora was loyal to the last, but would it prove a stumbling block?

Now was not the time for lectures. "Have you ever wondered why her own children refuse to come 'round? Don't you think she's tried to manipulate them, control them so they would stay? Some women are like that because they are terrified of living by themselves. Or they simply enjoy playing puppet master."

He rather suspected the widow was the latter.

"I don't know what to do." Cora pulled away and lifted her gaze to his. Moisture spiked her blonde lashes. A few tears escaped to her cheeks. "That woman in there needs me, Perry." She sniffed and accepted the handkerchief he offered. "All my life I've been in the middle. Amelia was the oldest and the capable one, calm in a crisis. Gigi was the youngest and the wild one without a sense of responsibility. I was the dependable one always willing to help. How can I do no less now?"

Bloody hell.

It had already happened. Mrs. Bromington had successfully trapped Cora into a twisted, gilded prison and had turned the key in the lock. Heated panic rose in his chest. "What if *I* need you too?"

"Stop!" Shaking her head so hard a lock of hair tumbled from its pins, she pushed out of his arms and took a few steps backward. "You are jealous and just as bad as she is, for you don't want me to send you packing as well."

"I'm not, but I *am* trying to tell you that she's lying." How could he make her understand without entering into a huge argument born of high emotion? "Because you have a good heart, because you see the best in people and want to try and save them all, because you wish to fix what's wrong, she is preying on that spirit. It isn't a failing or a character flaw on your part, but people *will* take advantage of you."

"Including you?" Her chin trembled as she fought off a wave of tears. "As you did on what should have been our wedding day?"

Damn, but she knew how to wound. Hurt cut through his chest as if he'd been flayed open by knives. "I apologized soundly for that, you have forgiven me, and I've made strides to change. Mrs. Bromington has not, and her behavior continues to worsen." When he tried to come toward her, she held up a hand, and he huffed. "Surely you must see this. You are quite levelheaded when you wish to be. Don't let her take advantage."

For a long time, she looked at him. Finally, she sighed and dabbed at her eyes with the handkerchief. "Please go," she asked in an agonized whisper. "There is much that needs done here, and a doctor should be called."

"All right." Obviously, she was too overwrought to think clearly, so he nodded. "Please send for me should you need help."

"I will." The delicate muscles in her throat worked with a hard swallow. "I hope she will be well after a rest."

"Mmm, time will tell." Peregrine grunted. He closed the distance, framed her head with his hands, then lightly kissed her lips. "I *will* call tomorrow. On you both." Then he plunged down the stairs and hoped to God Mrs. Bromington would make a mistake and that Cora would be able to see the truth.

If the dragon were a poker player, she had just upped the ante in the game he and she played, and the prize was Cora. Could he come up to the mark? Well, he had no intention of folding. If that woman was truly paralyzed, then he was Prinny's long lost and secret brother.

Yet Cora had chosen to believe her charge over him. Not that he blamed her. It must be hell to hold that position.

As he gained the front door, he slammed that panel behind him. *Bah!* The problems found on land were infinitely more difficult than they'd ever been at sea.

CHAPTER FOURTEEN

May 31, 1817
Bromington House
Manchester Square
London

CORA YAWNED AND couldn't quite hide it behind her hand, for it had been a busy two days.

True to his word, Peregrine had called yesterday, but just as Mrs. Bromington had instructed all along, he was denied entry. She'd taken comfort in the fact he had been there and left a box of expensive French chocolates for her with Mr. Riley, for her charge had remained in bed all day, apparently wrestling with the fact her legs had lost all feeling and refusing to see anyone except Cora.

Today, however, Mrs. Bromington had returned to her previous lambasting form, which meant she refused to stay confined to her private rooms. What was more, she somehow had procured a Bath chair because she didn't wish to let her infirmity keep her immobile. Now that she was back lording her presence over everyone beneath her roof, no one had a moment's peace.

Including Cora. She had been run ragged since her employer had first collapsed. If at any time she spent more than twenty minutes alone in her room, the widow immediately had one of the maids track her down and recall her to the older woman's side. There were suddenly so many things to look after, which included giving comfort to the two upstairs maids every time Mrs. Bromington blasted them with her acerbic tongue. Truly, there was every indication the maids would hand in their notices soon, and that would be horrible, for Cora's responsibilities would increase tenfold.

Throughout it all, the conversation she'd had with Peregrine before he'd left kept circling around her mind like ponies on a loop. Had he truly been right and she wrong? *Was* the widow pretending her injury?

It was impossible to know.

She yawned again. Tea wasn't far off, and for the moment Mrs. Bromington was content with her crocheting. That gave Cora time to look through her personal correspondence, which had sadly been neglected for the past several days. There was a letter from her younger sister Gigi dated two weeks prior, and for the next few moments, she read through the breezy, gossipy words with a slight smile curving her lips.

> *...I'm afraid Papa's mind continues to degrade with each month. He tends to forget words as well as the books he's read. Just yesterday, he forgot Nora's name and why she never spoke aloud...*
>
> *Mama is beside herself with worry over Emmaline, who was frightened by a visitor coming to the manor and locked herself in her room for two days...*
>
> *...I wish you would come home. Everything is much more manageable and calmer...*
>
> *...someone came by the other day asking about the taxes, which sent Papa into a rage. It looks more and more likely I'll take a position closer to home, perhaps as a governess...*

With a chuckle, Cora tried to envision Gigi as a governess, when she had spent far too much time trying to escape her own, but it was concerning how things were moving at home. Which meant it was even more vital to grin and bear Mrs. Bromington's horrid behavior.

Then she cracked the seal and pulled Mia's letter from its envelope.

> *...we are finally settled into Moss Cottage and are setting up housekeeping for the summer as a sort of honeymoon. Ireland is gorgeous, and the cottage is so dear! I have a true sense of my husband's roots here. Oh, Cora, I wish you could see this country; it's so green with the sea twinkling around.*
>
> *...should return to London by the first of September, for Wycliffe has duties to parliament...*
>
> *...I never thought being a wife at my age would prove so exciting. I suppose that depends on the caliber of the man. It's been about a month since I wed Wycliffe and already my life has changed forever. I have written to Mama, but she hasn't responded. I hope all is well at home. Though I worry, there is now this new life I need to give my attention to...*

As Cora huffed out a breath in frustration, she folded the letter without finishing the read. Hot jealousy stabbed through her chest. While she was glad her eldest sister was so happy within her new marriage, another part of her felt as if that life was a dream she would never realize for herself. Anger clashed with the jealousy, for Mia had more or less left the Hasting family to their own devices and their problems in order to be with her new husband.

Why is helping Papa now my sole responsibility? For she rather doubted Gigi would do well at any position she managed to secure. She simply didn't have the fortitude for such, and was too big a flirt to have a respectable family keep her on. When Mia came back to London, would she go back home to help with Papa? It was highly unlikely, for she would no doubt have responsibilities also that came from being a viscountess. Surely Nora and the younger girls couldn't keep on by themselves, to say nothing of Mama's wellbeing.

"If you continue to sigh like a damned windstorm, go upstairs so I don't hear you. It's becoming distracting." The annoyance in her employer's voice immediately recalled Cora to the present as well as her situation.

"I apologize, Mrs. Bromington, but I worry about my family." She stuffed both letters into a book then set it on a small round table near her elbow.

"If they have any fortitude, they can puzzle out their obstacles for themselves." And she continued to manipulate the crochet hook through the wool on her lap.

Clamping her lips together to prevent an unladylike response, Cora stood up from her chair. She moved over the Aubusson carpeting, and when she peered out of the bay window, she stifled a gasp, for Peregrine had just alighted from his curricle in front of the townhouse. Immediately, her pulse accelerated. She smoothed her hands down the front of her plain pink day dress. "If you will excuse me for one moment? There is something I must urgently attend to." For she would *not* have the butler turn him away from the door again.

Never had she moved so quickly down the wooden stairs while trying to go as silently as she could. As soon as she gained the lower floor, she dashed into the short entry hall just in time to see Mr. Riley open the front door. Peregrine's big form stood in the frame, and she knew an insane moment of wanting to collapse into his arms and hide there until her turbulent world righted itself.

"It is quite all right, Mr. Riley," she said with some breathlessness while she skidded to a halt near the butler's location. "Captain Wetherford *can* come in today. All is well, I promise." Then, before the man could rebut that, she gestured Peregrine forward.

"Shall I announce him to Mrs. Bromington?" Mr. Riley asked as he had no choice but to close the door.

"No, no. I'll escort him up directly." When Peregrine opened his mouth to no doubt question what was going on, she cut him off with a curt shake of her head. "Mrs. Bromington is in the drawing room," she said in a low voice.

"So I assumed. It will be good to see the old dear again." And he followed her up the stairs because she gave him no choice.

"I'm glad you are here," she admitted in a barely audible voice. "It has been quite the mess here for the last couple of days." Once they cleared the stairs and since there was no one in the corridor, she burrowed into his arms and clung to him. "I have been run ragged and feel like everything is unraveling."

"Shh. I'm here; I will help if I can." He wrapped his arms around her and held her securely against his chest. Though anyone could see them if they started up the stairs, Cora shoved that worry from her mind. "Take a deep breath. Surely it isn't as bad as all that."

"I don't know." The scents of sun, sea, and oak filtered through her nose, and she tried to take comfort in that as well as the strength of him as he shielded her, protected her. "I had letters from my sisters today. Gigi isn't taking our family's woes seriously, and Mia has all but abandoned the family for her husband and new life as a viscountess." Even to her own ears she sounded petty. "She's traveled to Ireland for a honeymoon as if Papa's health doesn't matter!" Her words were muffled by the folds of his cravat where she'd buried her face into.

"Ah, sweeting." The stroke of his fingers down her spine encouraged calm. "Amelia has every right to have her own life after spending so many years giving of herself to your family. There is nothing wrong with cleaving to her husband, especially if they are truly in love as I suspect they are." Those logical words rang in her ears and worked to soothe the storms inside. "Your sister had the courage to break away, to carve out something for herself. It doesn't mean she's abandoning the family."

Cora took a shuddering breath. "She is on her honeymoon without a care in the world." Now she *was* being petty, for she knew more than anyone Mia deserved that happiness.

"After that period is over, she will return, and I'll wager she'll find some way to continue helping your father. But let her have this for herself. Give her grace, Cora. And have faith."

Yes, his logic was sound, yet it didn't help her own situation. "But—"

His sigh ruffled the curls on her forehead. "Life is short, sweeting. You can't keep tossing those precious days away on other people because sooner or later you will wake up and realize the time allotted to you is gone." He gently rocked her back and forth. "Some of those people appreciate your efforts then use your help as a crutch, but alternately, some don't and will selfishly keep you with them, use you up until there is nothing left. Then they'll move on to the next person in line."

"You speak of Mrs. Bromington," she said in a whisper.

"Of course."

Cora sighed. "I… I think she isn't as bad as everyone thinks."

"And Prinny is a svelte, lean man," he said with humor in his voice. "Don't be fooled merely because you have a good heart. Things will only change when you do. When you stop allowing the people around you to treat you terribly. When you convince yourself that you deserve more, better."

"How, though? My family is in reduced circumstances. We are barely clinging to the fringes of society."

"That doesn't mean it's permission for others to treat you as if you are less than." He pressed his lips to her temple and released her out of convention, peering down into her eyes. "You are worthy merely because you exist. There is nothing that is out of reach for you if you have enough determination." As he cupped her cheek, he wiped away the moisture on her skin with the pad of his thumb. "Don't see yourself through the glass of the worst of people or their need. You are on this earth for a reason, and it is not to always fix others' problems."

She shook her head, for though the words were pretty and meant as encouragement, they didn't show her a way out of her situation. "I cannot walk away. I don't have that freedom." Not like men, who could go at will wherever they wished.

"Then it will eventually be your prison, if it's not already." The somberness in his eyes sent a chill down her spine. "Is there any change in Mrs. Bromington's condition?"

"No." A cloud of hopelessness descended over her. "She is in a Bath chair now."

One of his shaggy brown eyebrows rose in surprise. "On the orders of a doctor?"

"No." Cora shook her head. "She refused to have one examine her."

"I wonder why." He glanced toward the drawing room door. "Perhaps because there is nothing wrong with her?"

"I…" She frowned. As much as she adored having his calm, solid presence here with her, why couldn't he see how she was drowning in her duties? That she must keep her position at all costs? "Don't be like that. She's truly struggling and in pain. I can see it in her face, and I believe her."

"Oh Cora." He snorted and shook his head. "No doubt this isn't the first time she has dissembled to make the people 'round her stay. She consistently disrespects you, and will continue to do so while you allow it." When he tried to take her hand, she snatched it behind her back. "I wish you could see the situation as I do. As no doubt her own children do. Truly, I'm trying to help you, to *free* you."

The truth was terrifying as she stared it down, even more so because it was delivered by this man she was irrevocably falling for. "I know. Don't you think I'm not aware of that?" she hissed in a barely audible voice, for no doubt her charge was listening. "However, she *is* my responsibility. There is no one else here for her."

"Why do you think that is?" Annoyance flashed in his eyes. "Think it through, Cora."

For the space of a few heartbeats, she stared at him, balancing on the edge of the life she wanted and the life she needed.

Eventually, he nodded. "Let us shift the subject for a few

seconds." When he grinned, flutters danced through her belly. "Did you receive the flowers I sent yesterday with the chocolates?"

Oh, dear.

"I did, and the notes were much appreciated." Those little jottings of a romantic nature she'd hidden in her room. "Uh, but Mrs. Bromington tossed the flowers out the drawing room window." A waver entered her voice, for why would the woman take umbrage at gifts a suitor gave to her companion? "She demanded that I give the chocolates to the kitchen staff." But the notes were exclusively hers, and each one had removed one of the bricks in the wall around her heart. "The gifts were lovely."

"Hmm. I did not pay good coin for those things to have one disgruntled woman toss out." His gaze narrowed. "I would like to talk to your employer, for those gifts were yours exclusively." When he took a few steps down the corridor, Cora laid a staying hand on his arm.

"Behave."

"I will if she does." There was a hard set to his lips she didn't quite trust. "Her recent behavior is outside of enough, and she needs to be dressed down for it."

Knots of worry pulled in her stomach, but there was nothing for it except to trail behind the captain as he strode into the drawing room. "Ah, Mrs. Bromington, Captain Wetherford wishes to talk with you."

"Oh, I'll wager he does." The widow attempted to manipulate the wheels of her Bath chair but soon grew frustrated. "Miss Hasting, help me turn this contraption about so that I may face my soon-to-be accuser."

Cora frowned. "How do you know he wishes you any animosity?" But she came into the room, grabbed the handles of the chair behind the rattan head rest of the chair, and then pushed and pulled the chair until the widow faced Peregrine.

"How dare you come into this house against my wishes, Captain." Anger shook through the older woman's voice. "I am not a well woman, and I don't wish to have visitors."

"I can understand that, but I am not here to see you."

The widow stared him down. "Miss Hasting is my companion. She is not a guest, so therefore is not allowed to have visitors. As well, today is not one of her non-working days." One of her bony hands lifted and she pointed a forefinger at Peregrine. "I demand that you leave this instant."

"Had you not taken the gifts I sent Miss Hasting, I might have been inclined to follow the suggestion, but since you have been nothing but a cantankerous arse, I am not going anywhere until I'm convinced your companion is being treated well." He crossed his arms at his chest. "Being an employer does not give you the right to act with ill will to a member of the *beau monde*, in reduced circumstances though she might be."

Merciful heavens, they would soon come to blows if something wasn't done. Detesting conflict and especially not wishing to see Peregrine verbally blasted by the widow, Cora stepped around the Bath chair and positioned herself between them. "Please be decent, the both of you. We can discuss this in a calm, civilized manner."

"Enough, Miss Hasting." Mrs. Bromington cut the air with a hand. She glowered at them both as Cora crept unconsciously closer to Peregrine. "If you don't encourage this man out of my house right now, I will sack you on the spot." Anger flashed in her eyes. "Additionally, I will make certain that no one in London wishes to hire you on as a companion, a governess, or even a maid." Her voice rose with each new threat. "You are *here*, Miss Hasting, so do the job you are paid to do."

"I am, but—"

"No, you are two seconds away from dallying with the captain while you should be tending to your duties." The coolness in her tone sent frissons of fear twisting down Cora's spine. "I grow weary with him always hanging about, sniffing at your skirts as if you are a dog in heat." She narrowed her gaze. "You must choose between him of your position."

Why is this happening?

Horror scudded through her gut and sent gooseflesh racing over her skin. "Surely you can't mean that." She bounced her gaze between the widow and him, but they both stared back, and it was clear neither of them would yield.

"I am deadly serious, Miss Hasting," Mrs. Bromington said. She gripped the armrests of her Bath chair. "Choose. I am done with this foolishness."

"I am rather inclined to agree with the widow." Peregrine slowly nodded then met Cora's gaze. "I feared it would eventually come to this, and here we are. Perhaps we all need to have it out in order to move forward." A note of command echoed in his voice. "What is your choice, Cora?"

Her breath came in short pants. Confusion ran riot through her mind, and in many ways, she hated the intense interest fixed upon her. "Why can I not have both my position and a suitor?"

Mrs. Bromington made a tsking noise. "I'm tired of having your attention divided. I specifically hired you because you weren't attached, and you are a spinster. That means your time would exclusively be mine."

"Nine and twenty is hardly a spinster." Close to it, though.

The widow snorted. "You might as well be if you've been forced to make a living."

"I..." She pressed her lips together and glanced at Peregrine. He offered no help or encouragement, but there was an air of expectation that demanded an answer. The longer she looked at him, the more her heart felt as if it was being torn from all sides and would soon split asunder. Waves of heat welled over her, and she fanned her face with a hand. "Put on the spot, I have realized there *is* no choice for me." The urge to cast up her accounts climbed her throat. How saliva filled her mouth, and she swallowed in a desperate attempt to stave off retching. "I need this position as well as the income."

Shock and hurt reflected in Peregrine's eyes. "Have you thought this through?"

"Yes." As her heart broke into a thousand shards, she dropped her gaze to the knot of his cravat, for she couldn't bear to see the disappointment he must feel. "My family comes first, and they always will. Perhaps you don't understand this as all your family is gone." A half-stifled sob escaped her. "You need to leave, Captain." Tears welled in her eyes as Mrs. Bromington crowed with victory. "I'm so, so sorry."

The silence that brewed in the room after that announcement was deafening.

Finally, Peregrine nodded. "Very well. I shall abide by your decision." He didn't grin but merely stood there like a man wounded who doesn't realize he should fall. "At least let me tell you goodbye properly, for it's doubtful you and I will ever meet again."

Dear God, she hadn't thought of the consequences.

"Go on then, girl. Make your goodbyes and then bid him good riddance so we can get on with our lives." The widow nodded with much smugness. "We have plans to make, and none of them include a man."

Though the strength in her knees suggested she would collapse onto the floor at any moment, she followed Peregrine out of the drawing room. Once in the corridor beyond, she steeled herself for his inevitable speech where he would try to convince her to change her mind.

Yet he did none of that.

Instead, Peregrine swept her into his arms. He kissed her with such authority and intensity that she felt it all the way down to her toes. As tears fell to her cheeks, she returned his embrace, clung to the broad sweep of his shoulders. Cold regret built in her belly, and all too soon he pulled away.

"No, don't…"

"I must." Then he released her, and there was such infinite sadness in the hazel depths of his eyes that felt as if she'd opened Pandora's box and unleashed a thousand horrors and laments onto the world. A muscle in his cheek ticced while his Adam's apple bobbed. "I hope you find that you have made the right decision for you." As if he couldn't help himself, he cupped her cheek, gently brushed his lips over hers, and there was a final note of goodbye in the gesture that she wanted to sob from the heartbreak of it. He cleared his throat. "Either way, I am proud of you, and I wish you nothing but happiness in your life."

"Perry, I…" What else could she say? Almost she'd hoped he would have argued, for then she could have responded with anger and a break would have been natural, but this was horrid, like falling into a dark pit that had no end.

"Goodbye, Cora," he whispered. Then Peregrine turned about and strode toward the stairs. He didn't look back. Those broad shoulders never flinched, and he kept his back ramrod straight. Proud to the last, not once showing defeat.

And he took all her dreams with him again, but this time 'round, it was her fault.

"What have I done?" But no one answered the agonized whisper.

She sagged against the wall, put her hands over her face, and cried, mourned for everything she could have had if she hadn't erred on the side of perceived responsibility and duty instead of throwing caution to the wind in order to chase love.

CHAPTER FIFTEEN

June 2, 1817
The Albany

"WELL, MATEY, OUR life has become much less satisfying."
The beagle huffed and continued to watch Peregrine from his basket.

To be fair, they'd had this same conversation many times over the last two days. Two damned days since he'd last seen Cora, when she'd chosen the widow and her position over a continuing courtship with him as well as a possible married life.

Because of that, his life was in tatters. How stupid could he have been to fall in love with the same woman twice and still hadn't managed to win her?

When he'd called at Bromington House two days ago and the widow had shoved everything to the breaking point, he'd truly thought Cora would have chosen him. Hadn't he shown her he would never leave, that he would choose her again and again? That everything he currently did in his life was to help the foundation for a future between them? Yet she had been apparently blinded by guilt-fueled responsibility and duty.

He couldn't blame her, of course, for everyone had their own views and feelings regarding family, especially when they were in financial gray areas, but why couldn't she understand that they could have met those issues as a united front, that everyone would be a little better if they'd done it together?

A rap on the front door proceeded the arrival of Viscount Maubrey.

"Why are you not ready to go?" he asked as he swept his gaze up and down Peregrine's form, which only consisted of evening breeches, hosiery, his lawn shirt, and the same silver satin waistcoat that he'd worn a couple of times before. "As it is, even if we leave now, we will arrive late to the Seacrests' rout."

"Does it matter?" The last thing he wanted to do was put himself into society, mingle, and act as if he hadn't a care in the world.

"Yes, of course it does." With a frown, Charles bounced his gaze between Peregrine and the dog. "You need to stop moping and move forward with your life. Especially since you have opened your shop. Drop a few hints tonight throughout the assemblage and hopefully you drive potential customers to the place."

In fact, he'd opened his shop yesterday… and then proceeded to sit behind his counter all day without one person coming in. "Everything has fallen apart, Charles. What I thought was easy has proved problematic. The shop is a failure, and quite frankly, so is my courtship of Cora." He shoved a hand through his hair. "I'm feeling a bit lost." To say nothing of how broken his heart was. In fact, that organ ached as if it had received a mortal blow.

"I understand, but you cannot let such things defeat you." The viscount came further into Peregrine's dressing room. He snagged the black tailcoat from where Peregrine's valet had left it on the back of a chair when he was dismissed. "You could always go after Miss Beaufort again. She remains unspoken for and from all accounts has developed a tendre for you." Then he held up the jacket and looked at him with an expression of expectation.

Peregrine sighed. Clearly, his friend wouldn't let him dissolve into obscurity. "I would rather pluck out my eye with a dull spoon." With nothing else to do, he shoved first one arm into a sleeve followed quickly by the next.

"Ah, so then you believe the answer to rejection is to bury yourself here with your dog or worse, spend all your time at the shop until you move into the rooms upstairs, eating warmed over soup, moldy cheese and stale bread." The viscount huffed as he smoothed the evening jacket over Peregrine's shoulders. "I should never see you again."

When put in those words, the future was bleak, indeed. "Do you take exception to Matey?"

The beagle cocked one eyebrow as if waiting on the answer.

"I do, for he is a dog, not the sort of companion a man needs for certain other things in life." He snickered when Matey whined. "For the love of heaven, he licks his own balls and has a tendency to eat waste found on the ground."

"True." Peregrine blew out his breath, for it felt as if he were caught in a vortex that was spiraling downward into an endless dark depression. "What the hell else do I have, Charles? At least Matey loves me without condition." He yanked the length of a silk cravat from the top of a bureau. "I'm retired from the navy. I don't have a ship or the sea any longer, and without Cora? Without knowing I'll hear her voice or cajole a smile from her?" He shrugged and, in some angst, began twisting the length of fabric about his neck, and doing a piss-poor job of it, truth be told.

The viscount shook his head. "I don't know what to tell you. At times, life doesn't go the way we hope it will."

"I am aware of that." He paused in trying to tie the cravat in order to don his cuffs. "For years while I was away, I thought of her on the loneliest nights." If he wasn't careful and in complete control of his emotions, he would suffer a breakdown in front of his friend. "When I came back to England disfigured, she was the only one who didn't mind the scars. Every other woman I'd met shied away from the mess I represent, but Cora and I connected like we'd never done in the past." His voice broke. "Then she threw me over out of fear, I suppose. As if nothing we'd shared mattered."

But to give her grace, he'd done the same first, out of fear.

Perhaps there was no point in talking about it or obsessing over it. She'd made her decision, and it had been quite final. Yet he knew himself, and it wouldn't be so easy to forget a woman like Cora. He forced a hard swallow into his throat, glanced between Matey and the door. What would happen if he ran away from London? If he put distance between him and his biggest failure, but where would he go?

"I would like to take advantage of your offer and retreat to your country estate for a bit." Removing to Kent would allow him the time and space to lick his wounds in private. And Matey could run to his heart's content there.

"Of course, I would enjoy having you there. In fact, I'm leaving for the country at the end of the month." His grin held a sad edge. "It will be like old times when we were aboard ship. Two bachelors on the prowl."

"Yes." And it would be a way to move on. "I suppose no one wins every battle they enter. Lords knows we didn't while on the sea." It was merely a matter of needing to pull himself together and try again.

Sometime.

Once his heart healed.

But how to do that when all he'd ever wanted was Cora?

Charles snorted. Clearly, he didn't believe any of it. "Then you intend to give up." It wasn't a question.

Even Matey whined and picked up his head to stare intently at Peregrine.

"I beg pardon?" His patience for this conversation was waning. One of the damned cuffs gave him trouble, and gritting his teeth, he finally manipulated it.

"Consider this. While in the navy you were fierce, ran your ship with an iron hand, refused to back down in the face of danger, even when you were injured and left for dead." Charles met his gaze, and there was nothing but earnestness in his expression. "You battled an infection, healed your injuries by willpower, fought off public opinion when you dared to go out in society with your scars on display, went on to perceiver, to win. You are still sought after as a speaker as well as a favorite guest at society functions." Then he shook his head. "Yet here you are, running up a white flag, presumably waiting for death."

Peregrine scoffed. "I rather think death is far off." No solace there. When Charles didn't answer, merely raised an eyebrow, he sighed. "Why *should* I try again with Cora? Hasn't she made it abundantly clear where I stand in her esteem?"

"Why?" The viscount rubbed a hand along his jaw. "Because, quite simply, you love her. Why the devil would you toss that away? I suspect she feels the same for you, regardless of what she told you."

"Ha." A snort of derision escaped him. Love was a waste of time. "If that were so, she wouldn't have given me up for a dragon."

Charles pulled a face. "Put yourself in her place, my friend. The woman is frightened and worried, pulled in two very different directions. She no doubt feels the walls are closing in on her because everything is shifting and changing in her life." He shrugged as he rested his gaze on Peregrine. "By the by, where *is* the older sister?"

"Apparently on her honeymoon in Ireland."

"Ah. Rumor holds that Wycliffe is a completely changed man now he's married. If that is so, then the eldest Miss Hasting must possess magic or is some sort of a witch." Though amusement danced in Charles' eyes, when Peregrine didn't laugh, he sobered and continued. "Miss Hasting's marriage was probably the straw that broke the camel's back so to speak. Your Miss Hasting undoubtedly feels trapped, as if she is the last line of defense for the family's woes since her sister essentially left, albeit temporarily." With a sigh, he came close and took up the task of winding the cravat cloth around Peregrine's neck.

"That is exactly what I said when I attempted to convince

her..."

"Perhaps that power doesn't rest with you." The next few moments were spent in silence as Charles tied the fabric into an intricate knot that Peregrine had always admired. "Miss Hasting needs to decide for herself what her own destiny should look like."

"Whether that is with me or not?"

"Just so." He nodded. "Keep the faith, my friend, and hope fate isn't done with you."

"Bloody hell." The remainder of the joy faded from life as he spiraled farther and farther downward into despair. "And in the meantime?"

The viscount shrugged. "Keep yourself busy. Build your business and bring customers to your shop. Be the man I know you are when I pulled your sorry arse from the fire."

More than a grain of truth lay buried in those words. It both humbled and prodded him. "Why do you care so much what happens to me?"

"Besides being worried about my closest friend?" Charles shoved a hand through his hair, upsetting the carefully arranged blond waves. "Quite frankly, I cannot chase a romance of the ages like you almost have if I'm constantly concerned about you." When he flashed a grin, Peregrine's chest tightened with guilt. "I feel responsible for you after saving you. Don't try to dissuade me. That is how it is, and I want you to be happy."

"Right, but..." Peregrine scoffed. What else was there to say? "Romance is nothing but trouble. *Women* are certainly that." Even he heard the bitterness in his voice.

"You poor, disillusioned sot." Charles clapped a hand on his shoulder. "Troublesome women, strong women who know their own minds, *are* the best kind. Don't ever discount them or their loyalty and capacity for love." His expression turned rueful. "Would that I could find the same."

What a load of gammon that was. "You can have Cora, and gladly." If he accumulated too much more bitterness, he would turn into Mrs. Bromington.

Perhaps Cora would take me back then, since that is obviously what she prefers.

"That is quite unlikely." The viscount snickered. "You would challenge me to a duel if I were to so much as dance with her again."

"True." Or at least he would have… before. A weak grin curved his lips. "I might be a nodcock, I'm bloody tip over tail for her, but it doesn't matter. She made her choice."

"Coward. You haven't died yet, so there is still hope." Playfully, he cuffed Peregrine's shoulder. "Stiff upper lip and all that, now let's go." He shoved Peregrine toward the door. "I'm told the brandy is of fine quality and there will be cards in the offing. You won't need to socialize, but I *do* want you to get out of here before you start stinking of dog."

Matey whined at that then lowered his head and put a paw over one eye.

"Perhaps you are correct." Peregrine nodded. "Thank you for the consideration. I shall remember your words when a woman stomps on your heart and you feel like shit."

"I rather doubt that will happen, for I have learned from *your* mistakes." But the joking in his friend's voice went a long way in lifting his own spirits.

⊱⊰

A CRUSH OF people milled about the drawing room as the rout got underway. He and Charles visited with a few other men they were acquainted with, but when the viscount decided to pop into the card room for a couple hands, Peregrine decided to linger a bit longer to watch the dancing.

When he'd completed a circuit of walking the perimeter of the room, his gaze accidentally alighted on Cora. How could he have missed her? Once more, she wore that yellow gown—clearly her reduced circumstances didn't allow for a new gown or two—but he didn't mind for she was uncommonly beautiful in that jonquil color, and she stood out from every other lady in the room. As he raised his gaze, it collided with hers.

Surprise jumped into her face. Two spots of color blazed in her cheeks, but she quickly looked away. Had she delivered him a cut direct? Swift hurt stabbed through his heart, for she had deliberately snubbed him. Of course, Mrs. Bromington wasn't far from her, prowling and even more fierce in her Bath chair as if she were the dragon he'd likened her to, and Cora was the gold she guarded, holding her by an invisible lead. It seemed she would continue to cling to the Drury Lane act she'd assumed a few days ago.

Damn. He should have remained at home.

"You have the look of someone who has lost his very last friend in the world."

The sound of a woman's voice behind him jerked him out of his musings. As he turned about, he frowned to find Miss Beaufort standing there, fresh-faced and lovely in a gown of moss green. "Good evening, Miss Beaufort. How are you?"

"A good lot better than you, apparently." Her eyelashes fluttered as she looked up at him while on the makeshift dance floor, couples were assembling for a country reel. "What troubles you?"

"It is nothing." His heart, his attention, simply wasn't engaged with this conversation as well as the lady.

"Surely, it is, for you seem as if you wish to flee far from here or perhaps toss yourself into the Serpentine." She dared to lay a hand on his arm, tugged him closer to the side and away from the movements on the dance floor. "You don't appear to wish to dance."

"I do not." Hell, he didn't want to do much of anything after Cora had summarily dismissed him as if she didn't know him. "In fact, I'm questioning why the devil I even came tonight."

"Perhaps to see a particular lady?" she asked in a lowered tone.

Damnation. It would seem he needed to put a halt to anything further once and for all. "My dear Miss Beaufort, I am certain you are a lovely person, but you and I will *not* suit, so your pursuit of me is for naught." This didn't make him think any better of himself or his satiation. "You see, my heart belongs to another." Even if it was currently shattered and lying forgotten on the floor.

"Ah." She nodded with a faint smile playing about her mouth. "Miss Hasting."

"Yes." Shock rolled through his chest. "You know?"

Tinkling laughter filled the ear. The joviality sparkled in her eyes. "How could I not?" She patted his arm. "You never look at me the way you look at her, as if you would do anything to see Miss Hasting smile, as if she is the center of your world."

Had he once thought that? Perhaps. He sighed, and once more fell into the spiral of despair. "Things have crumbled in that quarter, so such thinking is obviously not true." Again, bitterness had entered his voice, but this time it was tinged with sadness.

"Oh, you poor man." Compassion shadowed her eyes as she laid a hand on his arm. "If I might give you some womanly advice?"

"It couldn't hurt. All is lost regardless." How soon could he leave this place?

She scooted closer to him until her form almost brushed his. "Most of us ladies are fearful of something; society puts much pressure on us to be one thing while our families don't help because they wish for us to be quite another thing." Truth lay stamped across her features. "Sometimes, *none* of those things are possible, for we are all different with wildly differing dreams."

He frowned. "Why are you telling me this?"

"We all must believe in the secret wants in our heart—men and women—but we only need one person to believe in us that will help break those shackles not of our making."

"Oh?" In an odd way, her words helped.

"Yes." Miss Beaufort nodded. "For example, I want something entirely different from what society says I must, but I don't want to disappoint my parents, which means I cannot be myself.

Not openly, anyway."

What the hell did that mean? Far too curious, he forgot to pity himself. Lowering his voice, he asked, "What *do* you want? To be married? Have a title, wealth? Turn London on its head?"

"It is lovely that you think such of me." One tiny wave of her hand dismissed all of them. "None of those lofty dreams, I'm afraid." If possible, Miss Beaufort drew closer. In a barely audible voice, she said, "I wish for a happy, peaceful life where I can live my truth, for I..." A blush went through her cheeks. "I want Deborah, Lord Davenport's eldest daughter."

For the second time that evening in her company, shock slammed through him. "But you chased me."

"I did." She shrugged and rested her rueful gaze on him. "I needed a shield, a cloak if you will, to hide my real feelings and intentions. I thought you would be a good candidate since you were in love with a woman you couldn't have. In the spirit of that, I thought you wouldn't mind wedding me because you'd given up the possibility of *her*." As she spoke, Miss Beaufort's cheeks continued to redden. "Don't do that, Captain Wether-ford."

"Don't do what?" His mind whirled from the information he'd been given in a short span of time.

"Give up." She squeezed her fingers on his arm. "Please, no matter what else you do in life, go chase after that love no matter the obstacles or odds. When that emotion is true and you believe there is no one else for you than Miss Hasting, that is fate." With a nod, her eyes reflected encouragement. "You won't feel like that with another."

"I..." Another shock hit him squarely in the chest. "No, I don't suppose I will ever change my mind on what I feel for Miss Hasting." Was he daft to act so defeated? It warranted thought, if nothing else. "Thank you for that." Despite being in public, Peregrine bussed her cheek then whispered into her ear. "I sincerely hope you are able to find happiness with your love too. Should you need a private place to talk or remove yourselves from the public eye, drop by my shop. I promise to look the other way if you want to tour the upstairs apartment." When he pulled back, he peered into her eyes that welled with tears. "Lord knows everyone can use a helping hand in this world, and love shouldn't be thwarted merely because it isn't sanctioned."

"I appreciate that." She clung to his hand for longer than was necessary. "Planning for a future will prove tricky and scandalous, but I feel it will be worth it."

"Of course it will." As he cast a glance about, a slow grin took possession of his lips. "Is your lady love here tonight?"

"Yes." Immediately, her expression softened, and her eyes went starry, made even more so by the tears. "She is standing at the far window, dressed in navy. I fully believe she would fetch me the moon if I asked."

His heart squeezed for her predicament and the gauntlet she would need to run merely to be together to live her romance. "Indeed, she is quite handsome."

Miss Beaufort nodded. "I am trying to convince my father to take a holiday to the Continent and to invite Deborah's family to travel with us." A sigh escaped her. "Perhaps I won't come back directly…"

"I wish you good fortune." Then he stepped away from her.

"Thank you. I wish the same for you." For long moments, she looked at him with a tiny frown. "Love is both frightening and wonderful, but I wouldn't have it any other way."

In that moment, he and Miss Beaufort were in perfect harmony. "Neither would I. Thank you for putting things back into perspective for me."

"Fight for her, Captain. You can do no less, I think." Then she moved off as the dance ended, and she melded with the crowd.

Tracing his gloved fingertips along the side of his scarred cheek, Peregrine exited the drawing room and went directly to the card room where he proceeded to fill the next couple of hours by drinking entirely too much, gambling even more—where he won some coin and lost some coin—in an effort to keep himself from thinking. When he finally went home, he promptly cast up his accounts and fell into bed with a horrible, pounding headache and not many new answers to the questions that plagued him.

Women. Bah!

CHAPTER SIXTEEN

June 10, 1817
Bromington House
Manchester Square
London

WHEN CORA CAUGHT her eyes misting with tears, she sternly berated herself, for it was vastly unbecoming to turn into a watering pot over a man.

It had been eight days since she'd last seen Peregrine, and even then, it had been at a rout where Mrs. Bromington had forbidden her from leaving her side, had lectured her on the folly of pining after a man. That night while the widow had made the rounds in her Bath chair, Cora had no choice but to remain within a few feet of her as she'd promised when she'd chosen familial responsibility and duty to her charge over Peregrine's suit.

Yet at that rout, she had once more broken his heart by giving him the cut direct. Shortly after that, he'd found comfort in Miss Beaufort. As Cora had stood witnessing them talk with their heads close together, she secretly died inside for she had all but pushed him into the younger lady's arms. When he'd kissed her cheek and they both seemed quite satisfied with themselves, Cora had wanted to flee the room, but Mrs. Bromington demanded she find her pride and forget him.

That was her life now, and she needed to square with that. If she didn't look after the widow or help her family's finances, who would?

Surely at some point she would feel justified in denying herself a happy future.

Wouldn't she?

In that following week or just over, she had fallen into a routine, for Mrs. Bromington was nothing if not predictable. There were people to receive, servants to bedevil, calls to make, errands to run, and operas to attend. To be fair, the widow remained intent to spend the winter in Rome, but thus far, she hadn't made any firm plans or booked passage.

Regardless, Cora had fought to keep her emotions tamped down and buried, for there was no happiness or joy, nothing to look forward to in her life, and definitely no teasing from the captain, and no visits from his dog.

It was lonely, and she missed Peregrine more than she thought she might. For too long, she'd hated him and what he'd done to her, but when he'd come back into her life, had won her over with his charm and determination, she'd fallen for him all over again… only to toss it away over one silly decision.

As the long-case clock in the second-floor corridor struck the noon day hour, Cora once more stuffed her thoughts away and shoved her feelings down as she walked toward the drawing room. It was time for luncheon and no doubt Mrs. Bromington would be growing peckish, but as she drew near to the door, the sound of voices within made her frown. Apparently, the widow had one of her friends in for a visit, a Lady Bronson, who was one of society's biggest gossip matrons. With indecision racking her, Cora paused outside the open door, still hidden behind the wall.

Should she interrupt?

While she waffled, the conversation within drifted to her ears.

Lady Bronson sniffled, for she'd just sneezed. "In any event, I wish to hire a companion like yours, Alice. Do you have any ideas where to acquire one? Perhaps with an agency?"

"Or you can take out an advertisement for help in one of the newspapers." Mrs. Bromington chuckled. "Be certain you hire a biddable one, older preferably, one who has all but given up on their dreams, and one who is responsible and duty bound." There was a pause, and presumably the widow was maneuvering her Bath chair. "If the candidate's family is of reduced circumstances, that is even better. Usually, they are already wracked by guilt but will embrace the challenge presented with their position."

"Oh? Is your girl in that category?"

"She is. Her father is Baron Landover, and you know how far that name has fallen within the *ton*."

The other woman made a sound of agreement, while Cora stood in the corridor with a hand pressed to her lips so she wouldn't betray her presence. "Has that helped you in getting along with yours? I can't believe she's stuck by you for so long where others have given notice or been sacked."

"It definitely has, especially now that some of the fight has left her." The widow chuckled. "Miss Hasting has been with me six months this week. I'm hoping to take her to Rome this winter and do some traveling through the Continent. I've a hankering to see the world and spend my inheritance."

A gasp issued from Lady Bronson. "How can you do that in the Bath chair? Won't that be a hardship for you both? I cannot imagine trekking through streets on a ship with contraption."

"I'll let you in on a little secret, Cecily." A rusting sort of laugh escaped Mrs. Bromington. "I haven't been completely honest."

"Oh?"

As Cora peered around the door frame and into the room, she stifled a gasp with both hands over her mouth, for Mrs. Bromington had stood up from her chair to walk about the immediate area with little to no strain, if a tad slowly, which was why she usually used a cane. Shock billowed through her chest while she stared in disbelief.

"I am only pretending to be an invalid to ensure Miss Hasting remains with me. She had some silly notion of throwing her life away on a retired sea captain."

"Ah, I know the one. That man with the horrid scars?" The other woman shivered. "I cannot imagine waking up to that face every day."

"Yes, exactly." The widow nodded before she returned to the Bath chair. "To make certain the girl stayed with me, I falsified my injury, had to run off the man before she tumbled tip over tail for him."

"Did she learn nothing from her previous failed engagement to him?" the other lady asked with another sniff.

"Who can say what goes on in the heads of young women who build castles in the air." Mrs. Bromington huffed. "Besides, she needs to get her living due to her family's financial problems and I need a companion whose will has been defeated by disappointments in life." Another creaky laugh echoed in the room. "Now we'll both be able to enjoy the Continent. In this way, I can show my ungrateful children I don't need them as they claim."

Dear heavens. In the corridor, Cora gaped, stood shaking in silence as shock continued to hold her captive.

"I thought your youngest daughter wished to move in with you and keep your house."

The widow snorted. "She does, but it's only out of pity, I'm sure." A hard note had entered her voice. "I refuse to be a charity to anyone."

"Be grateful, Alice. If one of your children is willing, best take advantage of that."

"The companion is more biddable than my daughter."

They both shared a laugh.

Then Lady Bronson spoke again. "Does Miss Hasting suspect any of this?"

"As far as I know, she does not. Now that the danger of her

running off with the captain has passed, I suppose I should begin putting out hints that the feeling is *miraculously* coming back into my legs." Another laugh issued from her. "I'll blame it on aging and the mysteries of a woman's body. No one will question it."

Out in the corridor, Cora curled the fingers of one hand into a fist within her skirting. *It had all been a lie?*

"You are quite clever. But won't Miss Hasting be upset?"

"I rather doubt it." The sound of the Bath chair being manipulated filtered to Cora's ears. "Though she's prone to outspokenness at times, she is too fearful to speak her mind or cause problems. Especially now the captain is gone. Of course, I did threaten to sack her without recommendation, so that is what guided her responses."

The two women chuckled.

"This has all been fascinating," Lady Bronson said with a definite grin in her voice. "Now, *does* she have a friend or perhaps another sister who is willing to be a companion?"

How dare her!

As the conversation droned on inside the drawing room, in the corridor, Cora was in the grips of heavy emotion. Hot anger and annoyance battered her insides, quickly followed by cold guilt, regret, and despair. Mrs. Bromington had lied to her to make her stay, just as Peregrine had suspected, but she—Cora—had refused to listen, had denied it was possible, had chosen to side with the widow.

Her breath came in quick pants. She leaned her back against the wall merely to remain upright. Because she'd believed the lies, believed that Mrs. Bromington had truly lost the use of her legs, she had given up a life with Peregrine. Out of false pretenses! She had thrown away her future for the sake of a paid position in order to save her family and provide companionship to a woman who not only didn't respect her but also would use her until there was nothing left.

Just as he'd feared, Peregrine had so much integrity that he'd let her make her own decisions without throwing a fit or trying to convince her out of it.

In everything, he'd been naught but a gentleman, had supported her in everything she'd wished to do with each step, and she'd been too blind to see the truth.

Oh, God, what have I done?

With nothing to do just now, Cora tamped down hard on the urge to sob. Knowing she risked discovery, she retreated along the corridor as quickly and quietly as she could then she ran up the stairs to her room, where she softly closed the door. Then she threw herself onto her bed, buried her face in her pillow, and sobbed out the contents of her heart. As she wept, she mourned for what she'd done, for what she'd caused to happen, the dreams she'd willingly given up, for everything she had lost.

And for what?

She didn't know how long she'd indulged in tears, but eventually Bridget came into the room, and by that time, the afternoon sunlight was slanting through the window.

"Miss Hasting? Are you well?"

"No!" A wail followed the answer.

"Oh, dear." The maid came into the room. She perched on the side of Cora's bed and grasped Cora's hand. "What happened? Mrs. Bromington is grousing that you neglected to join her for luncheon, but she's occupied enough with Lady Branson."

"Truth to tell, I honestly don't care what Mrs. Bromington thinks." In between bouts of tears, Cora told the maid what she'd discovered in the corridor. "She's not an invalid nor is she paralyzed. It has all been lies to ensure my obedience. Ensure that we all remain here with her!"

"I wish I could say that I'm shocked, but I'm not." Bridget hugged her. "I'm so sorry."

"Because of that woman, I gave up a future with Captain Wetherford. That poor man tried every day to call on me and was turned away nearly every time." Another round of tears beset her, and she wiped them away with her fingers. "I made a horrible mistake because I believed Mrs. Bromington needed me, and she only considers me a pawn to be used, as if I'm naught but a candle, there to provide light for her to read by. There will be another behind me, and another after that." The enormity of what she'd lost continued to press in on her chest, and she gasped for breath. "What am I to do? I can't stay here now."

Yet where would she go?

"Don't cry so." Bridget pressed a folded and starched handkerchief into her hand. "Things truly aren't as bad as you fear."

"How? I've ruined everything."

The maid tsked her tongue. "First off, you should beg the captain's forgiveness, grovel if you must." That lovely Irish brogue was heavy in her voice. "He loves you to distraction. Everyone thinks so, and he's handsome besides, even if his face is marred." She tucked an escaped strand of Cora's hair behind her ear. "Men like him don't flit from woman to woman. I'll wager he loves you still."

"I don't know about that. He was quite cozy with a young woman the last time I saw him." Then she frowned and stared at the maid. "Even if he somehow asked me to marry him, that won't help my family. He isn't well off."

"Perhaps not, but you will have each other, and *that* will make you happy. You will finally know peace." Bridget patted Cora's arm. "The rest can take care of itself later. Things like that usually do."

"I don't know." She wiped her eyes once more. "Surely, he will never forgive me. I betrayed him, Bridget. I *left* him. That hurt in his eyes will haunt me for the remainder of my life. I know how that feels." A shuddering sigh left her throat. "When I could have him, I chose something else—"

"That you thought was right for you at the time, just as he did when he went into the navy and left you behind." For long moments, Bridget held her gaze. Compassion lined her expression. "Now he knows it was a mistake, just as you know that you made the same." She shrugged. "If he loves you as he claims, he will forgive you, especially if you love him as well." The young woman paused, raised a red eyebrow in question. "You *do* love him, don't you?"

Did she?

As she peered at the maid, thought about everything Peregrine had done since they'd crashed back together all those weeks ago, she groaned with sadness. She could no longer deny it to herself. Yes, she loved him, and had never stopped even though she'd shoved that emotion behind anger, denial, embarrassment, and fear. "Oh, Bridget, I've been such a silly, stupid widgeon."

The maid chuckled. "We have all been made to feel such because love has twisted us about. There is no shame in it."

Despite the reassurance, heat rose into her cheeks. "I'm quite embarrassed, though."

"As soon as you make amends with your man, all of that will go away."

"Do you think he'll even consent to see me?" She glanced at the window where rain drummed against the glass and gray skies loomed as far as the eye could see.

"You won't know unless you try," Bridget said with a wink as she stood up from the bed.

"Right." This would be the most important visit and speech she would ever make in her life. Everything else fell away to the back of her mind. Perhaps it was time to put herself and her needs in the forefront for once. Afterward, she could address all her other worries, but she couldn't do any of that until she'd spoken to Peregrine. Struggling into a sitting position, she sighed. "Then we shouldn't delay. Find my prettiest gown. I'll need my hair set, oh and locate the ivory hair comb as well as that ivory ring on the chain." It had been something she'd given up wearing after she feared she'd lost him forever.

"I would be delighted, but it's raining, duckie. You'll ruin the hair and the gown."

"Does that matter when my future is hanging above my head by fate's string?" She squirmed off the bed and headed to the armoire. "When at any moment it can be cut, and this chance will be forever dashed from my grasp?"

"Perhaps not." Amusement sounded in the maid's voice as she joined Cora in contemplating the gown choices. "Will you leave Mrs. Bromington's service?"

"I'm not certain." Already, her stomach was full of knots, for if she didn't stay here, she would no longer have the coin to send to her family.

Papa will lose the hall.

Bridget heaved out a breath. "She'll undoubtedly sack you once she finds out that you've run off after the captain."

"Perhaps she will." Cora scowled at her small collection of clothing. "I'll hate to leave you here to fight alone."

"Oh, la." The maid waved a hand. "I will manage. There are always households who need maids, but you will have your man, and nothing should ever stand in the way of that."

"It's so frightening." Her insides were in a jumble. "What will I even say to him?" Would any words win back the heart of a man scorned and rejected?

"Speak from the heart and be honest. Men like the captain don't engage in games and riddles." Bridget grinned. "And a bit of kissing doesn't hurt either."

"I shall think of what I'll do on the ride over. Will you tell Mrs. Bromington I'm in bed with a megrim?"

"Of course, but if all goes as it should, I'll wager you'll be in bed with something far more pleasurable, my girl." Then she pulled at a few gowns. "Let's see what we can find."

"Good." Cora pressed a shaking hand to her heated cheek. *I must try.* For herself and the future she suddenly desperately wanted. Just as her older sister had taken a chance and stepped out with faith and hope, so would she.

God help me.

CHAPTER SEVENTEEN

*B*LOODY HELL.

Would this dismal day never end? He blew out the last lamp in the shop. It had been raining for seemingly forever, and since there had been no business in the shop for the last few hours, Peregrine had determined he would close early. Like the bitter man he'd become over the past handful of days, he wanted tea, a blanket, and Matey would no doubt be missing him. For a summer afternoon, there was a bit of a chill in the air thanks to the rain, and the dog tended to howl at the raindrops. That couldn't be good for his neighbors at The Albany.

Not that it mattered.

Since his last conversation with Viscount Maubrey, he hadn't pondered hard enough on a plan that would win Cora back or entice her away from the dragon who guarded her. And that had made him more disgruntled than before.

With one last look around, he crossed the wooden floor, opened the door, and went outside. The rain beat down on his top hat in a steady rhythm; water dripped from his brim. As he fumbled for his key, a hired hack pulled up in front of his shop. From the reflection of the door's window glass, he watched with consternation as a woman alighted from the conveyance. When the vehicle drove onward, he frowned, for that woman was Cora, wearing a magnificent gown in a raspberry color.

His traitorous heart squeezed, and his pulse accelerated. *Bloody, bloody hell. What the devil is she doing here?*

"Peregrine."

His shoulders drooped when she came toward him and his shop door. She hadn't worn a spencer, and aside from her plain straw bonnet, there was nothing to protect her from the rain. "What do you want, Cora?" Damn, but his heart hurt. Why the hell was he still alive if the organ in question ached so badly? Though he'd had over a week to square with the fact she had chosen her position over a possible future with him, it still stung. Deep down in his shredded soul, he had steeled himself for never seeing her again, especially after the cut direct she'd given him at that rout.

"I wanted to see you." Her voice sounded from close by, but he still hadn't turned around to face her.

"So you have. Now you can go. I am headed home, regardless." He'd lost and his planned second courtship of this woman hadn't amounted to much. Sometimes, regardless of how a man felt, or how much he'd prepared for, he didn't win the hand of his lady love. That was how fate worked, but the recovery from that failure would prove the real challenge.

Once more he was alone, and it was much like when he'd left her and London for the navy. The only difference between now and then was that this time, he'd foolishly had hope. Though Charles had told him not to give up on her and to try again, he hadn't been able to summon the strength such a feat would entail, for in his mind, he largely suspected she would tell him the same thing. Hope was gone, shattered and broken. Those pieces glittered among the remains of his heart.

"I won't go until you and I talk."

Damn impossible woman. Finally, he turned around and narrowed his eyes. "I have nothing else to say." Point in fact, he was the one who'd been wronged this time, and if she expected him to grovel or go to great lengths to come about, she could think again. "You have obviously made your choice."

"No!" She shook her head, wiped at the raindrops on her cheeks with her gloved fingertips. "It was the wrong one. I should never have picked Mrs. Bromington over you."

"What?" Peregrine couldn't help but gape at her. The rain rapidly dotted that lovely raspberry taffeta, leaving wet patches that soaked through the fabric. The low, rounded neckline showed a fair amount of her décolletage that gleamed with a sheen of rain, but it was her eyes that held him captive—unending despair seemed accumulated in those lake blue depths. "Why are you here?"

"I need to talk to you, Perry," she said and took another step toward him. "I have made a mistake, perhaps the biggest one of my life, and I would like the opportunity to try and rectify that if you will allow me to explain."

Did he even wish to grant her that? It would only prolong the pain, yet part of him was indeed curious. He crossed his arms at his chest. "I won't stop you, and you'd best do it quickly, for the longer we remain out here, the wetter we grow."

"Of course." A few muttered words fell from her lips that sounded suspiciously like, "Why must you prove so annoying and aggravating?" but he couldn't be certain since the tone was almost inaudible in the drum of the rain. "Do you promise to listen to what I have to say without interrupting or interjecting your opinion?"

"Ah, so then I'm not allowed to defend myself if necessary?" Peregrine shook his head as he peered at her. "From what I have managed to discern, this relationship has always been one-sided. It has been me trying to convince you to take a chance." He thrust the pretty picture she made with her cheeks pink from the slight chill and the ever-dampening tendrils of her blonde hair that lay pasted to her forehead and neck beneath the bonnet's brim. What would those raindrops taste like that clung heroically to her lips?

"Please stop. I don't have the strength to argue with you

while I gather the remainder of my dignity enough to move through this speech." The entreaty rang with desperation. "Once I'm finished, if you still wish to have nothing else to do with me, I will understand. We can both walk our separate paths and never think of this again."

"I was not the one who drove this wedge between us," he couldn't help but remind her.

"Don't you think I'm not exceedingly aware of that?" The words exploded into the air, propelled by extreme emotion. "It's why I'm here now." She shoved off her bonnet, no doubt the better to see him. Then his breath caught, for she wore the ivory comb that he'd given her. The teeth were buried in her beautiful, damp hair.

Rain continued to fall, and with each new drop, her gown continued to be more saturated and her perfectly upswept hair looked rather worse for wear. She didn't make a move to go into his shop, and he didn't invite her in, for why should he make yet another concession? "I…" The set of her jaw and how she held her head that exposed her throat—showing her vulnerability and trust—as well as the emotions in the depths of her eyes gave him pause. Perhaps she was dead serious and not here to taunt him or tease him with something beyond his grasp. *God strike me for a nodcock, but I'm willing to hear her out.* He gave a curt nod. "Very well. Say your peace."

"Thank you." Cora stood her ground as if she wasn't sure of her reception. It was good to have her on the offensive, for he wasn't ready to forgive her. Perhaps he never would. A man who'd been cut to the quick didn't forget that hurt, regardless of if he loved her. "I'm at a loss of where to start," she admitted with a shrug that only lifted one shoulder. The dull sound of the wet taffeta was added to the steady tattoo of the rain.

"You were the one who came, so I suggest you puzzle it out. I do have other plans this day." The response came out frostier than he would have liked, but his patience had been stretched already. There was only so much he could bear, and every second in her company was torture.

"I've always appreciated your penchant for not wasting time." With the rain falling around her and the fresh, bright raspberry color of her gown striking against the overcast gray day and the muted splash of carriage wheels against the wet street, he couldn't help but admire the picture. At another time, perhaps, he would have taken her into his arms and stolen a kiss, told her how brave she was after everything.

But that sentiment was long past. She had brought them to this pass.

"I… Dear heavens, I knew exactly what I wished to say on the ride over here, but now it's all flown out of my mind when presented with you in the flesh." The tip of her tongue darted out and whisked away the raindrops that had alighted on her bottom lip.

Peregrine stifled a groan. No longer was she his, for she'd rejected him at every turn, and he had to remember that. "Please arrive at the point. This delay is unnecessary, and we will both be drenched before too much longer." The ache around his heart renewed its torture, reminding him that he still lived and there was no future between them. Surely this was a nightmare he'd awaken from soon.

"Though I realize you have just cause to act ugly, I don't appreciate it while I'm struggling to find my bearings." A hint of tears wavered in her voice, but he steeled himself against it. She met his gaze without flinching. "Earlier today, I bore witness to something so egregious that it rocked my very existence."

"Oh?" Not relaxing his posture, he rested a shoulder against the closed door of his shop. The tiny overhang of the roof provided a modicum of shelter from the rain.

"Yes." Again, she whisked away the moisture from her lips with her tongue. Was she not aware of how erotic that gesture seemed? "I was on my way to ask Mrs. Bromington if she would enjoy luncheon when I paused outside the drawing room. She had a friend who wished to engage a companion." The delicate tendons in her throat worked with a hard swallow. "Mrs. Bromington suggested finding a biddable woman without purpose, generally, and then…"

"Yes?" Despite himself, he was desperate to discover the end of her tale.

Stifling a sob, Cora continued. "And then the widow revealed that she wasn't truly paralyzed. She stood up from her Bath chair, admitted to her friend it had all been a fiction in an effort to make me stay with her."

"What?" Shock moved through him so hard that he sagged against the shop door. "Then I was correct this whole time?"

"Yes." A sob escaped her, but she didn't bother to brush away the tears and they blended with the rain on her cheeks. "As I peeked into the room, I witnessed her stand and walk about the room as if there was nothing wrong with her at all. Additionally, she admitted to her friend that she'd done it to ensure my obedience and continued companionship."

When her damned chin trembled, the gesture tugged at his heart. He relaxed his arms, took a step toward her. "There is nothing wrong with her legs." It wasn't a question.

"No."

"Yet you tossed me to the curb as if I didn't matter, as if the history between us didn't mean anything." Not ready to forgive her just yet, he frowned.

"I won't deny what I said or what I did, for at the time, I thought it was the best decision. I thought she needed that assistance." A blush developed on her cheeks. "I have made mistakes, Perry, but none have been so great as choosing a liar and a generally foul person over what you and I could have had together."

"It certainly didn't sound like you regretted it that day. Those words still ring in my mind, and you have only just discovered that choice was the wrong one." Perhaps that was what truly stuck in his craw like a twisted dagger. She'd been perfectly fine living with her choice… until today while he'd agonized about it for over a week.

"Don't assume that I didn't berate myself every night since that afternoon!" Annoyance flashed in her eyes. "I hated what I'd done. I mourned for what I gave up for that woman."

"Perhaps." He refused to give quarter. No longer would he plead for her affections. If she continued to play him like a bowstring, never quite agreeing to a courtship that would end with a proposal, he wanted nothing more to do with her. His ego wouldn't allow such fickleness, and quite frankly, he was tired. She hadn't forgiven his mistake for over three years; he was owed a bit of that victory. "Why should I believe you? I have done my best to pour everything that I am into this relationship, but you haven't been entirely present, have always teetered, measuring me against your family or the widow." A muscle ticced in his cheek. "If I take you at your word, the moment I might resume what we had, you'll find another way to stab holes in my heart." At the very basis of everything, she needed to understand that he wouldn't put himself back up on the gallows for her to walk away as he swung.

"I've acted horribly. There is no denying that." For the space of a heartbeat, she silently cried while the rain came down. "And I understand how you feel. I should never have done that to you. No matter how many directions in which I've been pulled, you didn't deserve such poor treatment."

At least there was that. "Thank you. Though, to be fair, it was exactly what I'd done to you when I broke our engagement." He clenched his teeth then told himself to relax. "Good thing we hadn't made it to that point this time. Clean break and all that."

A shuddering sigh escaped her. She sniffed, for her nose was a bit snotty. Finally, she raised her gaze to his. "It's time to be honest. I have hidden from certain things for far too long." Tears pooled in her eyes as her gown was completely soaked through and her blonde hair lay more or less plastered to her head. "Please forgive me for the words I said to you out of anger, out of fear. I am solely responsible for the duties I placed upon my shoulders.

In the past week, it has been glaringly apparent that what I've lost is more valuable than what I have convinced myself I should be doing."

It wasn't exactly an apology, but it went a long way in straightening out his jumbled guts. "Meaning?" This time, there could be no misunderstandings, nothing used to hide behind or to replace real feelings.

She pressed her lips into a thin line before yet another sob wrenched from her. "I fell in love with you over three years ago, and when you asked for my hand, I was thrilled. You were dashing and charming, everything a navy man should be." When he raised an eyebrow, she rushed onward. "But when you broke our engagement, all of that crumbled into dust." As he opened his mouth to protest, she held up a hand that dripped with water. "I realized that what I felt for you wasn't love at all, but perhaps infatuation, for love would not have vanished at the first obstacle."

Fair enough. "I can understand that, but though I did love you—have always loved you—perhaps my heart wasn't as entrenched as it should have been, for I wouldn't have left in the first place had I been besotted." Still, Peregrine steeled his heart, for he had been disappointed before.

"We have both been foolish to let things in life that have no real roots tear us apart, make us forget that what we had could have gained the potential for a strong foundation." She wiped at the moisture on her forehead. Not that it made a difference. "Perhaps you would do better to pursue Miss Beaufort. I saw her with you at that rout, and you are quite a handsome pair." A tear fell to her cheek.

"Let us say her affections are very much on someone else who is not me." He ignored her distress; he had to for his own peace of mind. "Your point, Cora? I wish to move out of the rain." It wasn't well done of him to keep her in the weather, but he needed to know the depths of her commitment.

"When my little hope was taken from me, that loss hurt more

than anything else, for it was the final piece of you gone. And there was no one except my twin who knew, so I couldn't even remember that hope aloud for fear of the scandal that would embarrass my parents." A cry of either frustration or despair left her, and the sound slashed through his heart. "It wasn't until you arrived, and you accidentally misidentified me at that rout I knew my path wasn't done crossing with yours."

"And?" Despite himself and the hurt she'd caused, he wanted this bit finished. She was adorable in her agony. Heat built inside him; he no longer noticed the rain.

"As I said the other day in that library, you have left an impression on my heart, a fire in my blood, an itch beneath my skin, and the longer you kept coming, kept chasing, kept asking me, letting me make my own mistakes and discovering who I was, that impression only deepened." With a cry, Cora offered a hand to him, but he resisted taking it, for once he did, he'd be lost, and nothing had been resolved. "Perry, please. Grant me pardon. Say something so I'll know you don't hate me."

"No, I don't hate you. How could I? But I do remain wary." He cocked his head while a grin of amusement flirted with his lips. If he'd had to grovel for her, she could return the favor a bit. "The solution to this convoluted speech is quite simple."

"Perhaps you're right. Again. Damn you." The ghost of a grin met her lips as her hand fell heavily to her side. "It's time to lay bare my soul." For long moments she gazed at him while her chin trembled, and her lips shook. "I realized too late that what I truly want from life and *in* my life is you. If we forgive all the wrongs, excuse the less than favorable words, if we toss out all the secrets we've kept from each other, what's left is love." Twin tears slipped down her cheeks. "That is all that matters, don't you think?" The delicate tendons in her throat worked with a swallow. "To the depths of my soul, until the end of time, I love you, Peregrine Wetherford. You were the first man to have my heart, and I want you to be the only man to hold it now."

Oh, God. The honesty in her entreaty compromised his ability to remain indifferent, but he couldn't quite forgive her just yet. While uncommon happiness bubbled in his chest, he kept his expression hooded. "What of Mrs. Bromington? What of your intent to help your family?"

"I have made the decision to give notice to the widow. No longer can I remain as her companion in good conscience knowing she is only using me for her own ends, but I wanted to fix things between you and me first." Her chest heaved with the force of her emotion, which sent his notice dropping to her bosom. "As for my family, perhaps a new idea will come to them as a collective, for I realize now I shouldn't sacrifice my future for something I had no hand in making. Above all, I won't forget their plight and will help if I can."

While he was satisfied with those answers, there was still one thing he wanted desperately to hear. "I seem to recall that you promised me an answer by June fifteenth." God, he was a bastard for acting as if he were a player upon a Drury Lane stage, but he owed it to himself—and her—to make this ending, or rather their new beginning, as emotional as their history.

A smile tugged at the corners of her lips. "I still have five days."

"Ah. Well, you know my address. Please write to me there when you are certain." Then he maneuvered around her, as if he would start the walk through Mayfair toward a hack stand.

"Wait!" She moved into his path, blocking his forward momentum.

Her cry paused his steps. "Was there something else you wished to say?"

"Yes," she said on a gasp. "Dear God, yes I *must* lest I break apart from it." The darling woman dropped to her knees despite the rain and the mud that would ruin the remainder of her skirting. "I'm so ashamed for how I've acted, not only when you returned to London but in listening to Mrs. Bromington over your logic. Forgive me."

"Of course I do, for we both need it, but does the apology

come too late?" It was rather pleasant, this being courted, and he couldn't wait to hear what she would say next. Afterward, he would kiss her senseless, reassure her that everything they'd gone through would make them stronger.

"We've both made mistakes." Desolation reflected in her eyes and tone.

"We have." It was becoming more difficult to keep his humor of the situation hidden.

"No doubt we'll continue to make them." Though she wiped at the moisture on her face, with the continuing rain, it was a useless endeavor. "At least I will."

"That *is* what life is all about. Without mistakes, we would never learn or grow." When she still looked glum, he continued. "Sweeting, life is raw and messy and emotional. It has joyous moments and horrid ones. It will send you flying and lay you low. If you're not taking such risks, you're doing it wrong, and you will eventually end up as bitter as Mrs. Bromington."

"You've helped me to see that." Cora nodded. "I want a flawed man with annoying habits who I can hold, and kiss, and argue with."

"Ah, well there is no denying I'm quite flawed, and quite objectionable with my scars."

"You are everything handsome and lovely. I wouldn't have you any other way." She sniffed. "A man who will forgive me as I forgive him, and knowing we have more in common than we do not, and that our history will remind us to go gently with grace."

"The world is full of men like that," he said with twitching lips that desperately wanted to burgeon into a grin of pure happiness. "You should start your search with alacrity, for you are nearly a spinster, darling."

"Damn you, Peregrine." She scrubbed at the tears on her cheeks. "Don't be an arse. I am already beset with nerves."

"I can't help it, for the moment deserves some lightness." He couldn't hold back the grin he finally gave into. "What is it you truly wish to say to me? It is rather chilly and quite wet out here, and frankly, I'd like to go inside and see about relieving you of that sopping gown."

"Oh?" Hope sprang into her eyes. "I suppose this is the truth of it, and what I've only ever wanted." She dug into her reticule and pulled out the ivory ring he'd given to her years ago, held it up between her thumb and forefinger. "Captain Wetherford—Perry—will you marry me? No matter what we face, will you stand with me for the rest of our lives?"

Slow seconds went by, marked by the rapid beat of his heart. Perhaps he was a fool, but he believed her, and in that, he knew everything would work itself out. "Ah, Cora. You gorgeous, endearing thing." He put a hand beneath her chin and gently raised her head until their gazes connected. "Yes, I'll marry you, and why shouldn't I?" The pieces of his heart picked themselves off the ground and flew into place, held together by a love that had endured and strengthened and changed over the years. "I love you to distraction, always have, but I needed to be sure of *your* feelings for *me*. After everything."

"Understandable." Wonder reflected in her eyes as she stared at him. "You will marry me?" Astonishment lingered in her whispered inquiry.

"As soon as I can procure a license, and if I can't, we will have the banns read, either here or in the parish where your parents reside. It matters not to me." He grasped her hand and easily tugged her into a standing position. Then he took the ring from her, yanked the wet glove from her left hand, and carefully slipped it upon the fourth finger there. "I love you, Cora. Please don't ever doubt that."

"I don't. Not anymore." She wiped at more tears. "I should never have discounted it to begin with, for you have been nothing but truthful and supportive this whole time, where I've been naught but a silly widgeon."

"Not silly, but perhaps worried and lost. Everything will come out right. You'll see." Then he claimed her lips in a kiss he hoped seared his commitment to her into her brain and told her in no uncertain terms how much he adored her. When he pulled away, his breathing was as labored as hers. "Come. Into the shop with me. Let us get you warm."

She uttered a soft protest. "I am not done kissing you, though."

"I never said we were finished with *that*, love. And there will be much, *much* more between us than kissing this afternoon." With anticipation buzzing at his spine and his heart overflowing with victory from finally winning her as well as the love he held back out of fear from rejection, Peregrine led his soon-to-be wife into his shop and firmly closed the door behind them.

He didn't know what the future held, but he couldn't wait to meet every damned step of it. With her.

EPILOGUE

May 24, 1820
Landover Manor
Bedfordshire, England

CORA WETHERFORD NÉE Hasting couldn't help but smile as she removed her bonnet, then did the same with her half-boots.

In a month's time, she and Peregrine would celebrate their third wedding anniversary, but since they were at her father's property in Bedfordshire currently—and since this meadow was the place where Peregrine had first claimed her body before they were supposed to have been wed the first time—it only seemed right that they would enjoy a picnic here today.

After they had spent a honeymoon period at Lord Maubrey's estate in Kent, they had traveled to Bedfordshire and visited with her family, which they tried to do twice a year, and most definitely during the Christmastide season.

"Is this the spot, then?" her husband asked with a grin. He held a willow basket in one hand and an old quilt in the other.

"Yes." The green grasses were dotted with a wash of wild-flowers in a riot of colors that resembled an oil painting. In the far distance, blue-gray water from a brook sparkled in the sunlight.

"It's perfect, and I remember this place well."

"As do I." After setting the basket down, he proceeded to spread out the quilt that had seen better days. The edges were fraying. A hole had started in one quarter. Long ago the colors had faded. But there was still life in it yet, and while it was serviceable, Cora would always pull it from the cedar trunk in the attic and use it.

Like for such an occasion as this.

"The day is wonderful, and just smell the flowers, Perry. If all the year could be like this, everything else would be bearable, I think." Over the years since she'd married the captain, they had made amazing memories and had grieved together through dark and lonely valleys. But always, at the end of each cycle, they had each other.

"You speak of the child we lost." It wasn't a question, and though he was every bit as handsome as he'd always been, there were new lines that crinkled the corners of his eyes and framed his mouth. And during the last year or so, there had been shadows *in* his eyes.

"I do."

Eighteen months before, when her father had succumbed to the disease that had taken his mind, the news had been so shocking and sudden that Cora had gone into premature labor. Since she'd only been five months along, the babe was too small to survive and had perished immediately following the birth.

However, Cora had been told after the fact, for once she'd been delivered of the child—a daughter—there had been certain internal complications with her body. Once a horrifying bout of hemorrhaging had been stemmed and other measures had been administered to make certain she survived the ordeal, the midwife had gently broken the news to Peregrine that it was unlikely she would ever be able to conceive again.

"We still have a lovely life, though, don't we?" Yes, there was a wistful note in his voice, but his eyes were bright as he set the basket on the quilt and his grin had the power to weaken her knees just as it always had.

"Of course we do, and it's been enriched more than I ever thought possible." She met his gaze and offered a smile. "Please don't misunderstand me. The losses we have suffered temper the joys, but that doesn't mean there isn't so much in the offing for us to discover and rejoice over." When she joined him on the quilt, a squeak escaped her when he tugged her down to sit next to him. "We do not need children to make our marriage complete or fulfilled."

"A lovely sentiment and one I quite agree with." As he tossed his top hat to the edge where it joined her bonnet, he sighed. "But then, I expected nothing less from my lovely wife."

"You are too charming for your own good." Cora delved into the basket and removed a corked bottle of lemonade. "I am content with what we have."

Peregrine's shop, Charts and Springs, had slowly gained popularity. In those early days, since she'd been without a paying position, she had worked as his shop assistant, and months later, it had been a cozy arrangement spending her days beside him. They'd moved into the rooms above the shop and had made it into a happy love nest that suited them—and Matey—quite well. There was no need to immediately move, and perhaps they would find a modest townhouse someday, but that was for the future.

He had even brought on an assistant for those times when they were away. It might not be the glittering life that her oldest sister lived as a viscount's wife, but they were happy, and especially after the losses the family had suffered, that was all that mattered.

"As am I. We have certainly filled our little home with laughter and love." He delved a finger into the pocket of his waistcoat. "I have a gift for you."

"Oh?" It was rare, indeed, they had enough coin left over at the end of the month for such frivolity, so this was quite a boon. "Why?"

"Because it's time. It's needed. You deserve it." When he opened his palm, a band of silver filagree rested there, and in the center, square-shaped sapphire winked in the sunlight. "I finally had enough saved to buy you a proper engagement ring."

"You didn't need to do that." The ivory ring had been enough. She'd worn it every day until the metal band had developed a crack. Then she'd tucked it away lest she lose the whole of it.

"Yes, I did, and I want the world—and your sisters specifically—to know that I'm more than capable of caring for you even if I don't have a fortune."

"No one thinks badly of you." Her hand shook as he slipped the bauble onto the fourth finger of her left hand. "We live an honest life and there is nothing wrong with that."

"But I want to give you everything you deserve."

"You do, every day that goes by, and your income is nothing to sneeze that." She rested a hand to the scarred side of his face, and when his eyes briefly fluttered closed, she smiled. "In another two years, who knows what will happen? That is the fun of this journey."

"I'm glad we are traveling it together." He took her hand, brought it to his lips, and kissed each finger. "Did you know that there is quite a history in the wildflowers in England?"

"Oh?" There were times when he told her stories from his travels around the world, and in each one, there was such adventure and emotion that she felt as if she'd been the one to experience those travels. "How so?"

"Consider the corn poppy." He nodded toward one of the red flowers nearby. "Poppies were, along with wheat, the emblem of the Greek mother goddess Demeter, who presided over agriculture and the fertility of the earth. Associated with the fullness of the moon, she took care of the growing of crops, and poppies put vital nutrients back into the soil."

"They are rather pretty. I could see how a goddess became enamored with them."

"Indeed." Again, he brought her hand to his lips and kissed the back, but it was the gleam in his hazel eyes that sent anticipation skittering down her spine. "Cowslip, with its beauty-enhancing qualities and yellow hue, is attributed to Freyja, goddess of love and beauty in Norse mythology. It's said that the flowers represent the keys to open the door to her secret hall, and the treasure of inner knowledge."

"Isn't it interesting the lovely flowers are always given to goddesses, but never the common or the ugly?"

"Everything has its place, and nothing is ever overlooked or shunned in the world of nature." He peered into her eyes then slowly toed off his scuffed and much-used Hessian-style boots. "Would that humankind remembered such. The world would certainly be a better place."

"I adore it when you tell me stories." However, in this moment, she wanted so much more from him, since they were the only two around for miles.

"Collecting knowledge is a hobby of mine." With a crooked grin, he pressed feather weighted kisses to the inside of her arm. Gooseflesh followed in his wake. "The cornflower is linked to Venus and Saturn. There are two Greek myths that center on the flower's alleged curative qualities against poisonous venoms."

"Oh?"

"A nod to both myths is found in the flower's botanical name, *Centaurea cyanus*. The first part of the name comes from the tale of the centaur Chiron, advisor to Achilles, who healed Achilles' wound with cornflowers when he was poisoned by an arrow in his heel."

"What a lovely story."

"And what lovely eyes you have that resemble such an impressive bloom." Stretching, Peregrine reached over the edge of the quilt, snagged a cornflower, and when he came back to her, tucked the flower behind one of her ears. "Perhaps it will grant us good fortune in the future."

Her heart skipped a beat. "What is it you want?"

"Many long years with the woman I love." With little effort, he tugged her into his arms and brushed his lips over hers. "And you were right. It's not a bad life at all as long as I have you."

She slipped her arms around his middle. "Do you regret that?" There was always the sensation of coming home when she felt his arms around her.

"Absolutely not. I'm the most fortunate of men." He cupped her cheek and drew the pad of his thumb along her lower lip. "And like the varied colors and shapes of the wildflowers in this field, so go the days of our life together. Some are wilting and limp, but others blaze with color on strong stems. They all make up a wonderful bouquet."

How romantic he was! "How could I ever believe I was better off without you?"

"I ask myself that every day." His next kiss held a possessive note that ignited tiny fires in her blood. "Years ago, Miss Beaufort told me the person she loved would fetch her the moon if she but asked. I would give you the same, for I love you to distraction, more now that we are married."

Tears stung her eyes. "What use would I have of the moon in our cozy home? I only need you." When she glanced up into his dear face and the love and blatant need in those dark depths mirrored what she felt, Cora went once more into his eager arms. "Kiss me as if this is our last day on earth."

"As if you need to ask." With a growl, Peregrine treated her to a series of long, drugging kisses that made her forget her name and desire cloud her brain. One by one, he worked the laces at the back of her gown, and when the garment gaped, he helped her out of it. To be fair, she enthusiastically helped, too. "It wouldn't do to appear at tea with your sisters in a gown stained by grass." He stripped off his gloves and dropped them to the ground near her dress.

She snorted. "We are on a quilt."

"One never knows what will happen when we're lost to passion."

"Stop, you." But she could hardly speak for the excitement and anticipation playing through her insides. Even on the verge of celebrating three years together with him, he still made her giddy before bedding her. Once he'd divested her of the petticoat of thin cotton embroidered by her own hand at the hem with rose buds, she relieved him of his collar and cravat, and then shoved his tweed jacket from his broad shoulders. His tame waistcoat of brown velvet was the next to be shed. The garments randomly decorated the quilt around them.

"Come, Mrs. Wetherford." He pulled her down with him and his arms were warm and strong around her, and the heady scent of wildflowers teased her nose. "I'll wager you are even more beautiful than all of these wildflowers in this field," he whispered and covered her body with his.

Then she was lost on the waves of pleasurable sensation, for he set out to explore every inch of her skin, baring it all to the sun, sky, and his gaze as he kissed and caressed her curves. Once her stays and shift had fallen from his hand, she yanked his shirttails from the waist of his breeches, and with a growl, he pulled it up and off his body.

"Someone is needy this afternoon."

"Can you blame me?" Cora smoothed her palms over the ridges and contours of his flat abdomen. The light mat of coarse hair covering his chest tickled her skin and sent fires scurrying into her blood. "When I'm in your arms and you are loving me, I forget everything, but right now, I need to feel you against me. Urgently," she added in the event he didn't understand.

"Have I ever disappointed you in this regard?" After briefly leaving her to remove his breeches, he layered himself over her, and finally having him skin to skin with her was every bit as wonderful as it ever was. Over and over, he plied her mouth with kisses while he did magical and naughty things to her breasts.

Lips, fingertips, and tongues competed in a game as old as time to see which one of them could bring the other to the edge first. His body made a lovely playground, and she had long ago become familiar with the planes and angles of his form, but he was also an expert on her body, and all too soon they were both panting with need. Moans blended with the nature sounds of birds and the breeze in the tree leaves.

When he skimmed a hand along her hip and then caressed her thigh, Cora trembled, for she was well-primed for this next bit.

It took little time for her to encourage his fingers between her legs, and as he found the sensitive, swollen button at her center, a shuddering sigh escaped her. She broke his kisses long enough to whisper, "Send me flying, Captain. You know what I like." And as he claimed her lips in another mind-bending kiss, she crept a hand up the back of his leg and kept going to cup a bare buttock. How much did she adore him in this way?

"I do, indeed," he whispered and applied himself more fully to sending her over the edge of bliss, while she did the same to him.

She could hardly concentrate on her own exploration when he took a nipple into the warm cavern of his mouth. Her back arched and her legs opened wider, which gave him greater access. A moan left her throat, for he was quite relentless in his quest; never did he approach coupling with anything other than intense determination. Because of that, her mind was nearly gone, but she had enough wherewithal to slide a hand around to squeeze his impressive equipage, giggling as another moan escaped him, this one of surprise. "Even after all this time, you are not ready for that?" He was hard and hot in her palm, and very aroused.

So incredibly delicious.

"Your delight and encouragement are quite the aphrodisiac." Peregrine employed his mouth and free hand at her breasts, while bringing her to the heights with relentless friction on her nubbin. "By the time I'm done this afternoon, every living thing in this meadow will know how pleased I am to have married you." And again, he applied himself with vigor to that button as if he hadn't anything else to do with his time.

"Oh!" Bliss washed over her as she fell into a release. A shuddering sigh left her throat and ended with a stifled scream. Contractions rocked her core. She clung to his straining biceps as he held himself over her. "Perry, that was... You are..." Why wouldn't her brain turn over intelligent words? "Surprising and I adore that moment."

"Mmm, let us see what else you can manage, hmm?" He shifted his position until he settled more comfortably between her bent knees, his weight on his forearms. "Unless you are too tired?"

"I am absolutely not." She looped her arms about his broad shoulders and pulled him closer, went so far as to lightly nip his ear lobe. "I might need more convincing of your love for me." It was a game they often played, and he always came up to the mark beautifully.

One second, his cockhead flirted with her opening as he kissed her thoroughly. The next, with one fluid flex of his hips, he'd thrust into her and didn't stop until she'd been fully impaled. Their moans of pleasure blended, and he paused, smiling down at her.

With the sunshine gilding his chestnut hair and his shoulders, he was almost god-like. She shivered and her heart squeezed, for he was hers. "Is there an issue?" The words were a breathless affair, for he filled her so completely that if she took a few deep breaths, she'd spend right with little effort.

And she adored it every single time.

"I honestly never remember how I got along without you in my life. As much as I enjoyed my time in the navy, this phase of my life has been infinitely better." He smoothed the curls from her forehead and then pressed a kiss to the skin there. "I love you." Then he moved, employing slow and easy strokes that made her shiver with anticipation and pleasure.

"I love you too," Cora finally managed to pant out before giving herself over to his mastery. Planting her feet on the ground, she lifted her hips and matched his rhythm. Oh, he felt so good, so strong, and she couldn't have enough of him. It never grew stale, this part of marriage, and she absolutely delighted in joining with him both physically and emotionally—even spiritually. Everything she was went into his keeping. Tears pricked her eyes at the perfection of it and the thought they had years of this to enjoy together.

"Ah, sweeting." He pressed his lips to her cheeks, her nose, her closed eyelids, and when he claimed her mouth in a proper kiss and fenced with her tongue, the cadence of his thrusting changed to match. Frantic, hard, forceful, Peregrine stroked into her as if he wished to touch her soul.

A moan escaped her as Cora drew her knees up and wrapped her legs about his waist, and that sent him deeper. The crisp hairs of his chest rasped along her already sensitized skin. The friction added depth to their joining. Far too soon, her world tilted and fractured, but he didn't slow. "Perry, please…" She panted and her heartbeat accelerated. With every push, every thrust, waves of intense sensation rolled over her. "I need…" What *did* she need? Every thought in her brain flew away like butterflies in the wind. She opened her eyes and peered into his face. Such love and devotion were reflected there; those raw emotions stole her breath, and when she grinned, a tremble moved down her spine to help usher in her imminent flight.

"Tell the heavens, Cora. Shout how you feel, for I'm nearly done. I want the countryside to know." He paused briefly as he kneeled between her legs, took her hips in a bruising grip, and then continued working her body by going deep until she fell.

That wasn't the right term, not at all. It was more like she hurled through a spinning sky that was bright with rainbow-colored sparkles, and then she flew as bliss exploded all around her. "Peregrine! Dear God!" Out in the open with the privacy of nature, she shouted her exultation while contractions rocked her body. As she tumbled, her inner muscles sucked greedily at his length as he thrust once, twice. The third one pushed him over the edge, and he claimed his own release with a muffled shout.

"So good." His labored breathing rasped in her ear as his shaft pulsed. She reveled in the heavy press of his body that pinned her between him and the quilt-covered ground. "I will never have enough of you," he said with his lips in the crook of her neck while she looped her arms about his shoulders.

"I feel much the same." With a sound much like a purr, Cora stroked her fingers through the hair at his nape. "I sometimes think I live a charmed life."

A frown pulled at his sensual lips. Oh?" He kissed away the moisture on one cheek. "Are you unhappy about that?"

"No. The opposite. It all still feels exciting and new." Then she nestled into his hold, content to lay there while the sun warmed her skin and her breathing returned to normal.

"That is all to the good, for my fondest hope is that we'll never grow dull together."

They lay together for quite a while before the captain stirred.

"Perhaps we should dress. We need to at least investigate our picnic before we return to the house for tea. Cook will be quite offended if I don't eat at least three of her jam tarts."

"The staff does dote on you." She reached for her shift, and her muscles protested that banal movement. "Mama told me Mia and Wycliffe are scheduled to arrive today with their children." She adored those young ones, and spoiling them made her loss a bit less acute.

"Indeed. Sounds like the making of an entertaining evening."

"You have no idea. My sister Anna is home for a bit. She's been a governess to a family in Bath, but now the last child is grown, she's without a position."

"Ah, and she's bored?" He brushed his lips over hers.

Cora giggled. "Weren't we all at seven and twenty?" When she tugged him over, she kissed him soundly before letting him move away to dress. "Ah, Perry, there is nothing more I could ever want from our life together, so thank you for risking everything for that second chance."

"I would do it all over again, for you are more than worth it."

They shared a grin, and she lifted her face to the sun while breathing a silent prayer. Life was indeed surprising, and just when a person thought it would always be one way, fate shifted and thrust one into a new and astonishing path. The trick was never letting fear overrule bravery, for so many things could be missed if that happened.

Having a supportive and loving man by one's side didn't hurt either.

The End

About the Author

Sandra Sookoo is a *USA Today* bestselling author who firmly believes every person deserves acceptance and a happy ending. Most days you can find her creating scandal and mischief in the Regency-era, serendipity and happenstance in Victorian America or snarky, sweet humor in the contemporary world. Most recently she's moved into infusing her books with mystery and intrigue. Reading is a lot like eating fine chocolates—you can't just have one. Good thing books don't have calories!

When she's not wearing out computer keyboards, Sandra spends time with her real-life Prince Charming in central Indiana where she's been known to goof off and make moments count because the key to life is laughter. A Disney fan since the age of ten, when her soul gets bogged down and her imagination flags, a trip to Walt Disney World is in order. Nothing fuels her dreams more than the land of eternal happy endings, hope and love stories.

Stay in Touch

Sign up for Sandra's bi-monthly newsletter and you'll be given exclusive excerpts, cover reveals before the general public as well as opportunities to enter contests you won't find anywhere else.

Just send an email to sandrasookoo@yahoo.com with SUB-SCRIBE in the subject line.

Or follow/friend her on social media:
Facebook: facebook.com/sandra.sookoo
Facebook Author Page: facebook.com/sandrasookooauthor
Pinterest: pinterest.com/sandrasookoo
Instagram: instagram.com/sandrasookoo
BookBub Page: bookbub.com/authors/sandra-sookoo

9 781963 585506